TRUE BLUE ~ BOOK FOUR

SCREAM BLUE

AWARD-WINNING AUTHOR

SUSAN PAGE DAVIS

Scrivenings
PRESS
Quench your thirst for story.
www.ScriveningsPress.com

Published by Scrivenings Press LLC
15 Lucky Lane
Morrilton, Arkansas 72110
https://ScriveningsPress.com

Printed in the United States of America

Paperback ISBN 978-1-64917-274-7

eBook ISBN 978-1-64917-275-4

Editors: Erin R. Howard and K. Banks

Cover by www.bookmarketinggraphics.com.

1

C ampbell McBride opened her top desk drawer to get a paper clip and was confronted by a photograph staring up at her. The four faces smiled as though they knew good things awaited these young people.

Campbell grabbed a black binder clip and shut the drawer more firmly than was necessary. The photo had resided in her desk drawer for nearly a month now, and she still hadn't made a decision.

"Hey, Nell Calhoun just drove in next door," Nick Emerson said.

"She's probably showing the house today." Campbell squeezed the wire handles of the clip and applied it to the stack of papers she'd prepared for her father.

"Let's hope it sells this time," Nick said. "It's been on the market for, like, a month."

"More." Campbell didn't care if the house sold or not. Without close neighbors on the side their office windows overlooked, their days were mostly quiet and productive. Not to say boring.

"People are snapping up houses all over the county." Nick frowned. "I'm pretty sure no one's buying Tatton's place because of what happened to him."

"Maybe. A lot of people don't like the idea of sleeping in a house where a murder took place." Campbell rose and left the airy, pleasant room that had been the former owner's living room and crossed the hall to her father's private office. She tapped on the door. "Dad?"

"Come on in, Soup."

She smiled, resigned to keeping the nickname as long as her father was around. She stepped in and held out her papers. "Here's the printout you wanted on the Hasseltine case."

"Great. Thanks, honey. I set up a meeting with Mr. Hasseltine right after lunch."

"Nick says Nell's showing Ben Tatton's house this morning."

"Good. I hope she snags a buyer."

"Even if they have noisy kids or drive motorcycles?"

He laughed. "This street is too quiet. We need some young people."

Campbell scowled in mock offense. "We're young."

"No, you're mistaken there. You might be young, but I can't make that claim anymore. I've passed the half century mark. And if you're counting Nick, he doesn't live here."

She smiled. "Guess you told me."

"Yep."

"So, what do you want me to do now?" She'd been working for her father for a couple of months at True Blue Investigations and anticipated taking the exam that would give her credentials for the job of private investigator within a few weeks.

Bill let out his breath in a puff. "Take your pick. We've got four cases we haven't started on. Do you want an insurance case, a background check, or a legal file?"

"Hmm, I don't know as I'm experienced enough to do a legal case on my own. Why don't I take the background check to plug away at while you're out this afternoon? I'm getting pretty comfortable with those." Although she might be wiser to take on something more challenging to get her ready for the exam.

"All right, that's under Lassiter. Start the file and dig into it." He shoved back his chair. "Guess I'll get some coffee."

"We've got pumpkin spice in our office."

His eyebrows drew together. "Nah. Regular for me."

"You should try it."

Bill shook his head. "I want the good stuff, but nothing sweet."

"Okay."

They walked across the hall together.

Nick stood by the window looking out on their driveway and the Tatton house. Without turning around, he said, "Looks like the client's arrived."

"Which client?" Bill asked.

Nick jerked around to look at his boss. "Not ours. Nell's." He nodded toward the window.

"You shouldn't stare at them." Nick always found ways to annoy Campbell. She felt like shutting the drapes, but her dad was already at Nick's side, looking out beside him.

A woman had left her green Toyota and was walking toward the front entrance. The Realtor came down the porch steps and greeted her with a handshake. The two women stood for a moment in front of the light-colored brick house as Nell pointed out a few features, then they climbed the steps and went inside.

"Let's hope she likes it," Campbell said.

"A woman alone. I don't know." Nick shook his head. "She may be afraid of ghosts. Think Nell will tell her about the murder?"

"I'd think she'd be obligated." Campbell turned to her father for his opinion, but he stood gazing out the window with a vacant stare. "Dad?"

"Huh?" His gaze shifted to her face.

"What's the matter?"

"Nothing. I just ... I thought that might be someone I know."

"Who?" Nick asked. "The potential buyer?"

"Exactly. But it's been a while."

"So ..." Campbell waited.

"She looked like a friend of your mother's."

"Oh." She hadn't expected that. Her mom had died almost eight years previously, and she'd never lived over here, on the west side of Land Between the Lakes. "Did I know her?"

"I don't know. She was an old high school friend." Her father pulled in a deep breath. "Well, regardless of whether she's Emily's old friend or not, this is a good exercise for you. What can you tell me about her, based on what you just saw?"

Campbell wanted to protest but held back. If she was going to be a topnotch investigator, she ought to be noticing details.

"Well, she must be late forties or early fifties ..."

"You could tell that without seeing her, just from my saying she was a friend of your mother's."

True. Campbell frowned and concentrated on the memory of the woman who'd met with Nell Calhoun.

"Uh ... short hair, nice blouse, good fit on the pants. Not sloppy. High-heeled sandals, so she's somewhat fashion conscious." She scowled deeper, unable to recall if the woman had worn makeup noticeable from this distance, but she must have. Most Southern women did, at least those who cared about their appearance, especially when going out.

"Nick?" Bill said.

Campbell couldn't hold back a grunt of frustration. She had taken too long.

Leaning on the windowsill, Nick peered across the driveway. "Car's a new model—this year or last year—in the thirty-K range. That says she's not poor. Can't tell if it's a Kentucky plate or not from this angle."

Ammunition to aid her in the competition came to mind, and Campbell jumped in. "Her handbag. It's rose leather, and from here it looked like a designer bag—could be anywhere from four hundred to a thousand dollars or more."

Her father pulled back a little and studied her face. "Really? Women will pay a thousand bucks for a pocketbook?"

"You'd be surprised." Campbell pursed her lips, thinking of the worn vinyl one she'd used for two summers. She didn't believe in blowing your whole paycheck on frivolities, but someday she'd like to have a nice purse.

"I don't think she was overwhelmed by the house," Nick said.

"Why not?" Bill asked.

With a shrug, Nick turned to face them. "Her body language. She didn't look too enthusiastic when they were looking at the outside."

"Maybe she hates yellow brick." Campbell had to agree with him as to the client's demeanor, but she hated that Nick had seen it and put it into words before it had crystalized in her mind.

"Then she should stay away from Oz," Nick drawled.

"Or maybe Nell told her the last owner was murdered in the kitchen," Campbell snapped back.

"Children, children."

Bill's gentle chiding made Campbell's confidence plummet. She was older than Nick, and she had the benefit of loving parents and a great education. Why did she always respond to Nick's baiting in the most juvenile manner? Was it because he'd worked closely with her father for the last three years, while Campbell had been off in another state? It was foolish to think Nick had replaced her in her dad's affections. Or was he the son Bill had always longed for?

The only way to keep herself from falling into that emotional trap and wallowing in depression was to rise above it—above Nick.

"I'm sorry, Dad," she said. "And Nick, I'm sorry. I know this job isn't a competition."

Her father nodded. "You two work well together when you put aside whatever it is you don't like about each other. Now, please do that and get to your assignments."

———

That evening, Campbell retired to her room to study while her father watched the evening news in their upstairs sitting room. Western Kentucky was usually pretty quiet, and boning up on the law and the regulations for private investigators was more important than learning what Paducah's city council would be voting on next week or which streets in Murray were temporarily closed for repair.

She paused in making a list of privacy lines investigators shouldn't cross when her cell phone rang. Keith Fuller. She smiled and swiped the screen. "Hello, Detective."

"Hi. What are you up to tonight?" His warm voice sent a wave of comfort through Campbell. With Keith in her life, she could overcome most anything—this exam, her mild anxiety over her father's safety, even her thorny relationship with Nick.

"Just a little studying. How about you?"

"I just got home, but I may be called in again in the wee hours."

"Oh? Why?"

"There's a severe weather watch for our area. We're talking possible tornado threat."

Campbell grimaced. She and her dad had talked about that shortly after moving into their new home—where to take shelter if they got a tornado warning, which was more ominous and urgent than a tornado watch.

When a twister was imminent in the Murray area, a public service message went out to all local phones, warning residents to take shelter immediately. That meant grabbing her go bag and scrambling down to the Victorian house's dark, spooky basement. They'd stored sleeping bags, flashlights, a kerosene lantern, and a few other supplies down there for emergency use. Campbell had even stashed a couple of old favorite books she could reread to help stave off boredom.

"How likely is it?" she asked. Having grown up in Bowling Green and seen some pretty serious aftereffects of storms, she didn't take weather warnings lightly.

"Well, the storm will come through here for sure, but whether any funnel clouds will touch down is anyone's guess."

She gulped. So far, God had spared her family that horror.

"What about your folks?" she asked. Keith's parents had a lovely home on the shore of Kentucky Lake.

"Just talked to Mom. They're aware and ready."

"Do they have a basement?" She'd been out to Nathan and Angela's house a few times, but her introductory tour hadn't included things like a storm shelter.

"Yeah, they do. They're high enough above the shore to

have one, and Dad did it right. The house is sturdy too. But you never know."

"I'll throw a few things in my go bag before we go to bed."

"Good," he said. "I'll check in with you in the morning."

"Thanks."

"Hey, have you talked to Bill yet about that picture you found?"

Campbell scrunched up her cheeks. Keith would remember that. He'd been on hand when she opened the box of her mother's things. When her father moved to Murray six years ago, he had stored a lot of things from their old home in a storage unit for lack of space in the small ranch house he'd bought. Campbell, who was away at college when the move occurred, had no idea he'd rented the unit.

But now they were living together in the much larger Victorian on Willow Street. When her dad revealed that he'd stored a lot of old things, Campbell was surprised. He was so practical, she'd assumed he'd gotten rid of anything that wasn't in his small house. They'd gone together several weeks ago and retrieved her grandmother's rocking chair, some old dishes, boxes of her mom's books, and a couple of boxes simply marked "Em's stuff."

After several days of procrastination, she'd finally opened one of those boxes. When the photo had fluttered from between several envelopes, Keith had snatched it up before it hit the floor.

"Who's this?" he asked.

Frowning, Campbell took the photo and studied it. Two teenaged boys in suits and two girls between them, gussied up for a big night out, smiled out at her. "Well, that's my mom. I don't know who these other people are."

"Prom night?" Keith suggested.

"Maybe. I guess those are friends of hers." She paid special attention to the young man beside her mother. Not Bill, that was certain.

She flipped it over. "Phil, Em, Jackie & Shawn."

"Huh." Keith leaned in close over her shoulder, and she was very aware of his nearness. "Do you know any of them?"

"Nope. Must have been high school friends." Campbell wished for the millionth time that her mother had lived longer. So many questions flooded her mind that she longed to ask.

"You should ask Bill about that picture," Keith said over the phone.

Uncanny how he could almost read her mind. She wished she'd brought the photo up to her room, instead of leaving it in her desk down in the office.

"I don't know," she said. "I don't want to hurt him."

"How would that hurt him? I'd think he'd be glad to talk about your mother."

"Eh. He's been pretty quiet about her. I didn't even know about the storage unit. There's still a lot of stuff over there."

"I thought you brought it all home."

"Not nearly. There's furniture and more books and even some of her old clothes. I know he donated a lot of stuff to a charity shop in Bowling Green, but I was amazed at how much he kept."

"Maybe he did it for you."

"I think some of it he did. I'd been feeling kind of slighted that he'd dumped all of Mom's things without asking me, but we just never talked about it. And then he told me about the storage unit. It was like Christmas."

Keith chuckled. "And you get to open the presents."

She wished fiercely that he was in the room with her. If so, she'd kiss him for sure. She was beyond blushing just from thinking about it. She'd met him about three months ago, when her dad was missing and she desperately need help.

9

Their relationship had grown to a strong bond of appreciation of each other and even more—contentment. Unless she was mistaken, they both hoped it would continue to grow beyond the few actual dates they'd had.

"I've gone through everything we've brought home and found places in the house for most of it. Maybe it's time to go to the storage unit again and empty it out. We could have a yard sale if there are things we don't want."

"Bill would hate that."

"Oh, I don't know. It might be hard for him to see some family things being sold, but Dad loves going to sales and chatting with the people he meets."

"Think about it," Keith said. "Meanwhile, would you want to go over to the lake Friday? I'm off that day, and we could go to Mom and Dad's and take the boat out."

"Sounds like fun."

"Great. I'll touch base with you again with the time."

They signed off, and she was about to go back to her studying when a soft tap came on her door.

"Come on in." It wouldn't be anyone but her father, or she'd have heard the doorbell or voices in the hall.

Sure enough, Bill opened the door and poked his head in. "Busy?"

"No. Keith and I were talking, but we're done."

"Sounds like we're in for a storm tonight."

Campbell stood. "Yeah, Keith mentioned it. I guess I should check my go bag."

"I think I'll go downstairs and put all our latest files on a flash drive, in case we lose power. That way, we can take our laptops somewhere else and work on them if we have to."

"Good idea." She almost mentioned the storage unit but decided that could wait. If a tornado ripped through Murray, there might not be a storage unit tomorrow.

She wasn't usually so pessimistic. Two things had dragged her down lately. The upcoming exam and the photo.

"I think I'll run downstairs too, and grab a few things from my desk." She definitely didn't want to lose that photo of Mom, from a time she knew little about. If she and her father wound up huddled in the basement tonight, she could ask him about the other kids in the picture with Emily. Maybe. She wasn't sure she was ready.

Why wasn't the picture in her mother's old photo album, along with several others from her teenage years? Campbell didn't enjoy looking at a picture of her mom with another guy. They were kids, but still, it might make her dad feel bad to see it. She didn't want to do that, but she did want to learn about her mom's past. She slid her laptop into its carrying case and headed for the stairs.

2

Campbell jerked awake to an annoying buzz from her cell phone. She fumbled for it, staring at the digital clock. It read 2:40. She swiped the phone's screen and put it to her ear.

"Tornado warning in your area. Take shelter immediately. This warning will be in effect until 3:05 a.m. Repeat ..."

Her father's knock was louder than the one he'd used earlier.

"Campbell! Get up, kiddo. Tornado warning."

"I'm up, Dad. I'll be right there." She switched on her lamp, stuck her feet into her slippers and reached for her robe. At the last minute, she'd shoved a complete clean outfit into the tote bag she used for these times, so she wouldn't have to worry about getting dressed or being without shoes if the worst happened.

Wind buffeted the tree outside her window, so loud it sounded as if a big truck was passing. She stuck her phone in her robe's side pocket, grabbed the tote and her laptop case, and opened the door. Her dad was standing just outside with an olive green knapsack and his laptop in his hands.

"Let's go." He strode to the stairway and glanced back at her.

"I'm right behind you." Campbell hurried down the steps and followed him through the kitchen to the cellar door.

Bill flipped on the lights in the basement and went more slowly down the narrow staircase. The kitchen windows rattled. Campbell trailed her father, shutting the door at the top of the stairs, but leaving the lights on behind her. They had put a couple of armchairs left from the previous owner's furnishings down there. Tonight was the first time they'd felt the need to shelter in the basement, and Campbell was glad they'd had the foresight to prepare.

"Just like being in the bunker." Bill laid down his burdens and sank into an ugly, mustard-colored chair.

Campbell winced at the reminder of her father's time in forced solitude. Though the memory was painful for both of them, it had prompted Bill to stock their own cellar with bottled water, non-perishable food, a battery-operated weather radio, a few books and games, and enough furniture to keep them somewhat comfortable.

They'd stashed food and bedding for three, in case a warning came in daylight hours and Nick was with them. Campbell was glad he wasn't. She couldn't imagine being confined for very long with Nick.

"So," Bill said.

She smiled. "Yeah. Here we are."

"I guess we could read e-books."

"Or play cards."

"You want to?"

She hesitated. "I'd rather just talk for a while."

"Okay."

After another ten seconds of silence, Campbell turned to

see his face in the glare of the bare bulbs overhead. "Dad, I'm worried about the test."

"You'll ace it."

"What if I don't?"

He shrugged. "Study some more and take it again?"

"Maybe."

"Having second thoughts?"

She let out a sigh. "Not really. I love working with you, and it seems we're getting enough business for you to pay two employees."

"We sure are. I've never been so busy. I think it's the publicity we got from the last couple of high-profile cases."

"You mean, the psychic?"

He pursed his lips, nodding. "And the writer."

"You're probably right. A lot of people still ask about Katherine."

"You're good, Soup. You've got a real knack for this."

She studied his face. "Do you really think so, Dad? I mean, I thought I had a knack for teaching. But now I think I just loved literature. More than I did the students, maybe, and that's not good. I mean, I'm supposed to love people and—and show God's love to them."

"You can do that as an investigator. I think you have."

"Not much."

"Some, then. You can't come on full blast at people you're working for. But if the client's situation is difficult, which it usually is in our profession, then sometimes you can ease into a discussion about God and how He's in control."

"Yeah." She sat for a moment pondering that. Was she too reticent to broach spiritual topics with other people? Was she scared of breaching ethical guidelines? Or was she just afraid people wouldn't like her if she did that?

The light bulbs flickered and went out. Neither of them spoke for a moment.

Campbell swallowed hard. "Dad, what if I can't pass the test, do you really want me to stay on?"

"Of course."

"As what? A receptionist?"

His hand found hers in the darkness. "Campbell, you're always welcome here. I love you, and I'm happy you chose to live with me. Even if you went back to teaching, or if you had a different job, I'd still be pleased to have you here. But you are not going to fail that test."

"That's easy to say."

After a pause, he said, "You were always a little timid. Even as a child, you were afraid of failing. But I can remember very few times when you did."

"I didn't make the basketball team."

"Okay, there was that."

"Or get the part I wanted in the senior play."

"What part did you want?"

"Cinderella, of course."

"But you got to be in the play."

She sighed. "As an extra, to dance at the ball. And I had to have private dancing lessons to do that right."

"You dance beautifully now."

"How do you know?" She turned toward him, although she couldn't see him. "You haven't seen me dance since that play."

"I remember."

"Well, I haven't done it in years. I've probably forgotten how."

"I think it's like riding a bike."

Meaning, she supposed, that you never forgot. When you went back to it, the technique returned to you. Fairy godmother magic? Muscle memory, more likely.

"Dad?"

"Yeah?"

"If I wasn't here, would you have asked Nick to move in with you when you bought this house?"

"No way."

His instant response brought her some relief.

"He'd drive me crazy," Bill added.

Campbell smiled and turned on her flashlight. "Should we turn on the lantern?"

"If you want. Talking in the dark isn't so bad, is it?"

No, it wasn't. In fact, she'd found it easier to voice her fears knowing her father's sharp gaze couldn't find her face.

Campbell turned her flashlight off. She wrinkled her nose at the pervasive scent of the earth floor.

Her father shifted in his chair. "I intend to give you a raise after you pass the test, you know."

"No, I didn't."

"You should get the same pay I'm giving Nick. You do at least as much work as him, and you're nearly as good. In fact, I predict you'll be better than he is within a few months."

"Why do you say that?"

"You're a quick learner. That girl they picked for Cinderella—"

"Audra Pagels?"

"Whoever. She stumbled over her lines."

"Yeah, I guess she did a few times."

"You wouldn't have."

Campbell smiled in the darkness.

Above them, a roar burst through the air. The house shook, and the joists creaked. Her heart thudded.

Her dad's flashlight came on. Flecks of dust floated in its beam. "I don't like the sound of that. Let's move."

She jumped up, grabbed a foam mattress, and ran to

crouch beneath the stairs, next to the wall of the old coal bin they didn't use. Her dad plopped in beside her and held his foam pad over their heads.

———

Half an hour after the noise stopped, Campbell and her father emerged from their nest. In the beams of their flashlights, the basement looked the same.

"Let me take a look topside." Bill headed for the stairs.

"I'm coming too."

He didn't protest, so Campbell followed him up the steps. At the top, he opened the kitchen door and paused, flicking his light around the room.

"Looks okay in here."

As she emerged from the cellarway, the pattering of rain against the windows greeted Campbell, along with the lingering scent of coffee. Her dad was right, everything in the kitchen looked fine. They ventured into the hall and checked the dining room and the big office. Bill opened his office door, looked around, then closed it.

"Upstairs?" Campbell asked.

"Yeah. I think it may have missed us, but we'd better make sure. There could be a broken window or something."

She let her father lead the way, and they separated on the landing, checking their bedrooms, the sitting room, bathroom, and guest room.

"Okay here," she told him when they met again in the hall.

"Just let me take a look at the attic."

Campbell flipped the light switch in her bedroom while he was gone, hoping but not believing the power had been restored. Nope, still dark. She went to the window, shut off her flashlight, and looked out. The trees tossed eerily, and she could hear a constant moaning of wind. The sky was still black, and rain drummed on the porch roof below, but it wasn't a deluge.

Willow Street was out there, but she couldn't see it. No streetlights. No comforting glow from the Hills' house across the street.

Her father came to the doorway. "The attic looks okay. I don't think there's any damage to the roof, but I want to rig up and scout around outside, just in case."

She smiled. "I can't make coffee, but I'll rustle up something for a snack."

"Don't open the refrigerator."

"Right." That would put a serious cramp in her efforts.

Down in the kitchen, she rifled the cupboards and came up with small bottles of root beer—not cold, but they'd have to rough it—a few no-bake cookies, and the remains of Nick's morning doughnut run.

She lit a candle and placed it in the middle of the small pine kitchen table. She thought of setting their places as if for a formal occasion but decided not to. No telling when they'd be able to run the dishwasher again. She settled for a couple of paper plates and two glasses.

Bill came in through the garage door, took off his rain jacket, and hung it on a hook. "Looks like a limb from that big oak came down on the garage."

"Is it leaking in there?"

He shook his head. "I don't think so, but we'll know by morning. I'll have to cut up the limb and get rid of it."

"Fireplace wood?" Campbell looked forward to chilly evenings in the fall when they'd have an excuse to use the fireplace. They'd never had one in their previous homes.

"Yeah, maybe. It won't be dry, but I can stack it in the garage." He surveyed the table as he spoke then nodded and sat in one of the chairs. "If the roof needs work, I'll call someone in the morning. But that's not the worst thing."

"Oh?" Campbell picked up her root beer. "What else?"

"You know that tree in Tatton's yard?"

"The big willow?"

"Yeah, the one the cat liked."

"What about it?"

He grimaced. "A big chunk of it fell on the house. I couldn't see very well, but I'm thinking there's a lot of damage."

Campbell sucked in a breath. "We should call Nell and tell her."

"Yeah. And thank God no one was in the house."

Campbell's phone rang, and she pulled it from her pocket. "Hey, Keith."

"Are you okay?" he asked without greeting her.

"We're fine. I guess you are?"

"I'm all right, but I'm worried about my folks. Word is, there's a lot of damage here in town and on up toward Aurora and the lake. I haven't been able to get through to them. I don't have details yet, but I'm heading up there with a squad. We'll be going door to door."

"Wow. Can we do anything?"

"Not until daylight, I'd think, but all the firefighters, EMTs and officers who aren't essential to the station are going. Stay in and stay safe tonight."

"Okay. Keep us posted."

She relayed what he'd said to her father, who had just come down the stairs with his own cell phone.

"The land line's out," he said.

Campbell frowned. "Usually we have it even when the power goes out."

"I know. This is bad, Campbell. They're saying on the radio that some businesses on the west side of Murray were hit, and several dozen homes. It ripped over to the Land Between the Lakes. They don't know how bad it is yet. It could have done some damage in LBL, or even on the other side of Lake Barkley."

"Well, Keith says a lot of rescue workers are out there."

"We're supposed to shelter in place, but I think we should check on the neighbors."

"Yes, especially the elderly ones. Miss Louanne must be terrified. Do you think her house was hit?" The sweet, older woman lived just beyond the vacant Tatton property.

"I don't think the twister got that tree. I think it was the strong winds. But, yeah, we should check on Miss Louanne. You want to go there, and I'll go over to the Hills' place?"

"Sure. I'll run upstairs and get her key." Louanne Vane had given Campbell a key to her house after a mishap that gave them all a scare. She dashed up the stairs and back down again. Her dad was just about to go out the front door.

"I've got my phone," he said with a wave. "I'll call you if anything's amiss."

"Ditto." She put on her rain jacket, tucked her hair up under a baseball cap, and pulled up the vinyl hood of her jacket. Without electricity, resetting the security alarm was pointless. She wasn't sure whether Bill had taken his keys. With some misgiving, she left the door unlocked and scuttled out to the sidewalk.

The wind buffeted her as she hurried toward Miss Louanne's house. She pulled the side of her hood around to better shield her face from the rain. Willow Street in complete darkness felt like an alien world. As she slowed her steps and dodged around a fallen branch, she caught a glimmer of light on the other side, farther down the street. Someone was lighting candles in one of the homes down there.

As she passed the vacant house, she swept her flashlight's

beam over it. She couldn't see very well, and only a bit at a time, but her dad was right. The tree had definitely breached the roof on the kitchen end of the house. She looked ahead. Miss Louanne's gray house beyond was engulfed in darkness.

Campbell hurried up the driveway, fighting the wind. She splashed through a puddle and winced as the water penetrated her sneakers. When she gained the front porch, she pounded on the door with the side of her fist. She'd have to make noise if she wanted to be heard over the wind and rain.

"Miss Louanne!" She rapped again, hard. "Miss Louanne, it's me, Campbell." She paused and listened. When she received no response, she resumed her knocking. After a minute, she stood back, panting. Maybe it would be better to go around back, to the kitchen door. She knocked again, so hard her knuckles hurt.

A noise behind her caught her attention. She turned and swept her flashlight beam over the front yard.

"Hey!" Her father was running up the driveway, his light bobbing. He detoured around a fallen branch and hurried up onto the porch. "She's over at Fred and Vera's."

"Miss Louanne?" Campbell stared at him.

"Yes."

She let out a big breath. "What about Blue Boy?"

"She's got him over there in a carrier."

"Okay. Well, it looks like her house is all right." Deflated, Campbell walked with him out from under the shelter of the porch roof, down the steps, and around the fallen branch of Miss Louanne's oak tree.

When they reached the street, she was about to speak when lights appeared at the end of the block.

"Squad car," Bill said, as the headlights topped by a flashing blue beacon approached.

They stopped on the sidewalk, halfway between Miss

Louanne's and the empty house. An officer rolled down the window nearest them and ran his flashlight beam over them.

"That you, Mr. McBride?"

"It's me, Officer Ferris. Just checking on the neighbors."

Bill and Campbell both stooped to peer into the car. Officer Denise Mills was in the passenger seat.

"Hey, Denise," Campbell called.

"Hi. Anything we should know?"

"Miss Vane is holed up over yonder with the Hills." Bill pointed toward Vera and Fred's house. "A tree came down on this house behind us, but it's vacant. I thought I'd call the real estate agent and tell her."

"Good idea. We're looking for lights—candles, lanterns. If we don't see any, we check on things," Mel Ferris said.

"Well, if there's anything we can do, call my cell phone," Bill said. "Our land line's out."

"Everybody's is," Denise said, leaning across Mel. "It could be a few days before we get the power back. You're on city water, right?"

"Yeah. We don't have a generator, I hate to say. We have some bottled water, but we'll probably go through that fast."

"They'll set something up tomorrow," Mel said.

"Any really bad damage?" Campbell asked.

"We don't know the extent of it yet, but we're patrolling street by street. Reports are starting to come in, and they're telling us by radio. They sent a couple of cars over toward Aurora. There's more damage on the west side of town, but I think a funnel cloud touched down near the lake."

"Everything okay at the hospital?" Campbell asked.

"We just came from there," Mel replied. "They're coping."

"Give us your cell phone number," Denise said.

Bill complied, and the officers rolled on down the street. Campbell watched them and was glad to see that more lantern lights and flickering candles were appearing in her neighbors' windows.

"If the power's still out in the morning, I'll go find us some water," her dad said.

Campbell swiped her phone's screen. "I can't believe it's only four o'clock."

"I'll give Nick a call, and then what do you say we hit the hay?"

"Sounds good." She trudged up their driveway with her father, thankful for the solid house. Their basic needs were met, but how many people out there needed help?

3

Campbell was amazed to see so many people outside the church on a Wednesday morning. Her father found a parking spot on the far end of the lot, and they both got out. Campbell stood looking around. She saw a few people she knew from the congregation, but most were strangers, and the two large box trucks sitting on the pavement were definitely not the usual sight in that place.

"There's Pastor Flynn." Her dad pointed, and Campbell spotted the lanky man. He was dressed casually, in khakis and a short-sleeved maroon shirt.

He looked up as they approached, peering at them through his dark-framed glasses. "Bill, Campbell. Thanks for coming. Everything all right over your way?"

"We're fine," Bill said. "We spent yesterday cleaning up and sorting things out."

"Was your house damaged?"

"No, just the edge of the garage roof, but it's not serious. With so many people needing more help, I went ahead and did the repairs myself. The house next door got smacked by a tree, but it's vacant right now. Otherwise everything's good."

"Glad to hear it."

Her father was downplaying their difficulties, but Campbell didn't blame him. With so many people hurt or homeless now, the inconvenience of the power outage and a bit of minor damage to the garage seemed insignificant. They'd checked on all their clients by cell phone and assured them they'd continue to work on their cases. The attorneys and insurance companies from which her dad often accepted jobs were all closed for the time being.

"We heard on the radio that people were coming here to help distribute water and food," Campbell said.

"That's right. Nancy's organizing things." He nodded to the side, where his wife was seated behind a folding table with another woman. Clipboards and papers covered the surface before them.

"Is the church all right?" She couldn't see along the side of the building.

"A couple of broken windows from flying debris. We're thankful it wasn't worse." The pastor smiled. "Our house was spared too. We're trying to help those who fared worse."

"How bad is it?" Bill asked.

"Real bad over Aurora way and along the western lake shore. They've got a lot of rescue workers over there. We're trying to provide bottled water and bag lunches for all the crews and families who really need it. Of course, the power's out all over, but some people have lost their homes. They've got nothing."

"Wow. Do you know how many houses were hit?" Campbell asked.

"Not yet, but I'm told thirty at a minimum were destroyed. That includes half a dozen on the west side of town, but it seems it's worse near the lake. And a lot more have severe damage. Maybe hundreds of structures."

Bill frowned. "How can we help?"

"Well, the city's lining up places for people to stay—hotel rooms, apartments, campers—anything as a temporary lodging. The church is providing water and a little food, along with information on where they can find shelter and clothes—the basic needs. You can help with the distribution."

"We'd be happy to," Campbell said. "Do you know if anyone was hurt in the storm?"

Pastor Flynn nodded soberly. "They haven't confirmed it officially, but I heard there are at least three dead, and quite a few who were taken to hospitals. I'm heading to Murray-Calloway myself. Those with more serious injuries are being taken to Paducah or Nashville."

Bill patted his shoulder. "You get going, Waldo. We'll check with Nancy and see where we can help out."

"Thanks." Pastor Flynn nodded and walked away.

"I didn't think it was so bad," Campbell said. "I guess the fact that it didn't rip through the middle of town was deceptive. A few trees down, some roof damage ..."

"Yeah. Let's see if we can make a difference here." Her father led the way toward Nancy Flynn's table, and they got in line behind two other people.

"Hello," Nancy said with a smile when it was their turn.

"We're here to help," Bill said.

"Wonderful." She looked down at her clipboard. "Can you drive over to Kentucky Lake?"

"Sure."

"Good. There are several crews working over there, checking on people and searching damaged houses for casualties. We're sending them bottled water and food, for the volunteers, mostly, but of course you can give some to anyone out there who needs it."

"Do you need food donations?" Campbell asked. "Or people to cook?"

"Oh, no. We may hold a supper here later for the volunteers, but we've got several restaurants donating bag lunches—the Barn Owl, Dumplins, Papa John's, Panera Bread —quite a few, actually." Nancy looked up as a young woman slipped a sheet of paper onto the table in front of her. "Thanks, Gina."

Campbell recognized the volunteer as a church member and exchanged smiles with her before Gina hurried away.

"If you could take some of the donated food out there, it would help, and we're sending cases of bottled water for the crews to distribute."

"We can take a dozen or more cases," Bill said.

"Great."

"Where are you getting the bottled water?" Campbell asked. Her father had scouted stores in the area the previous day but hadn't found any open for customers because of the power outage.

"Several men from the church drove to Paducah yesterday. We got a great response on donations." Nancy stood and pointed toward one of the trucks, where the back doors were open and men were unloading flats. "I'll give you authorization, and you can take it over there, to the fellow in the green shirt. He'll show you where to pull your vehicle up so they can load for you."

While her dad moved his car closer to the truck of donated water, Campbell went to collect two dozen bag lunches from a van marked *Applebee's*. A woman gave her a carton with the first dozen.

"Take these and I'll hold the second batch until you come back."

"Thanks." Campbell edged between people, carrying the box toward her dad's car. He had the trunk open, and two young men were filling space with cases of water. Her father stood beside the car, talking to a dark-haired woman whose back was to Campbell.

"Excuse me, Dad. Where do you want these?"

Bill jumped forward to take the carton from her. "I'll put them in the back seat. Oh, Jackie, I don't think you've met my daughter."

The woman turned toward her with a broad smile. Campbell grinned back as she handed over the lunches to her dad.

"Oh, you're the one who was looking at Ben Tatton's house yesterday."

"Yes, I did view the house. Your father was just telling me it was damaged in the storm."

Campbell winced and took the woman's extended hand. "It was. I hope you weren't planning to buy it and move right in."

"No, I'd crossed that one off my list, but I'm sorry to hear about the damage."

Her dad was back, and he looked expectantly between the two of them. "Campbell, this is an old friend of your mother's —Jackie Fleming. Jackie, my daughter Campbell."

Jackie. Campbell studied her face intently. Friend of her mom's. Yes, it was her. The girl in the photo with her mom and their dates. She should say something, but her lips wouldn't seem to operate.

She cleared her throat. "I hope you find the house you're looking for soon."

"Thanks," Jackie said. "I went out to look at a place on the lake a few days ago, and it was a great location, but it was too pricey. I hope to find something here in town."

Bill nodded. "If we hear of anything, we'll let you know."

From that, Campbell assumed her dad had Jackie's phone number. Of course, he was a private investigator—it probably wouldn't take him two minutes to find it if she hadn't already given it to him.

"Well, I'd better let you get going," Jackie said as one of the young men shut the trunk. "Bill, it was great to reconnect with you. Maybe we'll meet again." She hurried off.

Campbell turned to her dad, still a bit shell shocked.

"All set?" he asked.

"Oh! No, there's another box of lunch bags. Hold on." She turned and dashed back to the restaurant van.

"There you are," said the woman who'd helped her earlier. "I almost gave your box away." She lifted another cardboard carton and placed it in Campbell's hands. "Good luck, and keep safe."

"Thanks." Campbell plodded back to the car.

Her dad was waiting with the back door open. "I'll take it." He eased the carton from her arms and slid it in beside the other.

Campbell went around to the passenger side and got in, still trying to process the new information. "So," she said as he started the engine. "Jackie. Did you say her last name is Fleming?"

"Yeah. Used to be Lowe, I think."

"Oh, so she married some guy named Fleming."

"That's right."

"Do you know his first name?"

"I don't think she mentioned it. Why?"

"Nothing. I just—I didn't see any Mr. Fleming with her when Nell showed her the house."

"No, I don't think he's in the picture now. She told me she was thinking of moving over here to be closer to her daughter's family."

Already, Campbell was planning to do some research when they got home. Was Mr. Fleming's first name Shawn? That was the name of the boy standing next to Jackie in the photo. Interesting. If she did have another encounter with Jackie, maybe she'd ask about the high school foursome.

They rode in silence for several minutes, up Route 80 to Aurora, then up 68. It seemed like trees were down everywhere, and they passed two crews dragging limbs and other debris off the road. Several houses and businesses looked unscathed, and then they'd roll past one with severe damage. One garage's roof had apparently peeled off during the storm.

When her dad turned off onto a gravel road toward Kentucky Lake, she took notice.

"This is the road Keith's folks live on."

"Yeah."

She looked over at him, suddenly fearful. "Keith would have called us if their house was hit, wouldn't he?"

"You tell me." Her dad drove onward without looking her way. "If he was too busy, maybe not."

"Oh, Dad."

"You've been praying for the people who are affected by this, right?"

"Yeah."

"Well, keep praying. We'll know soon if the Fullers were hit."

Keith had checked on them by phone the previous morning, but he'd been in a hurry and had said nothing about his parents.

A half mile from the lake, they passed less expensive dwellings than those on lots with shorefront. Several modest summer cottages stood uninhabited and a bit forlorn looking. As they rounded a bend, Campbell caught her breath. She was sure a small house had stood there, but now it was gone. Scattered fragments lay here and there, but the site of the dwelling now consisted of foundation blocks and part of one wall jutting upward. Beyond it, trees were uprooted and tossed to the ground like a child's building blocks.

"It passed through here," her father said grimly.

A short distance ahead, flashing lights put them on the alert. Bill slowed the car to a crawl and pulled up behind a patrol car.

"Stay here." He got out and walked to the place where a gaping foundation showed where another cottage had stood.

Much of the scattered debris was so broken and battered that Campbell couldn't identify it, though she did see a large piece of metal roofing leaning upright against a tree, the top half of which had been snapped off. Chunks of siding and sheetrock lay here and there, mingled with bits of clothing or furniture. Something metal—a tray, perhaps—was wrapped tightly around the trunk of a scarred oak tree.

Bill had found a county sheriff's deputy and was deep in conversation with him. Campbell rolled down her window but couldn't hear what they were saying.

After a couple of minutes, the deputy walked with her father to the car.

"We'll leave half a dozen lunches here, and a case of water," her dad said and went to open the trunk.

She got out and took six lunch bags from the back seat and handed them to a second uniformed man who'd come to help.

"Just pull around us and keep on," the deputy said. "I'm sure you'll find him. And thanks!"

As soon as her dad was back in the car, Campbell said. "Find who?"

"Keith."

"He's out here? It's not his jurisdiction."

"Anybody who can help is out here," Bill said.

"We're nearly to his parents' place. Did the deputy say anything about Nathan and Angela?"

"Not much. But you can be sure Keith's with them, unless someone else needs him more urgently." He edged his Camry around the patrol car and eased on down the dirt road.

The closer they got to the lake, the fewer trees remained standing. Campbell's stomach roiled as she saw evidence of several demolished dwellings.

Then she spotted him. Keith, in jeans and a sweatshirt, stood with his parents at the end of their short driveway. Beyond them she glimpsed the roofline of the Fuller's year-round house with a gaping hole on the end nearest them. The lake below, which was actually a widened section of the Tennessee River, didn't hold its usual shimmer. Today, the turgid water looked muddy and broody, and certainly less inviting than usual.

"I wonder what this did to the fish."

"Who knows?" Bill pulled in behind Keith's SUV.

As soon as their car stopped moving, Campbell leaped out and ran to them.

"Are you okay?"

"Well, hi there," Nathan said with a tempered smile. "We're fine, little lady."

Campbell grabbed Angela's hand. "Were you out here Monday night?"

"We were. The basement is sturdy, and we were safe." She looked sadly toward their house. "We'll have some major repairs to do, but thank God we lived through it. Our house is still standing. Some of our neighbors weren't so fortunate."

33

Campbell glanced around. From where she stood, she could see evidence of at least two demolished houses.

Bill explained their errand, but Keith's father shook his head. "We drew water when we heard the storm was coming, and we've got several barrels full. We've got plenty of food, too, but thanks. Take it to someone who's worse off than we are."

Keith leaned close to Campbell. "I was going to call you, but I came out here to check on the folks, and then I couldn't get cell service. I was on duty all day yesterday, but I managed to touch base with them, so I knew they were basically okay. I'm off today, and I came out to help Dad get started on closing in the end of the house."

"Our phones worked in town," Campbell said. "Do you think the cell towers are down?"

"Some of them, for sure. Dad and I have set up his generator, and we're trying to figure out which circuit breakers to turn off for the wrecked part of the house."

Bill shook his head. "I knew I should have bought a generator."

"There'll be a big run on them this week," Nathan said bleakly. "You probably won't be able to find one by the time you get back to town."

"No, but when this is over, a lot of people will sell them," Angela said.

Nathan sighed. "Probably true. Some folks think lightning never strikes the same place twice, but we know better." He looked off along the shore. "Keith and I are heading next door. Those poor folks got it a lot worse than we did. We went over yesterday to check if anyone was in there when the storm hit, but the fire department crew is checking under all the mess to make sure. Care to join us, Bill?"

"We'd better stay on our round. But maybe the crew over there can use some refreshments and water." He turned to

Campbell. "Grab a few of those lunches, Soup, and I'll get some water bottles. We can have a looksee."

Angela walked with her to Bill's car, while the three men headed for the destroyed cottage.

"I'm glad your house is still standing." Campbell smiled and opened the rear door.

"Oh, yes, we're so thankful!" Angela accepted two of the lunch bags, and Campbell pulled out four more. "That cottage next door was for sale, you know."

Campbell shook her head.

"That's why we're pretty sure nobody was in there when the tornado hit." Angela walked slowly toward what had been her neighbors' house. "The owners only came out here twice this summer. They told us in June they were thinking of selling, and the next thing we knew, it was on the market. We figured it would sell fast, but ..." She looked bleakly ahead to the rubble.

"That's sad," Campbell said. "I suppose the insurance company will reimburse them, but still ..."

"A woman was out here Saturday, looking at it. Nell Calhoun has shown it at least a dozen times in the last week."

"I know Nell. Who was the other woman? A local buyer?"

"I'd never met her. She said she was from over Bowling Green way. Jackie something."

Campbell stopped walking. "Jackie Fleming?"

"That sounds right."

"I know her too."

Angela frowned. "That's right, you folks used to live in Bowling Green."

"Dad said Ms. Fleming was a friend of my mother's. I met her this morning at the church, when we went to volunteer. I don't think I'd ever met her before—or if I did, I was too young to remember."

"Small world," Angela said.

"Very." They started walking again. "So, you talked to her?"

"I was outside when they came, and Nell introduced us."

"Nell's good that way." Campbell stopped twenty feet from the heap of rubble.

One of the volunteer firemen left the work crew and came to meet them.

"This is terrific. Thanks!" He took the water bottles and lunch bags and distributed them among his crew of four.

Angela went on toward what was left of the vacant cottage, and Campbell followed.

Nathan stood at the edge of the rubble with his hands on his hips. "They're pretty sure nobody was in there, just as we thought."

"Good. I was surprised nobody had made an offer on it yet." Angela glanced at her husband.

"Maybe they priced it too high." He shrugged.

"Oh, look at that next cottage." Angela stared toward a spot beyond the men, closer to the lake.

"I didn't notice how bad that one was earlier," Keith admitted, frowning. "I guess I thought what little is there was bits that blew over from this lot."

"There used to be a whole cottage there," Nathan said.

Angela shielded her eyes. "It's just gone."

"I remember, now that you say that," Keith said. "That was a rental, wasn't it?"

"Yes, they have it on Airbnb," Angela said.

"Do you know if they'd rented it out this week?"

"No idea."

Nathan shook his head. "I don't either. I don't recall seeing anyone over there Monday, but I was more concerned with making sure our place was battened down."

"Let's go take a look," Keith said.

Bill and the Fuller men walked toward the spot. Campbell wasn't sure what to do. She looked back at where she'd given the food to the firefighters.

"The crew's leaving." She could barely see the men walking toward their truck on the camp road.

"I wonder if they realized there was another cottage down here." Angela started across the ground strewn with pine needles, dodging a ruined window frame and some broken tree limbs.

Campbell gazed up into the ravaged trees, wondering if the squirrels and other animals had escaped.

They headed toward the next lot, surveying the storm damage. In a swath about twenty yards wide, every tree was uprooted or snapped off a few feet above the ground.

"It's awful here," Campbell said.

"Yes, Keith said at least twenty houses were destroyed in Marshall County alone. There's a lot of debris in the lake."

Campbell looked back toward the Fullers' house. "After seeing all this, I can hardly believe your house was almost spared."

"Me either. And the firemen said that around the point, everything looks almost normal. A few trees and limbs down, but nothing like this devastation."

Ahead of them, her father, Keith, and Nathan were in the middle of what had been a foundation, throwing pieces of debris out on the far side. Campbell wondered if the owners would rebuild the vacation cottage. It had been a source of income for them, not their primary residence like Nathan and Angela's.

Bill gave a sharp cry, and the others hurried to where he stood by a pile of broken building components. Keith and Nathan started throwing off the chunks of debris. Their air of urgency sent a surge of adrenalin through Campbell. She walked a little faster.

"Nathan," Angela called, and her husband paused with a piece of a broken plank in his hands. "What's going on?"

"We think there may be somebody here."

"No!" Angela quickened her steps, and Campbell hurried with her to the spot.

4

The men had partially uncovered a recess in the ground, and Campbell surmised that the cottage hadn't had a full basement, only a space beneath it. Splintered ends of beams and planks stuck up above the ground level. Broken pieces of wood, soggy chunks of wallboard, mangled metal, and shredded fabric remnants lay scattered about. Off to one side, a small box stove lay upturned. How could the wind pick up something that heavy and throw it?

She sidled up to Angela on the edge of the pit. Smells of leaf mold and wet trash filled her nostrils.

Keith stood in the hole below them beside her father. With Bill's help, he pulled a large piece of wood free and handed it to Nathan. With effort, Keith's dad tossed it out the far side of the site. The three of them gazed into the heap for a long moment.

Keith took his cell phone from his pocket and turned on the flashlight feature. Stooping over, he shone it into the collapsed debris and then spoke to Bill and his father. They renewed their efforts to remove the rubble.

Angela looked at Campbell, her mouth gaping open. "What should we do?"

"Just wait, I think. Keith will know." Campbell itched to be down there, helping the men, but she didn't want Angela to wade into the rubble or to be left alone watching. She placed her hand on her friend's shoulder.

Leaning to one side, she could see something then— something that shouldn't be there, where her father was rooting in the mess. A foot clad in a high-end sneaker. A bit of stocking-covered ankle and the hem of a pair of jeans was visible beyond.

"There's someone," she said.

"Oh, dear." Angela stood beside her, hugging her herself and focusing on the activity.

Keith leaned in beneath an overhang of debris, his head and torso out of sight. A moment later, he backed out. After the three men conferred for a moment, he had his phone out again.

In spite of her dread, Campbell stepped closer. Her father picked up pieces of boards and clumps of trash from near the body, examined each one, and threw it aside.

Nathan climbed out of the hole and lumbered toward Angela and Campbell. When he was close enough to be heard speaking in a low tone, he said, "There's a dead man in there."

Angela clapped a hand to her mouth.

"Is it anyone you know?" Campbell asked.

"Don't think so, but we're not sure. Probably a renter. Keith's trying to call it in, but he may not be able to from here."

"Does he have a radio in his SUV?"

"No."

"There are officers just up the road. They'd have one."

"Yeah." Nathan looked up toward the road. "I guess the fire crew's gone."

"They just left," Angela said.

Nathan turned back toward the demolished cottage.

Keith walked toward them, but Bill had stayed behind, crouching near the recess in the rubble that shielded the body from their view.

He eyed his mother closely. "Dad told you?"

"He did. What now?"

"I'll go find someone with a radio and call for a team of officers to investigate. Bill's going to stay down there and make sure nothing's disturbed."

Campbell nodded. Her father was a former police officer, and he knew the drill.

"I'm sorry, Mom," Keith said. "There'll be a lot of activity out here for a few hours."

"Do whatever you need to." Angela smiled grimly. "I'm sorry we can't be of more help."

When Keith set out for his vehicle, Campbell said, "Do you want to go back to the house? Maybe we can do a little cleanup."

"Don't go into the side where the damage is," Nathan said. "The kitchen end is okay, but I don't want any chances of you two getting hurt."

"Why don't you come with us?" Angela turned wide eyes on him.

"Thought I'd keep Bill company."

———

When they got home that afternoon, it was nearly five o'clock. Campbell was surprised to see Nick Emerson's Jeep still in their driveway.

"Have you been here all day?" Campbell asked as she set her purse on her desk.

"Yeah, pretty much. I went out to get some lunch, but

41

everything's closed because the power's out. So I came back here and raided your fridge."

Campbell wanted to scold him for opening the refrigerator, an act she and her father had avoided that morning. But, she supposed, they might as well eat up the perishables in it as quickly as possible.

"I couldn't do much," Nick confessed. "A couple of people dropped by to see if you were okay. I called the clients on today's schedule and tomorrow's to change their appointments."

"Thanks," Bill said. "Let's hope the power and the landline are back up soon."

"Yeah. I found I could get cell service if I went upstairs in your living room, near the window, or if I went outside and walked down the driveway."

"Did you talk to your folks?" Campbell asked. Nick's parents lived in Florida.

"Yeah, my mom called. They'd heard about the tornado on the news and wanted to know if we were all right. I told her we're fine. So, how's everything in the outside world?"

"Not good," Bill said. "We found a body in a flattened cottage over near the Fullers'."

Nick's chin jerked up. "What? And I missed it?"

"Sorry. We couldn't get phone service at all out there, or I'd have called you."

"Who is it?"

"They don't know yet." Out of habit, Bill headed for the coffeemaker. "Oops. Guess I'm not getting any brew today."

"You could set up the camp stove," Campbell suggested.

"Great idea. Is that in the garage?"

"I think you put it in the cellar."

"That's right." Her father paused on his way to the

doorway. "Nick, want to stick around and help us eat what's left in the fridge—or did you clean it out?"

"There's some stuff in there. Cold cuts and cottage cheese. I ate some leftover casserole, but I didn't eat all of it."

"Great. Let me get the propane stove. We can set it up in the garage. Coffee first, then whatever you two want out of the fridge or the pantry." Bill headed for the cellar door via the kitchen.

"You didn't open the freezer, did you?" Campbell asked as soon as her dad was out of the room.

"Nah, I know better than that."

"Good. I hope we'll have power back by tomorrow and we won't lose anything." She plopped down in her office chair. "Although, we could barbecue if we could get in the freezer. I know there are brats and a steak in there."

"What I wanna know," Nick said, "is how those restaurants made lunches for you to deliver if they don't have power."

"They said they couldn't open for business, but they had stuff that they didn't want to spoil, so they made sandwiches and things like that—things that didn't require cooking. And some of them have generators to run their appliances, but they still can't open yet."

Her cell phone rang, and she dug it out of her purse. The screen showed Rita Henry, their once-a-week housekeeper.

"Hello, Rita! Everything okay at your house?"

"Yes, we're fine, other than having no electricity. I'm just touching base, Campbell. tomorrow's my day to work for you, and I wondered if you wanted me to come in if we don't have power." Her voice faded in and out, but Campbell got the gist of it.

"Oh. Uh ..." She walked into the hallway and toward the front door. She could picture Rita sweeping the uncarpeted floors and trying to cobble up a meal for the three investigators. Out on the steps, she said, "What do you think, Rita? We can manage without you until the power's restored if you think that's best."

"Well, if you can get by, that's fine. But if it's back on, I'll be there."

"All right, that's settled," Campbell said with some relief. "Why don't we call each other when we get our power back."

They signed off, and she went back inside.

"So, what's the deal with the body?" Nick asked.

"They hadn't identified it when we left. The medical examiner came. Keith said they'll fingerprint the dead man and see if that will tell them who he is. But he also said autopsies will probably be backed up for a few weeks. Apparently there were other people killed in the storm."

Nick nodded soberly. "I heard three dead and something like twenty people unaccounted for. That was maybe an hour ago."

"So it may take them a while to I.D. him."

"Was it a summer cottage or year-round?"

"I think it was winterized. I saw insulation in the debris. And the Fullers know the owners. In fact, Dad said he knew them slightly. Anyway, Keith got hold of them. They were fine, and they said they'll check on their extended family, but if any of them were out there, they weren't aware of it. They've been renting out the lake house, but there was nobody booked for it this week."

"Huh."

"The police asked them to take a look at the body once it's in the morgue, and I guess the owner said he would, to see if it's anyone he knows. On a brighter note, we met that woman who looked at Tatton's house yesterday. She came to help the volunteers at the church."

"Oh, yeah?" Nick quit rocking his chair back and forth. "Was she who Bill thought she was?"

"Yes, and ... well ..." Campbell opened her desk drawer and gazed down at the photograph that had troubled her. "As a matter of fact, I'm pretty sure it was her." She took out the picture and carried it over to Nick's desk.

He took it and frowned over it for a moment. "That's a pretty old picture."

"Yeah. And that's my mother beside her when they were juniors in high school."

"No joke?" Nick looked up at her and then back at the photo. "Where'd you get this?"

"It was in a box of Mom's stuff from the storage unit. I told you we brought home some boxes."

"Yeah, and a million books. And this was in that stuff?"

"Yes."

Nick studied the picture. "I guess that's the house lady, with the dark hair, so that must be your mother."

"That's right."

"That's not your dad."

"No. I think it's a classmate."

"All dressed up for prom."

She looked over his shoulder at the four teenagers. "That's what I think."

"Who are the guys?"

"I don't know. Their names are on the back, but I didn't recognize either of them."

Nick flipped it over. "Phil and Shawn."

Campbell nodded.

"Did your mom have an old yearbook? You could find them."

"Why would I want to?"

He shrugged. "Curiosity?"

45

"I could ask Dad if he knew them."

"Why haven't you? You must have had this picture for a couple of weeks, at least."

"I'm not sure. I just wasn't ready to bring it up."

"Oh, you're afraid he'll be jealous? Bill isn't like that."

"You're right." She took the photo back. "I don't really look like her."

"Mm, your face is the same shape, but you have Bill's eyes."

"People say that." She leveled her gaze at Nick. "There's more about the body."

"What, the one out near the lake? Something important?"

"Dad thinks so. I'll let him tell you."

"Tell him what?" Bill asked from the doorway.

"The other stuff about the body. You know."

"Oh, right. Soup, do you know where the camping coffeepot is?"

"Wasn't it with the stove?"

"I didn't see it."

She sighed. "I'll go down and look for it."

"So what's up with the corpse?" Nick asked.

"Oh, I thought there wasn't enough blood."

"For what?"

Her father lifted his shoulders. "There was blood on the guy's shirt and his face and neck, okay? I didn't get a good look at his wounds, but it seemed like he'd bled enough that there ought to be blood on some of the boards and things, too."

"The stuff that clobbered him in the tornado?" Nick asked.

"Yeah. But I didn't see any blood on the pieces that were touching him. Or on the ground under him when they moved him."

"Wasn't he in a basement?"

"No, that place didn't have a cellar. But there was a crawl space under the cottage."

"And that's where he was hiding from the twister?"

Campbell lingered in the doorway. That part hadn't sounded credible to her, either.

"I just don't know," Bill said, sinking into Campbell's desk chair. "If he was hiding in that cottage, I'd think he would have either been swept outside it by the wind or have some stuff under him—parts of the floor, for instance."

"And the stuff on top of him wasn't bloody." Nick scowled. "So, what happened to him?"

Bill leaned back in the chair and looked up at the ceiling. "Well, my theory is that he didn't die in the spot we found him."

"So ... he got mortally injured somewhere else and crawled in there?" Nick eyed his boss. "That's not it, is it?"

"I don't know. But I think it's possible he died elsewhere ..."

"And someone hid the body under the debris." Nick sat there with his mouth open slightly and nodded slowly. "They used the storm to cover up what happened."

"I'm just saying it's possible." Bill flicked a glance toward Campbell. "So, kiddo, coffeepot?"

"I'm on it." She hurried to the cellarway and grabbed the flashlight.

5

Keith knocked on the McBrides' front door at eight thirty that evening. Campbell hurried to let him in.

"Hi." She gave him a quick appraisal and decided there was no sense telling him he looked exhausted. "Long day, huh?"

"Very." He pulled her in for a quick hug. "It's good to be here. I just got in from moving three families into temporary housing."

"On your day off."

"Yeah, well, that's the way it goes."

As they talked, they meandered into the large office and settled on the sofa in front of the fireplace. A kerosene lantern burned on Nick's desk, giving off plenty of light.

"Dad says we can light the fire if we want to. What do you think?"

"Might be nice."

Campbell had laid the tinder and kindling earlier. She took a long match from the holder on the mantel. The cool weather after the storm had kept the house a bit chilly, and she welcomed the bright blaze that sprang up.

"Where is Bill tonight?" Keith asked.

"He went over to check on the Hills."

"Is Miss Louanne still with them?"

"I think she and Blue Boy went home last night."

Campbell grimaced, thinking of the hardships older women who lived alone, like Louanne Vane, faced with the prospect of a prolonged power outage. Her dad had brought some large containers of water back from the lake, so they could flush the toilets occasionally. If she knew him as well as she thought she did, he'd probably offer to perform the service for a few select neighbors.

"Yeah, that cat wouldn't like it if she wasn't there to spoil him." Keith stretched his arms and yawned. "There's talk of the National Guard coming in to help remove debris. And FEMA will have representatives on site in the morning to help people apply for assistance."

"We've surely been blessed here. All we need to do is wait for the power company to get things up and running. How are your folks doing?"

"I didn't go back tonight, but I think they'll be okay. I saw that Bill and my dad got tarps covering the worst of the breach on the end of their house."

"Yeah, your dad thought they could survive until the insurance inspector can look at it." Campbell smiled. "He sure was eager to start the repairs, but your mom told him not to."

"That's right. If they want to be properly reimbursed, the inspectors need to see it at its worst." Keith sighed and sank back on the cushions. "Their bedroom is a mess. If they hadn't got up and gone down to the cellar ..."

"I know." They sat in silence for a few seconds. Campbell tried not to think about what-ifs but sent up a quick prayer of thanks. "Are you hungry?" she asked. "Dad rigged up a camp kitchen in the garage so we could heat things up and make coffee."

"I'm all right."

"I don't suppose there's any new information about the body you guys found?"

"No, nothing yet."

"Who's investigating?"

Keith's eyebrows rose. "Well, the Marshall County Sheriff's Office was first on the scene officially. As I understand it, they've talked to the state police but were told to wait and see what the autopsy says. They're swamped right now, and if there's no evidence of foul play, the county sheriff will handle it."

"And he didn't have anything on him to tell who he was?"

"Nothing obvious."

She studied his face for a long moment. "Dad really thinks that man didn't die in the tornado. At least not where y'all found him."

"I know. And I think he's got a valid point. But it's outside my jurisdiction."

"But you told them what you think, right?"

"Yes, I told the sheriff's deputies, and I told the medical examiner."

"What about the coroner?"

"Again, it's not in our county."

"Right." She mulled the situation for a minute, staring into the fire. "What about those missing people?"

Keith nodded. "There still at least eight people unaccounted for in Marshall County. Four confirmed deaths now, and about a dozen in the hospital."

"Have you checked on missing people in Calloway and other counties?"

"It did cross my mind, but I haven't had a chance yet. I think I'll swing by the station before I go home."

"If it's not too much trouble, could you call me if there are any in Calloway?"

"Sure, if you think you can get the call."

"If it's something significant and the call drops, try texting."

"Okay." Keith ran a hand over his eyes.

"Are you positive you don't want some coffee?" Campbell asked. "It would only take about ten minutes."

"No, I'd better get going. I'm on duty tomorrow, and I have a feeling it will be a long day." He stood.

Campbell jumped up. "Do they have generators at the station?"

"Yeah, they do. They probably have some coffee brewed too." He leaned down and gave her a quick kiss. She started to step back, but he pulled her in for another, longer kiss. "Talk to you later."

———

Bill called a strategy meeting as soon as Nick arrived Thursday morning. Since the power was still out, they concluded they couldn't do much in the office.

"We should check on the people involved in the insurance cases we're working on," Bill said. "Find out if they were affected by the tornado."

"I'll take the Benson case," Nick said. "If he's put in a fraudulent claim, this might be a good time to find out."

"Okay. I'm thinking Campbell might run up to Paducah."

Startled, she asked, "What for?" The trip was at least an hour each way.

"They've got power. You can take your laptop and do some work on those background checks we need."

"Oh, right. Isn't there anyplace closer?"

"Well, I tried to call the McDonald's in Benton, but they don't have power this morning either. Can you think of anywhere else?"

She shook her head.

"We'll probably get electricity back within a couple of days," Nick said. "There's not a lot of damage in this part of Murray. Just a matter of connecting us, I'd think."

"Assuming the power plants weren't hurt," Campbell said.

"It's mostly downed lines." Bill huffed out a big breath. "I shoulda bought—"

"A generator," Campbell and Nick finished with him.

Her dad chuckled. "Guess I've said that enough times. Meanwhile, I'll go around to the legal offices and the insurance agent's. If any of them are doing business today, I'll touch base and assure them we're working on their cases, even if we're out of juice here."

Although she didn't especially relish making the tedious drive to Paducah, Campbell was glad when she arrived. She was back in the world of open restaurants and stores. She not only spent time working on the background checks True Blue Investigations had contracted to do, but she had a great lunch and was able to pick up some bottled water and food that needed little preparation.

She'd just returned to the office that afternoon and was putting away the groceries when the ringing wall phone startled her. Dropping a bag of clementines on the counter, she grabbed the receiver.

"Hello?"

"Hey, it's Dad."

"Where are you? The phone's working. Obviously."

"I'm over at church. The phone's back here, too, so I decided to try ours."

Campbell stretched toward the light switch and flipped it with no result. "Well, the power's still not on. Is it over there?"

"Not yet, but this is progress."

"I got some food we don't have to cook much, and more bottled water. Oh, and I got you some root beer."

"Thanks. I'll be home soon. If Nick's not there, can you give him a call and tell him the phone's back? He doesn't have to come back to the office unless he's got something significant to report."

They spent a quiet evening by lantern light. Because of the widespread power outage, Bill had been told some of their cases could be put off for a few days. They laid out their plans for working on the "must-do" cases the next day.

"You didn't hear anything about that body at the lake, did you?" Campbell asked.

"No. I went by the police station. Keith says there are a couple of open missing persons cases that were filed before the tornado, but they're pretty sure everyone in Calloway County is accounted for on the day-of."

"I guess that's good." Campbell scrunched up her face. "Dad, did you go to your high school prom?"

He blinked at her. "Well, that's a bit out of the blue."

"Not really. I found a picture of Mom in one of those storage unit boxes. She's with that Jackie woman, and it looks like they're all dressed up for a prom or something."

"That Jackie woman is Jackie Fleming."

"Right." Campbell lowered her gaze, ashamed of herself for letting her slight prejudice against her mother's old friend show.

"I saw her again today," her father said.

Why did that make her apprehensive? Campbell gave

herself a mental shake. This was not the time to analyze her feelings toward Jackie.

"Oh, yeah? Where was that?"

"She was coming out of the Pride and Calhoun office."

"They're open for business?"

"Apparently they're carrying on with hotspots and showing houses for anyone who wants to look. Jackie said she's going to make an offer on a small house in Almo."

Campbell took a deep breath. "Dad, did you know Jackie very well in high school?"

"Not really. I mean, she and Emily hung out together a lot, so I saw Jackie quite a bit. But they were both a year behind me."

"Why didn't you take Mom to the prom?"

"My junior year we weren't going together. And my senior year ..."

"Weren't you going steady?"

"More off and on at that point. We didn't get serious until I went to the academy."

The police academy. Campbell thought about that.

"And her senior year, I wasn't around. I think she went with someone else."

"Do you remember his name?"

"Sorry, no. It wasn't important at the time."

"Wow." She sat still, trying to process that. "For some reason, I had this idea you and Mom went together all through high school."

"No. We dated a few times my senior year, but then I took two years of university. Criminal justice—it was a new program then. And then I went to the academy. That's when Emily and I reconnected and got serious."

"I see."

"I'm sorry if getting the stuff out of storage stirred up anxiety for you."

"No, it's just … well, I'm getting used to the idea of Mom dating other guys." She looked at him sharply. "What about you? Did you ever date other women?"

"Of course. I wasn't hugely popular in high school, but I did have a steady girl for a while."

"Not Jackie?"

"No, a girl named Mary Ellen Hayes. She went off to college and met the love of her life, or so I was told. He's a lawyer. I think they live in Virginia now."

"Huh. What about college?"

"I dated a few times, but I mostly concentrated on my studies. When I went to the academy, Em and I started writing, and I saw her every time I went home. We got married the next summer."

Campbell decided she would have to write this all down in her journal and ponder it. Maybe she'd go through the old photo albums again and see if she found any more high school era pictures of either parent. What was the earliest photo of Bill and Emily together? She still wondered about the boy with her mom in the prom picture.

"Was there a guy named Phil in your school? High school, I mean."

His eyes went out of focus and he shrugged. "Probably. Why do you ask?"

"Do you want to see the picture?"

"What picture?"

"The one of Mom and Jackie and their prom dates."

"Not really."

"Oh. Okay."

Her dad got up and stretched. "I think I'll head for bed."

"Take the lantern," she said.

"No, I'm good with my flashlight. You can use it."

He went out into the hall. Campbell sat there for several minutes wondering if she'd put her foot in it. Her instinct to keep quiet about the picture was right. Or did she just want to think that because it would mean Nick was wrong? When she looked at the conversation as objectively as she could, she had to admit that her dad didn't seem troubled by the fact that Emily had dated other boys before settling down with him. So why should she care?

"Hey, Nick." Campbell had waited until her dad's office door was firmly closed before she turned to her coworker for help on Friday morning.

"Yeah?" He bent over his desk, loading his day pack.

"How would I get hold of a Bowling Green yearbook?"

"Go to Bowling Green."

"Seriously. I meant without driving two hours."

"Well, some might be online." Nick straightened and met her gaze at last. "Is this about that picture?"

"Maybe."

"Hmm. Well, doesn't your dad have his old yearbooks?"

"I don't think he kept them."

"Your mother's ...?"

"They could be in the storage unit, but I haven't seen them yet."

"Is this about that Jackie person?"

Campbell grimaced, remembering her father's mild rebuke when she'd said something similar. "Actually, it's about the boys in the picture. I wondered if Jackie eventually married that guy, Shawn, she was with then."

"Okay. What's her married name?"

"Fleming."

"So search for a Shawn Fleming in Bowling Green."

It was so simple, she hated that she'd had to ask Nick to come up with the idea.

"Right. Thanks."

"Anytime. I'm heading out. Hey!" He looked up at the ceiling then grinned at her. The overhead lights had come on.

"Woohoo! I wonder if Dad knows."

"Go give him the good news. I'm out of here. Surveillance this morning." Nick swung the strap of his pack over his shoulder and slouched toward the entrance.

Campbell gave a perfunctory knock on her father's door and pushed it open. "Dad! The power's back."

He was halfway from his desk to the door already, with his coffee mug in one hand. "I know. I'm booting up the desktop, and I thought I'd get coffee."

"Yes!" She seized his mug. "What kind do you want?"

"Make me one of those mochas, and I'll go check the breaker box."

"Good. And flush the toilets." She wouldn't remind him that he'd said he didn't like sweet coffee.

"I will," he said. "Anything else?"

"Maybe draw more water, in case we lose it again?"

By the time he returned, his coffee was ready and Campbell's was dripping into her mug.

"Everything looks good." Her dad took a sip of his steaming drink and sat down in an armchair near the fireplace.

Campbell waited for her pumpkin spice java to finish brewing and carried it to the sofa near him. "Does this change what we'll do today?"

"I'll go through the cases we have open and on hold. I'll let you know if anything is urgent. Otherwise, just try to finish up those backgrounds, okay?"

"Got it. I only have a couple more things to check on, and the ones for the grocery store will be finished. We can send them out today."

He nodded. "Follow up with the clients afterward to be sure they received the files. Some people in town may not have their power back yet."

They sat companionably for another ten minutes, discussing cases and neighbors. Bill's cell phone rang, and he answered.

"Oh, hi, Vera. Campbell and I were just talking about you. Are you folks all set? Good. All right, let me know if you need anything. 'Bye, now." He tapped his screen and smiled at Campbell. "The Hills are in good shape, and Fred's going to check in with Miss Louanne." He lumbered to his feet. I'll start catching us up."

He'd barely left the room when the doorbell rang. Campbell jumped up and hurried into the hall. She swung the door open to find herself facing a man whose face held despair yet, at the same time, a kernel of hope. His short hair looked as though he'd rumpled it by running a hand through it repeatedly. In gray slacks and a light blue Oxford cloth shirt, he might have been anything from a store clerk to a surgeon.

"Hello. May I help you?" Campbell asked.

"I would like to speak to Mr. McBride if I may."

Polite, grammatical, and definitely worried.

She strove for a neutral smile and stepped back. "Of course. Come on in, and I'll tell him you're here. Mr. ...?"

"Kellum. Drew Kellum."

"Come have a seat, Mr. Kellum."

She led him into the large office and gestured toward the

61

seating area near the fireplace. When he'd headed toward the sofa, she strode across the hall to Bill's office and tapped on the door. She opened it, and her father looked at her with quirked eyebrows.

"Did I hear the doorbell?"

"You did. A Mr. Drew Kellum would like to speak with you."

"Kellum? That's the fellow who owns the cottage out near the Fullers."

"Not the crime scene? Or do you mean the one in between them?"

"The one where we found the body, although I'm not convinced it's the actual scene of the crime. Show him in here. I'll call you in if I think it would be beneficial for you to hear what he has to say."

She nodded and went back to the other room. The client was leaning toward the fireplace, hands outstretched toward its warmth.

"Mr. McBride will see you now." She smiled as he rose and walked toward her.

"Are you his daughter? I'm sorry, I don't mean to—I'm Nathan Fuller's neighbor, you see, at the lake. He recommended Mr. McBride, and he said that his daughter works with him."

Her smile felt more genuine now. "Yes, I'm Campbell McBride. It was kind of Mr. Fuller to recommend us."

"Well, I don't know how kind—to you, anyway. This whole thing is a mess. But Nathan's a smart man, and I figure anyone he trusts is worth talking to."

She nodded. "Right this way."

With the potential new client ensconced with her father, Campbell went back to her desk, but she couldn't focus on the background checks. She had a feeling they were about to embark on something more exciting. She ought to wrap up her mundane assignments and be ready.

She forced herself to go through the motions. The restored electric power and phone line helped, and within twenty minutes, she had the information she needed. After adding it to her reports, she routed them to the printer and via email to the business that had commissioned them.

Her father's door was still closed. Slightly disappointed that he hadn't called her in, she leaned back in her chair and closed her eyes. Her mind drifted back to Jackie Fleming and Nick's words.

At a ping from her computer, she opened her eyes and checked her email file. The reports had been received. She got up and went to the oak file cabinets. Her dad insisted on both electronic and paper files for all their cases, and that had saved their bacon more than once.

Fleming. An image of the pretty woman flitted through her mind. Why not look for her online? Not that she would do a background check per se, but surely it wouldn't hurt to take a peek at Jackie's social media.

It seemed Ms. Fleming was more cautious than Campbell had supposed. Her Facebook page was limited to people Jackie approved as "friends," and she didn't seem to have an Instagram account or any of several others Campbell checked.

She drummed her fingers on the desk. If Jackie's husband was dead, she would surely be able to pull up an obituary. If not, then perhaps a divorce record.

Before attempting that strategy, she did a general search for Jackie Lowe and then Jackie Fleming in Kentucky. She got a few hits. While none of the Jackie Lowes seemed right, she found more than one with the married name—a Jacquelyn Fleming in Lexington, a Jackie in Somerset, and two Jack Flemings, besides Jacklyn "Jackie" Fleming of Rockfield. That was close enough to Bowling Green for Campbell. She checked out the URLs for the woman in Rockfield and was immediately convinced she'd found her target.

One of the references led her to an obituary, which was no surprise. Campbell gave herself a mental dressing down for not trying that route first.

She stared at the screen. She'd expected to find a Shawn Fleming, hoping Jackie had married the young man she'd gone to the prom with. But no, she was listed as the surviving wife of Philip R. Fleming.

Could Jackie have married Phil, the boy her mother had dated? Campbell felt a little lightheaded. Had her mom's best friend stolen her boyfriend? She wasn't quite sure why that thought upset her. After all, if her mother had married Phil, then she wouldn't have married Bill McBride, and Campbell wouldn't exist. She scowled. It probably wasn't even the same man. Still ...

Her father hadn't wanted to see the old picture, and she'd taken that for indifference. Was it more than that? Or maybe Shawn was her mom's date all the time, and they were simply standing in the wrong order when the camera caught them.

Her dad's door opened, and voices murmured. She copied the obituary to a file she could peruse later and quickly brought her email to the screen.

"Campbell," Bill said as he entered the room, "We'll be doing some work for Mr. Kellum."

She stood and faced them as Kellum came in behind her father and stood next to him. Extending her hand, she crossed the room. "I hope we can help you, Mr. Kellum."

He was holding a folded sheet of paper, which she assumed was a signed contract.

"I hope so too," he said. "It's bad enough, all the paperwork we have to fill out for the government and the insurance company. We can't even start cleaning up the lot yet. But then I got the feeling the police had us on their suspect list."

Campbell tried not to show her surprise. Was Mr. Kellum deemed suspicious simply because he owned the cottage where the corpse was found? "Surely not."

Kellum shook his head helplessly.

"I think we can help you turn up what you need," Bill said. "We'll do our best to find evidence that someone else is responsible for the death and you're not. It will be a challenge, but I believe True Blue is up to it." He turned slightly toward the door. "We'll be in touch, Mr. Kellum. I'll email you a report daily, and we'll plan to meet again on Monday. If something conclusive comes up before then, I'll contact you immediately."

"That sounds good. I appreciate it." Kellum followed his lead and moved into the hallway.

He was soon out the door, and Campbell waited for her dad to come back from the entrance.

"What are we doing for him? I've sent the background checks and got confirmation. Is there something I should start on right away on the new case?"

"I think so. I take it you gathered Kellum and his wife owned the destroyed cottage where the body was found."

"Yes, you mentioned it. But what can we really do? I mean, the body hasn't been I.D.'d yet, and the state police are handling it, right?"

"As I understand it, yes."

"I guess you have some friends in the S.P. you can touch base with." She raised her eyebrows.

"I do, and right away I want to extend our inquiries about missing persons, to include all of western Kentucky. If that doesn't turn up any possibilities, we'll go on to northwest Tennessee and southern Illinois."

She nodded. "So, phone calls?"

"Mostly. I can check a few databases and call in a favor or two from friends who might help."

They worked for an hour and compiled a list of people unaccounted for. Campbell went to her dad's door. He was typing on his computer keyboard.

"Hey," she said. "I sent you an email. They're still looking for two people in Marshall county, and I got a couple of names from Weakley County, Tennessee, but they don't fit the profile. One's a teenager and the other is a retired woman."

Bill pursed his lips and nodded. "I got a couple from beyond the lakes—one in Hopkinsville and one in Cadiz."

"That's not far away."

"Right. And another report has been filed in Calloway since yesterday. There's a man who left home the evening of the tornado and hasn't returned."

She stared at him. "Why didn't the family report him sooner?"

"He lives alone, here in Murray. His mother's been trying to reach him, and she asked the rescue workers to check his place."

"Dad! That could be our guy."

"It could. His apartment building wasn't damaged, but he wasn't there. I think it's the best possibility so far. I just found out about it, and I thought I'd call Keith and see if he's aware of it."

"Good."

"Well, it could be that he just packed up and left to stay with friends after the power went out." Bill ran a hand through his hair. "I suppose it might be a good idea to drop by the church again. See what the scuttlebutt is among the volunteers."

"Do you think we should help this afternoon?" Campbell

asked. "I heard they're setting up a clothing drive for the tornado victims."

He clenched his teeth for a moment. "I think they probably have a ton of volunteers right now. If I thought we could save lives, then yes. But I don't. It's mostly going to be cleanup now. Government reps are setting up for business at the county courthouse here and at the one in Benton for victims in Marshall County. It's a matter of making sure they have housing and file for relief and compensation from insurance companies and FEMA and all of that."

"Okay. Because I can throw debris for a few hours if it will help."

"I think we'll do more good right here, doing our job for Mr. Kellum. My friend at the courthouse said they have a few families they're putting up in hotels, and they're trying to find vacant apartments or trailers they can put them in. We're not qualified to help with that kind of effort. And the National Guard is coming in to help with cleanup. Let's keep to our business."

She waited while he phoned Keith. So many people were hurting right now. Having a loved one missing and waiting for news was harrowing, as she well knew. A few months ago, she'd been through it. Looking down at her list of missing people, she prayed silently for each one and for the families who waited, not daring to hope but not willing to grieve.

Her dad came back into the main office. "Okay, before I forget, Keith says he'll call you later, and if he's able, he'll come by here tonight."

"Thanks."

Bill pulled over one of the extra chairs they kept to one side for clients and sat down facing her. "He says this missing man from Murray is definitely a possible match for the body, and he's going to contact the state police and maybe the Marshall

County Sheriff's Office—whoever he needs to, until he's certain who's in charge of the case. Meanwhile, we need to find out all we can about the man whose mother reported him missing."

"Do we have a name?"

"Clifton Morris. I'm going to get on that, and I want you to find out everything you can about Drew Kellum."

"The client."

"Yeah."

"I thought you were sure he knew nothing about the body."

"We can never be certain someone's telling us the whole truth. I tend to believe him, but we need to know, even if he's not involved, why someone left that body at his cottage. Was it just convenient, or was the killer already aware of that building being destroyed?"

"So, it could have been someone Mr. Kellum knows who put the body there?"

"Right now, anything's possible. It could have been someone who'd been to the lake enough to know there were some cottages out there that were often empty during the week. Or simply someone looking for a somewhat isolated place to unload a corpse. But if Kellum's associated with anyone shady, we need to know it."

"Okay, I'll find out whatever I can."

Bill nodded. "I opened a new client file and put in what details he gave me. Let's spend the next hour on those questions, if we're not interrupted. Then we'll get lunch, and I'll have you mosey over to the church afterward for a little chitchat, while I follow up on anything we find, or loose ends."

Campbell set to work learning about Drew Kellum. He was on Facebook, and she sent him a friend request. Since he'd hired her father's firm, she hoped he would accept it.

From what she could see as an outsider, she gathered that he was married. A few quick forays told her his wife was Marnie, and they had at least a couple of kids, in Calloway County schools. At least the client lived in their home county. The cottage was in Marshall, but her dad had assured her that wasn't a problem as far as their investigation went.

Marnie's social media was much more productive than Drew's. As Campbell gleaned information, she made notes. Soon she had enough details to allow her to search for other mentions of the Kellums. Their lakeside cottage was still posted on the Airbnb website, and she saved the photos she found there of the intact structure. It looked like a great place to spend a quiet weekend, much better than she would have guessed when she saw what was left of it.

Drew was employed in the city's public works department, and Marnie worked part time at a gift shop on Twelfth Street. She found Marnie's name in a news brief about a fundraiser for a summer reading program for children. Other than that, the Kellums didn't seem to feature much in the news.

She looked at the clock. Still ten minutes left until the hour expired. Tempting as it was to do more searching on Philip Fleming, she decided it would be more productive to start a load of laundry, now that they had the electricity back. She dashed up the stairs for her clothes basket. When she emerged from the laundry room a few minutes later, she met her dad in the kitchen.

"Just washing some clothes," she said.

He nodded. "Find out anything on Kellum?"

"Well, he's in public works. I'm not sure what that means."

"Probably patching potholes and mowing the parks."

"I think he's some sort of supervisor. He was listed with an email contact button on the city's website."

"Okay. Yeah, that makes sense. I wouldn't expect a run-of-the-mill laborer to be able to afford a waterfront cottage."

"On the other hand, he probably has access to things like backhoes. Equipment that would let him put that body in a place where it would be much less likely to be found. Why bother to take it all the way out to the lake?"

"Maybe, but he'd have to account for using that equipment. Easier to dump it in the path of the tornado." Bill frowned. "But why at his own property? He'd have to realize that would throw suspicion on him."

Campbell shrugged. "Yeah, it seems unlikely to me. His wife, Marnie, has a part time job in retail. They've got kids. There really wasn't a lot online. I sent them both friend requests on Facebook. Maybe I could go see Mrs. Kellum."

Bill glanced at the kitchen clock. "Well, let's get some lunch. What are you up for?"

"Is everything open? The power's only been on a couple of hours."

"Good point. Shall we cruise Twelfth Street and see who looks welcoming?"

"I'm guessing some of the fast food places are up, or the Panera Bread. Maybe the Barn Owl?"

"Yeah, something over near the campus should be open."

Along their route, everywhere they saw evidence of downed trees and limbs being removed. Lines at gas stations wended toward the fuel pumps that had been useless for three days. A lot of businesses still had not reopened, however, and they pulled in at the diner, where an OPEN flag fluttered near the door and the parking lot was full.

"Hello, Mr. Bill. Hello, Miss Campbell," said their waitress, Lily. "We have a limited menu today."

"Thanks." Bill looked up at the chalkboard over the counter. "I see you have plenty of sandwiches listed."

"There wasn't enough time to cook much for the lunch traffic," Lily said. "We're planning to have meatloaf and beef stew at suppertime, though."

The owner was flitting from table to table, greeting regular customers and nudging the wait staff.

"I see Ray is on the ball," Campbell said.

"Oh, yes. The minute the power came back, he called us all in to help get the kitchen ready and set up for lunch."

"I'm glad he did." Bill smiled up at her. "I'll have coffee and a turkey and Swiss cheese."

"Any salads today?" Campbell asked.

"No, the grocery stores aren't restocked on fresh produce yet. Sorry."

"Then I'll have the ham salad sandwich and sweet tea."

"You got it." Lily grinned and headed for the counter.

As they waited for their orders, Campbell looked around. The diner was nearly full. All of the tables and booths were occupied, and only a couple of stools at the counter were open. The customers kept Lily and two other waitresses in constant motion.

"Do you still want me to go over to the church after we eat?" Campbell asked.

"Sure. Don't spend a lot of time there, unless you get wind of something pertinent. And call me right away if you do."

"Got it."

Lily set their drinks on the table. "Your sandwiches will be right up."

When they'd finished eating, another couple claimed their table as soon as they stood. On the way out, Bill paused to speak to an off-duty police officer.

"Hello, Matt. Campbell, you've met Matt Jackson?"

"Yes, hello." She smiled and bit back the impulse to call him "Detective Jackson." Maybe he didn't want the world to know he was a police detective when he was off duty. On the other hand, Murray was a small enough town that anyone up to no good probably knew him by sight.

"Miss McBride," Jackson said. "All well at your place?"

"We got our power back this morning," Campbell said.

"Consider yourselves lucky. Mine's still out, but seeing progress gives me hope."

Bill laughed and patted Jackson's shoulder. "See you around, Matt."

They went out to Bill's car. He drove home so Campbell could get her own vehicle to take to the church. She ran upstairs first and sorted quickly through the clothing in her closet. She pulled out a nearly new top and a sweatshirt from Feldman University, where she'd taught for two years.

When she arrived at the church, she found the attached gymnasium had been set up with racks and tables of donated clothing. One of the social committee members was seated at a table just inside the door.

"Hello, Campbell."

"Hi. I just brought a couple of items."

"Great. People need casual clothing right now. Just hand those to one of the volunteers."

"Okay." Campbell hesitated. "Have you heard anything about more victims?"

"I think they've found most everyone in Calloway County. I'm not sure about Marshall. I guess you heard about the man they found dead in the debris over there?"

"Yeah. So tragic." Campbell headed for the area displaying women's clothing and was surprised to see Jackie Fleming sorting through the blouses and T-shirts.

7

"Oh, hi, Campbell," Jackie said with a big grin. "I'm just trying to find a few things to take to a single mom with a seven-year-old daughter. Their trailer was demolished in the storm, and they lost everything."

"Is the mom my size? I've got a couple of things here."

"Those look perfect for her. Thanks." Jackie took the top and the sweatshirt from her.

"Have you found a place to live yet?" Campbell asked. "I think Dad said you've made an offer on a house."

"I have, but I'm staying with my daughter and her husband until the closing. We're a little cramped, but we're getting by. How about you and Bill?"

"We're fine. Keeping busy. We have some active cases we're working on."

"Let's see, wasn't your father a cop when he married Emily?"

"That's right. He kept that job in Bowling Green for a long time, but after Mom passed away, he left it and moved over here."

Jackie nodded and held up a striped T-shirt. "This looks about the right size. What do you think?"

"It's fine. I'd wear it."

"Me, too, especially if I was as desperate as Rhonda." Jackie added it to the tote bag she was filling. "I'd better find some things for her little girl. She needs some clothes she can wear to school." She turned around to where the girls' clothing was laid out by size. Lifting a pair of jeans, she checked the tag. "Too big." She put them back on the pile. "The church has done a great job, collecting so much in such a short time."

Campbell followed along with her as she made her way down the table.

"Did you know my dad when you were in high school?"

"Not well. I knew who he was. He wasn't in my class, and I don't think he and Emily were dating then." She pounced on a pair of red shorts. "Perfect. Oh, and here are some long pants the same size. Now we need shoes."

"Your husband—he was Phil, right?"

"Yeah."

"Because I found a picture in my mom's stuff of you and her and two guys named Phil and Shawn."

Jackie's face lit up. "Really? Sweet. That must have been from the time we double dated to the spring dance. Funny, though. Emily went with Phil that night. Shawn was my date."

"So, that Phil was the same Phil you married? There weren't any last names on the picture."

"If he's a cute boy with blond hair and big blue eyes, he certainly was."

Campbell nodded. Jackie didn't seem to be embarrassed about ending up with Emily's date.

"Now, let's see ... they've got new undies and socks over there ..."

"Well, I should get going."

"See you around," Jackie said with a distracted air.

The pastor's wife was working her way among the tables with a clipboard in her hand.

"Hi, Campbell," she called.

"Hi, Nancy. You look busy."

"Terribly so. We're letting tornado victims come in and pick what they need, but we're also taking lists and trying to fill orders for those who have a hard time getting around right now. Several people's cars were ruined, and some are being housed some distance away from where they lived."

"That's rough."

Nancy nodded. "We were told the county's looking for RV trailers people want to sell or donate, for temporary housing. Most of Murray proper escaped the damage, but a few neighborhoods were hit hard."

"Uh ... is there a collection spot for donations? I mean cash."

"Cash is very helpful," Nancy said. "It allows us to buy specific things people need, like over-the-counter medicines and baby formula. I've heard some of the stores are starting to reopen. We're hoping Wal-Mart and Kroger and some of the others will be open for business by tomorrow. Waldo made a run to Paducah this morning to pick up some things we couldn't get locally."

Campbell opened her purse and unzipped the compartment for her wallet. "Wow. Yeah, I'd like to help. I need to get back to the office, but here." She pulled out all the bills she'd been carrying and handed the twenty-two dollars to Nancy. It wasn't much, but it would buy a few things someone needed badly.

"Thanks so much, Campbell. I'll make sure this gets into the right place."

With a nod, Campbell headed out to her car. She hadn't

exactly found any information that would help with their case, but Jackie and Nancy knew her father had found the body. She was sure they would have mentioned it if they'd heard anything connected to the incident.

"If that money isn't in my account by tomorrow—"

Campbell froze. Someone was speaking vehemently, and she thought she knew who. She looked cautiously around. Sure enough, Jackie stood between a red pickup and her green Toyota. Her back was turned, for which Campbell was grateful, and she held a cell phone to her ear. Not such a good place for a private conversation. Her acid tones, however, were anything but private.

"No, you listen to me. I've had enough of this stalling. If you can't hold up your end of the bargain—" Jackie gave a grunt of disgust and lowered the phone.

Campbell hunched down and opened her car door as quietly as she could. She needn't have worried. Jackie was stalking back toward the church, never giving a glance around the lot.

As Campbell adjusted her seat belt, her own phone rang— her dad's ringtone. She quickly responded.

"Listen, are you done at the church?" he asked.

"Just going to head home."

"Well, Keith called, and they may have a lead on Clifton Morris."

"That's the man reported missing in Calloway, right?"

"Yes. He didn't give me any details, and I'm stuck here. I've had two calls in the last hour from local insurance companies that would like us to help them verify some claims. One of them's sending an agent here to meet with me in about five minutes. Uh-oh, the doorbell. That's him. Skip by the police station and see Keith, okay?"

"Will do." Campbell started the engine. She'd gladly visit

Keith. Her job assignments usually had her doing tedious online research or watching people who claimed to have been injured, as Nick was doing today. She seldom got to track her favorite guy down at his workplace. She smiled as she turned toward Fifth Street.

She and Keith both had demanding jobs, but they managed to find bits of time to spend together. They'd met when she first moved to Murray to live with her dad and started working with him. Over the past few months, they'd grown close.

At first she'd thought she wouldn't stick around long. Her father's house was a stopping place until she could find a new job in the teaching field, preferably at the college level. But the deeper she got into investigating, and the better she got to know Keith, the more she wanted to stay in Murray.

Her thoughts drifted back to Jackie's overheard words. It sounded like a fight over money, but with whom? Her husband, Philip Fleming, was dead. Was she having money troubles with her daughter? A few minutes ago, she'd sounded as if she got along fine with her daughter. She'd mentioned being crowded but hadn't implied any real problems.

And she was moving over here from Bowling Green to be near her daughter. Surely they weren't at each other's throats over money. Campbell pulled into the lot before the police station and grabbed her purse.

The officer on the front desk called Keith, and he came to the lobby to take her back to the office he shared with three other officers. He got coffee for them both and sat down behind his desk.

Facing him, Campbell thought how comfortable he looked in this environment, and he should. He was good at the job, and he had enough experience to be confident in that ability.

"Dad said you had some information."

"Yeah. It's not really much, but we're working on it." He

pecked a couple of keys on his computer. "Clifton Morris was reported missing by his mother this morning. She lives in Mayfield, which is in Graves County, but she'd been trying to get hold of Clifton for a couple of days. Since the tornado, in fact."

"That's understandable, considering how badly Mayfield was hit by the 2021 tornado."

"Right. After she couldn't get him on the phone for twenty-four hours, she started to panic. Yesterday afternoon, she drove to his apartment. It's over off 16th Street."

"Okay. Did the storm do damage over there?"

"No. Well, not much, just heavy wind damage. The usual fallen trees, power lines down, and so on. We took a couple of reports over there. A car was hit by a big oak limb, and a roof was damaged, those sorts of things. But his apartment seemed to be okay."

"Did his mother have a key?"

"No. She called us, and we were really busy, but in light of the body being found and people unaccounted for at the time, the sergeant sent a patrol officer to go over and check things out. He got the landlord to open the door, and everything seemed normal, but Morris wasn't there."

"So, maybe he just went away for a couple days but didn't tell his mom where he'd be?"

Keith nodded. "That's what we're thinking. His mother told us where he worked and gave a list of friends she knew of. At this point, we're following up on that when we can, but we don't have any evidence of criminal activity."

"Did his mother look at the body?"

"We didn't ask her to do that. We took some fingerprints from his apartment and compared them to the dead man's. They weren't a match."

"So, that pretty well rules out Morris for being the body in the cottage."

"It does. Officer Mills also got two photos of Morris from his mother. She put them in our system with her report, and I looked at them. He's not our victim."

"What now?"

"We keep looking, but frankly, we're so busy right now, that we don't have a lot of time to be looking for someone who may be missing of his own free will. Morris could have gone off camping with some buddies or be staying with a girlfriend. His boss told us he had this week off, so that's our guess. He's on vacation and didn't bother to tell Mom his plans."

"Maybe she's an interfering mother, and he wants his space."

Keith smiled and gave a little shrug. "You may be right. Anyway, there was one bit of a surprise. Morris has a record. We've had him in before on drug charges."

"Huh. Did Mom know about that?"

"She knew he'd had a run-in with the police once before. She didn't know it was actually several times. Anyway, we've taken note of it, and if his name shows up anywhere, we'll be right on it. In the meantime, there's not enough there to justify us putting much time in on it when we have so many other things to do."

"Okay. I'll tell Dad. Thanks."

Keith rose when she did. "I wish I had more for you. At least you now know not to waste a lot of time trying to figure out if the dead man is Morris."

He walked with her to the hallway. Before opening the door to the lobby, he looked over his shoulder and whispered, "Can I see you tonight?"

Campbell smiled. "Sure."

"I don't know how many restaurants are open yet, but ..."

"I know the Barn Owl is, but it was packed this noon. Why

don't you come and have supper with Dad and me? We can watch a movie if you want, or just hang out."

"I think I'd like that." He reached for her hand and gave it a squeeze.

From the look in his rich brown eyes, she suspected he wanted to kiss her, but Keith was a stickler for rules, and he wouldn't do that here at the police station.

"I should be able to get off by six, but I'll call you if I'll be later."

She smiled. "I'll be looking forward to it."

————

"There. *Good* coffee."

Campbell smiled and accepted the mug her father handed her. He was definitely happy they had the single-cup coffeemaker up and running instead of the old camping coffeepot.

She detailed what she'd learned from Keith and was telling him about her visit to the church when the house phone rang. Her dad picked up the receiver.

"True Blue Investigations. Yes, Hayden."

Campbell recognized the first name of attorney Hayden Nesmith, of the legal firm Lyman and Nesmith. The agency had handled several cases for them since she'd arrived in Murray.

"Is that so? Hold on a second, Hayden. My daughter, Campbell, is with me, and she's working with me on the Kellum case. Do you mind if I put you on speaker?"

After a second, Bill pushed a button on the phone base, and Mr. Nesmith's voice boomed into the room.

"Mr. Kellum says he told them repeatedly that he doesn't know who the dead man is, or why he was on his property. But they kept at him, so he clammed up and asked for me."

"Sounds like a wise choice," Bill said. "But you said they're questioning Mrs. Kellum too?"

Campbell raised her eyebrows, and her dad nodded.

"Yes, two state policemen picked her up at home after they'd pulled Drew off the job."

"Where have they got them?"

"We're in Benton. They're using the county sheriff's facilities here."

Campbell puzzled over that. The Kellums lived in Murray, which was in Calloway County, but the dead man was found in Marshall County. She supposed that accounted for their choice of venue for questioning people. Still, she thought it would have been much simpler to talk to Mrs. Kellum in her home. It almost seemed the officers were trying to intimidate the couple.

"When I got here," Nesmith continued, "I was allowed to speak privately to my clients, of course, but separately."

"They won't let Mrs. Kellum be with her husband?" Bill scowled.

"That's right. Kellum's adamant they're being framed. Mrs. Kellum is just confused and scared."

Bill sighed. "Well, I suppose they want to make sure the two aren't in collusion."

"You've got the officer's insight into that," Nesmith said. "To me, it seems heavy-handed."

"Maybe a little. But it does tell us one thing."

"What's that, Bill?"

"The state police are taking the death seriously as a murder now. If they still thought that man was a tornado victim, they wouldn't be pushing so hard on the property owners."

"I think you're right."

"Look," Bill said, "Campbell and I have done some digging on the Kellums. We haven't talked to Mrs. Kellum in person yet, but so far we haven't turned up anything suspicious. They've been renting out the cottage for a couple of years now, and they both have decent jobs. Anyone could have driven out there and seen the empty cottage—or the flattened cottage, for that matter, if they were desperate to dump a body during the storm or right after it went through."

"It seems to be common knowledge that the Kellums didn't actually live there."

"Yes," Bill said. "From what Drew told me, they went out there sometimes if it wasn't booked for a few days, but mostly it was an income property for them. They'd put a lot into decorating and maintaining it."

"If we knew who the dead man was ..."

"We had hopes for an I.D. A man was recently reported missing in Murray. But a contact of mine at the Murray P.D. told us this afternoon that the dead man wasn't the one reported missing."

"Bill, if anyone can find out who that guy is, you can."

"Thanks for your confidence, Hayden. We'll keep on it and hope the autopsy's completed soon. The police aren't holding the Kellums, are they?"

"No, they talked to Mr. Kellum again after my confab with him—with me present, of course. He had nothing new to tell them, and they let him go. His wife had already been released and was waiting for us in the lobby. They're both home now, but they're shook up."

"Understandable."

When he and Nesmith had signed off, Bill huffed out a big breath and met Campbell's gaze.

"I don't like them putting pressure on the Kellums."

"What can we do?" she asked.

"Work harder at finding the truth."

8

That evening, Keith was determined not to bring up the case of the dead man at the cottage. Instead, he hoped for a low-key, relaxing time with Campbell. However, Bill pretty much monopolized the conversation during dinner, and he hadn't gotten the memo on topics.

Campbell didn't seem to mind. She let her dad take the lead in catching him up on their findings and probing about the police's work on the missing persons case.

"Well, if Clifton Morris turns up somewhere else, I don't know where to look next for the dead guy's I.D.," Bill admitted.

"We're pretty sure Morris is not the dead man," Keith said. "There are still a couple of folks not accounted for in Marshall County, though."

"Yeah, and a few east of here. I guess we look harder at those."

Keith looked over at Campbell, and she smiled at him.

"Rita Henry didn't work this week, but I scraped up a dessert. We had some canned pie filling on hand, and I made us a cherry pie. Frozen crust, I'm afraid, not scratch. Nowhere as good as your mom's, I realize, but ... Are you up for it?"

"I'm up for anything you cooked." Keith stood and picked up his empty plate.

Campbell took hers and her dad's and led the way to the kitchen.

"Coffee?" she asked as she set the dishes in the sink. "It's ready, and I know Dad wants some."

"Sure."

She took two mugs from the cupboard and handed them to him. "Could you get it, please? I'll dish up the pie."

A couple of minutes later, they returned to the dining room with the dessert and coffee. Bill was scrolling on his cell phone.

"Nick's pretty well wrapped up his surveillance case," he said as they placed his plate and mug before him. "Oh, thanks. That looks really good." He went for the coffee first.

Keith and Campbell resumed their seats, and Keith dug into his pie.

"That's delicious. My compliments to the chef." He winked at her.

She smiled. "So, Dad, we thought we'd watch something tonight. Maybe a mystery. Want to join us?" Campbell took a bite of pie and gazed invitingly at her father.

Bill laid down the phone and picked up his fork. "Aw, no thanks. I think I'll close out the report and the invoice on Nick's case."

"You should take some time off and relax in the evening," Campbell said.

"I want to get a jump on things in the morning. We got a little behind this week, with the power outage. You kids go ahead."

Campbell arched an eyebrow at Keith.

He grinned. Man to man, Bill treated him as an equal, but when considering Keith and Campbell as a couple, he often designated them "the kids." It usually annoyed Campbell, but Keith didn't mind. Bill was at least twenty years his senior—and besides, when he was old and his daughter was middle-aged, Bill would probably still think of Campbell as a kid.

A few minutes later, he retreated to his office. Keith lingered at the table with Campbell.

"So, how are you doing with your mom's stuff?" he asked.

"I've unpacked everything we brought home. I guess I'm ready for another load, whenever Dad and I have time."

"Did you talk to him about your mother's friend?"

"Jackie? Yeah, we talked about it. He seems to like her. And he didn't really remember the guy with Mom in the picture—Phil. Did I tell you that he's the guy Jackie married?"

"You did. That seemed to bother you."

"Well ..." She sighed. "I guess I don't like to think of some calculating girl stealing Mom's boyfriend. Jackie seems nice, but—"

"But."

Her face wrinkled.

"You don't like her."

"I'm trying not to let the prom picture thing influence me."

How hard was she really trying?

"Are you sure it's not just the idea of your dad being interested in another woman?"

She sat there for a moment with her mouth slightly open. "I don't think he's interested in her *that* way."

"Don't you?"

The skin between her eyebrows furrowed. "Should I?"

"Let me ask you this. Has Bill gone out on a date since you've been home?"

"No."

Keith nodded.

"What?" Campbell eyed him almost with distrust.

"I'm not saying this is bad in any way, but I happen to know he's had at least a couple of dates within the last ... oh ... two years, let's say."

"With whom?"

He smiled at her painfully correct grammar. He'd have shouted, "With who?"

"I'm not sure. There was one woman he met at your church. He told me another time that he went to dinner with a lady, but he didn't tell me her name."

"So, two different women?"

"I think so. Bill and I are friends, but we're not besties, if you get my drift. I think his old buddy Mart would be the one he'd pour out his troubles to."

Campbell nodded slowly. "Dad and Mart are still close, even though they live a couple hours apart now."

"They worked together a long time in Bowling Green, and Mart came running when your Dad was missing and you needed help."

"Yeah. He's my Uncle Mart, even though we're not really related."

"There you go. And you've known Mart all your life."

"Just about." She glanced quickly at him as a thought struck her. "I wonder if he knows Jackie Fleming."

"Hmm. You could ask him, if you feel that strongly about it. But you'd never met Jackie Fleming before this week."

"I don't think so. If she and Mom were still good friends when I was a teenager, I'd have known."

"I rest my case." Keith picked up his mug and sipped the tepid coffee.

"Keith?"

"Hmm?" He met her gaze.

"There's something else. About Jackie, I mean."

He waited patiently. Campbell always told him what was on her mind, but in her own good time.

"I heard her talking on the phone to someone. Just a few words. I didn't try to overhear, but it was in the parking lot when I left the church today." She frowned, thinking about it. "She sounded really angry."

"It happens."

"Yes, and I have no idea who was on the other end of the call. But ..."

His raised an eyebrow, still waiting, and she pulled in a deep breath.

"They were fighting over money."

"Okay." Keith took another sip of his coffee then set down the mug. "Ordinarily, I'd say forget it."

"Ordinarily, so would I. I mean, it's none of my business. But—but she could be ... you know."

"A person of interest?"

"Exactly. I mean ... she knew where that cottage was. And she was very upset."

"Do you remember her exact words?"

Campbell grabbed her mug and took a sip of her coffee. "It was something like 'You better put that money in my account by tomorrow.' I don't think that's exactly it." She shook her head. "But she sounded belligerent. She said, 'No, you listen to *me*.' Like that. She was definitely arguing."

They sat in silence for a long moment. Keith tried to make something of it, but it could be nothing—a domestic squabble, a scolding to her adult child. Or something more sinister. He could understand Campbell's unease at hearing that bit of conversation.

"She's house shopping, right?" he asked.

"Yes, and she'd told me a few minutes earlier that she's found a place. Dad had said she was going to make an offer on a house in Almo, but I'm not sure if that's the one she's settled on. I didn't ask for details. She did say she's staying with her daughter and son-in-law until she closes on her new place."

"Where do they live? In Murray?"

Campbell nodded. "Somewhere over near campus, I think."

"Have you met the daughter?"

"No." After a moment, she said, "Do you think I should? I could go talk to her, I suppose. Maybe I could think of a reason to go there. Taking something to Jackie, or whatever."

"I don't know if it's a good idea or not."

"Well, so far, most of the information I have about her is what I've heard from Dad, which is minimal, and her husband's obituary."

"What was his name?"

"Philip Fleming. He died about eight years ago."

To her surprise, Keith fished a small notebook out of his pocket and wrote in it.

"Daughter's name?"

"I don't know," she said. "I copied the obituary file, but I can't remember her name. The file's in my laptop."

He nodded and replaced the notebook in his pocket. "I'll look up the obit."

"I don't want to be nosey or pushy," Campbell said.

"I know. But it does sound a little ... not suspicious exactly, but as if not everything is peachy keen with her."

"Yeah." She let out a quiet sigh.

Keith was glad she'd told him about her misgivings. Campbell wasn't usually one to borrow trouble. There could be something there to worry about, and not the simple fact that her mother's prom date had gone on to marry Jackie.

He reached for her hand. "Let me know if you find out anything else that tells you she's pertinent to the case—or completely removed from it."

"I sure will." She smiled. "So, do you want to watch a movie?"

"If you do."

"That sounds like 'not really' to me."

"No, it's fine, if that's what you want to do. I thought you might want to talk some more."

She eyed him closely for a moment. "Thanks for taking me seriously. Is Jackie Fleming a suspect in that murder?"

"I'm not investigating, remember?"

"No, but you hear things."

Keith leaned back a little, but he couldn't put real distance between them. "Okay, I believe Detective Roland is keeping an open mind, especially since they haven't identified the victim yet."

She pounced on it. "Detective Roland? He's state police, right?"

"Yes, he took over from the Marshall County Sheriff's Department."

"I'll bet they loved that in Marshall County."

Keith shrugged. The law enforcement agencies usually worked together without a lot of wrangling, but sometimes personal jealousies came into play. He drained his mug. "Shall we load the dishwasher? I pictured us getting a little time not talking about murder tonight."

"Sure." She smiled and stood.

Keith moved around the table, took her dad's pie plate from her hand, and put it on the table. He slipped his arms around her and drew her close. Campbell returned his kiss warmly. He held her for a long moment.

"There, that's more like it," he whispered.

———

When Nick arrived the next morning, Bill strolled into the main office.

"Good morning. We've got a missing persons case I'd like you to handle." He placed a memo sheet on Nick's desk. "You'll need to set up the file and enter everything you check as you go. Campbell and I will be gone all morning."

Campbell said nothing, but her pulse accelerated.

Frowning over the memo, Nick said, "Missing heir?"

"That's right. The testator died three months ago, and the law firm hasn't been able to locate the principal heir. They want us to take a crack at it. You're good at this kind of thing, so see what you can find out."

Nick nodded. "On it."

"Great." Bill turned to Campbell. "Could you fix a couple of coffees to go?"

"Sure, Dad. Where are we heading?"

"Cadiz." He turned and walked across the hall to his private office.

Nick's eyebrows rose nearly to his hairline. "You think that's about the d.b. from the tornado?"

"I don't know, but there was someone unaccounted for over there." Campbell hurried to the kitchen for travel mugs.

By the time she had her cup and her father's ready, he'd come into the kitchen carrying his laptop case. He opened a cupboard and scrounged a half box of granola bars.

"Is this going to be a lengthy surveillance?" Campbell asked. Usually, if they traveled out of town they ate out.

"I don't think so, but we don't know what the situation is over there."

"True. Was there a lot of tornado damage in Cadiz?"

"Not so much in town, but I understand there was quite a bit on the side nearest Lake Barkley, and the farm we're going to is over that way."

She caged her curiosity until they were in Bill's car and on the road toward the Land Between the Lakes. To reach Cadiz, they had to cross both Kentucky Lake and Barkley, not to mention the recreational area between them. In less than half an hour, they rolled off the second big bridge and passed a marina and a few other businesses along Route 68.

"So, you said we're going to a farm." Campbell hadn't spoken during the first part of the journey, as her father had seemed deep in thought. Driving and thinking were enough for him to worry about, she'd decided when they set out, but she couldn't stand it any longer.

"That's right." He glanced at her and then back at the road. "That unaccounted-for person we heard about the other day ..."

"Is he still not found?"

"They haven't found a trace. Crawford Steele."

Campbell cocked her head toward her shoulder. "And he's a farmer? Help me out a little here, Dad." He was usually much better at briefing her on cases.

"He's got soybeans growing this year. The day of the tornado, he left to go over to Murray. Said he was going to look at a tractor. The next morning, he wasn't at the farm, and his pickup was missing."

"So, he went tractor shopping and didn't come home?"

"Right."

"Was there damage at his farm?"

"Some. We'll see the extent of it when we get there, I guess." Bill put on his turn signal and slowed, then turned onto a smaller paved road.

"Who reported him missing?"

"An employee who showed up to work the next morning. He couldn't find Steele, and he saw the damage. He reported him to the county sheriff over here."

Campbell looked around. They were passing a large cornfield on one side and a wooded area on the other. A swath of downed pine trees cut across the road diagonally, and on the other side, the corn was flattened in a fifty-yard strip for the width of the field.

"Looks like the twister came through here."

"Yeah, I think several touched down." Bill grimaced and slowed for another turn, eyeing the phone he'd set up to use for GPS. A mile farther on, he turned the opposite way, onto a gravel lane.

"I see a barn." Campbell leaned forward and squinted. "Looks like the roof is damaged."

"Yeah." Bill drove slowly, surveying the land and buildings as they pulled into the barnyard.

A dusty brown pickup sat before a small brick ranch house. When Bill parked a few yards away, a man in jeans and an MSU Racers T-shirt got out of the driver's seat. Campbell walked toward him, beside and a half step behind her father.

"McBride?" the man asked.

"Yes. Bill McBride." He flipped an arm toward Campbell. "My daughter, Campbell."

The man nodded. "Jason Hawley."

"You reported Mr. Steele missing."

Worry lines creased Hawley's brow. "Didn't know what else to do. I tried to call him after the tornado came through, but I didn't get an answer. When I drove over, nobody was here. Now it's been three or four days, and I still haven't heard from him. That's not like Crawford."

"Mr. Steele lives alone?" Bill asked.

"Yeah, his wife left him a while back."

"How far back?"

Hawley huffed out a breath. "Maybe five or six years."

"Do you know her name?"

"Lindsey."

Campbell pulled out a pocket notebook and wrote it down, along with Hawley's name.

Bill flicked her a sidelong glance and resumed his questions. "When was the last time you saw him?"

"Monday afternoon, like I said. We'd been working together most of the day. I left around six. We'd heard the severe weather watch, and we kind of joked about it. Not too funny, though, considering the history in these parts. Just kind of nervous joking, you know. Around four, Crawford said he was going to look at a used John Deere over in Murray. I finished up what I was doing and went home."

"And what were you doing?"

Hawley swung around and jerked his head toward an old tractor with faded red paint sitting in front of the barn. "Working on that thing. He really needed a better one."

"So, was the one he went to look at a new one? At a dealership?"

"No, he saw an ad and called the guy."

"Okay," Bill said. "Do you know where, specifically, it was located?"

"Not really. He said Murray, but I suppose it was probably outside of town."

"Hmm. Where'd he see the ad?"

Hawley shoved his hands in his pockets. "Don't know for sure. Online, I'd guess. There's a couple of forums farmers get on. And there are ads on bigger sites. You know, Craig's List and all that. But I don't think he'd go looking for a tractor there."

"All right. You said it was a John Deere?"

"Right. I don't know what model. Does it matter?"

"It might."

Sighing, Hawley looked off toward the bean field beside the barn. "He said it was about ten years newer than this one—which would put in around 1990, I guess, and maybe a little bigger. I dunno."

"That's helpful. Thank you."

Campbell glanced up from her note-taking and caught Hawley giving her a once-over. He quickly shifted his gaze back to her father.

"Does Mr. Steele have any family over in Calloway County?" Bill asked. "Or particular friends he might have gone to when the bad weather came up?"

"Not that I know of. He might, I s'pose."

"I see the barn was damaged."

"Yeah, he'll need to do some serious repair on that one side of the roof. I don't think this place was directly in the path of the twister, but we got some real strong wind."

"Where do you live?"

Hawley gave his address and noted it was about four miles away. "My house wasn't damaged, but the wind took some shingles off my shed, and a couple of trees in my yard lost some branches.

"Do you have access to the house?" Bill nodded toward Steele's ranch.

With a little smile, Hawley said, "Crawford never locks the back."

"Have you been inside?"

"I went in before I called the sheriff, just to make sure he wasn't in there. And when a deputy came by, he went in and looked around."

"I wonder if I could take a look? You could come with me. I

just want to see if he left any indication of where he was going."

"I s'pose."

Campbell followed her father and Hawley around to the back of the house.

"You take a look in the kitchen, Soup," her dad said. "I'll go on into the living room."

Not really sure what she was looking for, Campbell looked around the none-too-neat counters. Dirty dishes were stacked in the sink. Steele apparently had no dishwasher. The table was cluttered with dishes, food packages, and newspapers. Gingerly, she began to sort through them. Three newspapers emerged, with the latest one dated Monday, the day before the tornado.

Her father had said he would try to find an indication of where Steele went. She leafed through the newspaper to the classified section, but no ads were marked. She looked for an agricultural category but didn't see one. The "for sale" column contained dozens of ads, and she skimmed them as fast as she could. Nothing.

Bill and Hawley came in from the next room.

"Find anything?" her father asked.

She lowered the newspaper. "No. I was checking the ads in here. Apparently he takes a Hopkinsville paper."

"Well, if he was heading for Murray, I doubt he was chasing a Hoptown ad. I'm guessing he either found it online or heard about it by word-of-mouth."

"The cops took his computer," Hawley said.

Bill nodded. "I think we're done here. Jason, I'll call you if anything comes up."

"Thanks. I hope you find him. I don't know what to do."

"Are there any animals here on the farm?" Campbell asked.

"No, he just did row crops and wheat." He shook his head.

"I just don't understand it. I mean, where's his truck? You know what I'm sayin'?"

"We do," Bill replied.

As they drove out, Hawley headed toward the disabled tractor, his shoulders drooping.

9

Leaving the Land Between the Lakes, Bill drove off the Eggner's Ferry Bridge and signaled to turn right toward Aurora.

"Thought we'd drop in on Nathan and Angela for a minute and see how they're doing."

Campbell liked that idea. All she'd heard about them since the day the body was discovered was in brief reports by way of Keith. As much as she trusted Keith, she wouldn't mind seeing the couple for herself.

As he made the turn, a green Toyota passed them, heading the other way, toward the bridge.

"Hey! Was that Jackie?" Campbell craned her neck, but the car was too far past them for her to make out any details.

"I didn't notice," her dad said.

"Why would she be out here in the tornado zone? You know she looked at that cottage in Aurora, next to the Fullers'."

"Well, she didn't turn this way, did she? Most likely she's headed back to Bowling Green. She said she made an offer on a house. She probably has things to settle up over there before she moves."

Campbell faced forward, still frowning. He was probably right. She shouldn't be so quick to jump to conclusions. She watched out the window as they passed the Hitching Post, a motel, and a campground entrance. At the Aurora One Stop, a big sheet of cardboard with the words "NO GAS" painted on it was fastened to each fuel pump. A big Closed sign hung on the door of the store. Across the street, the Dollar General was closed too.

"What are all these people doing for gas and food?" she asked.

"Donations," her father said grimly. "I guess they'd have to go at least as far as Benton or Murray for gas."

"We have it pretty good, considering."

"You got that right." He glanced her way. "We've been blessed. Only three days without power and water, and now everything's back to normal for us."

"Well, sort of."

A short distance beyond, a crew was cutting up and removing fallen trees at the side of the road. When they reached the Fullers' camp road, Bill swung the car onto it. Campbell was silent as he slowly drove over the gravel road. They passed the dwellings with obvious damage they'd seen on their previous visit. So far, it seemed no one was beginning renovations. Orange flags warned people not to approach the place where a power line was down between the road and a cottage.

At last, Nathan and Angela's home came in sight. The two demolished cottages to the left looked almost the same as they had that first day—piles of wreckage. The one on the opposite side of the Fullers' house, away from the destroyed ones, seemed untouched.

Nathan was on a ladder, hammering something near the damaged roofline of his house. Bill parked and got out, waving to his friend.

"What are you doing up there?"

"Trying to fix it enough so the roofers can do their job next week," Nathan replied.

"Can I help?" Bill asked.

"Sure. Hand me that stud."

As her father fetched the board Nathan needed, Campbell strolled around to the steps leading up to the screened porch.

She found Angela inside, folding a basket of clean laundry.

"That looks promising," Campbell said.

Angela chuckled. "I went to Keith's this morning to take a shower and wash some clothes. We've got the generator keeping us going, but it's not big enough for me to run the dryer and the microwave at the same time, so we're being cautious."

"Oh, I see. No power yet out here, then?"

"No, and they're saying it could be weeks before they get all the downed lines up again. We don't usually think about how fragile our infrastructure is."

"True." Campbell snatched a bath towel from the basket and began folding it. "We only had to make do for three days, and it was too long. Listen, you're welcome to come to us anytime for stuff like that, you know. In fact, why don't you come have supper with us tonight? We'd be happy to give you a home-cooked meal."

"You're a sweetheart. I'll tell you what I'd love most."

"What?"

Angela's cheeks scrunched into an apologetic smile. "Showers tomorrow morning before church."

"Done. Come whenever is good for you."

"Is eight o'clock too early?"

"No, that's perfect. I'll have a hot breakfast for you. And you have to come home for dinner after church too."

"That's too much."

Campbell shook her head vigorously. "It's not too much. And if Keith's not working, he's invited too. I'll call him and let him know."

"We should just go to his house, but he's working tonight, and I don't want to bother him in the morning. And he only has the one bathroom." Angela pulled out one of Nathan's T-shirts and shook out the wrinkles.

"You come to us, and that's final. Anything special you'd like to eat? Anything you've been missing?"

"Not really."

"Okay, I'll use my imagination."

Bill and Nathan came through the screened porch, with Nathan carrying his toolbox.

"There, I think the roofers can get on with it, whenever we can get them out here."

"They said next week." Angela hovered between hopeful and dismayed.

"I know, but there's so many people needing them right now." Nathan set down the toolbox. "If they make it here on Monday, I'll be ecstatic, but I'm not going to count on it until I see them drive in. Meanwhile, I'll work on the guest bathroom. I don't want to start Sheetrocking until I know we're good and dry in here."

"You're doing the inside work yourself?" Campbell asked.

"I hope so. Can't afford to hire it all done."

"We should get some money from the insurance company, but that could take some time." Angela handed each of them a bottle of water. "Sorry it's not cold. We don't have any ice."

"Hey, we've got to get going." Bill waved away the water

bottle, and Campbell thought it was mostly so he wouldn't deplete their stock.

"I've invited Angela and Nathan over tomorrow for showers in the morning and dinner after church." Campbell was relieved to see her father's smile.

"Great. And if you need help Monday, let me know, Nathan. I can rearrange my schedule."

His offer surprised Campbell, but it was like him to inconvenience himself for a friend.

"Keith promised to come bright and early Monday morning," Nathan said. "He's got the swing shift and doesn't go in until three. We should be all right until we get to the finish work. Then I could really use you, Bill."

"Sure. I'd be happy to help."

They said goodbye and went out to the driveway. Bill paused, looking over toward the ruined cottages.

"I keep praying for the Kellums, and the people who owned that other cottage," Campbell said.

"Me too. If I'd thought about stopping in here, we could have brought the Fullers more water and something fresh to eat."

"I'll work on the meal prep tonight and get a few extra things ready for them to take home after Sunday dinner."

Her dad nodded. "Good. Better invite Keith too."

"I will."

They got in the car, and Bill said, "I'll see what we've got for containers. Nathan said they're using lake water to flush toilets. The incoming line was damaged, but he rigged the generator to pump lake water. They could get some jugs of our tap water tomorrow for other stuff—washing dishes and tooth brushing, stuff like that."

"He sounded as though they had it under control."

"I suppose you're right. We'd best get home and start working on what leads we have on Steele, the farmer."

———

Campbell planned the meals she would serve the next day with the care of a writer plotting his next novel. Nothing heavy for breakfast—they would all be dashing around, getting ready for church. She decided on cinnamon rolls, scrambled eggs, and bacon. She could set the dough for the rolls and cook the bacon tonight. Their midday dinner would feature pot roast, which she took from the freezer and started cooking in the Crockpot.

When she was satisfied with her menus, she tapped on her dad's door. "Any luck on the tractor ads?"

"I've narrowed it down."

Campbell set a plate with a sandwich and a few carrots and chips on her dad's desk.

"Look here." He pushed his chair back a little and waved toward his desktop's screen. "That one down Hazel way has got to be it. After I eat, I'll drive down there and see if I can find it."

"Have you got enough gas?" Campbell asked. "I'm not sure all the stations are up and running yet. Remember how everything was still closed in Aurora?"

"I'll take care of that first."

"Okay, what do you want me to do while you're gone?"

"You mean after you fix me a travel mug of coffee?"

She grinned. "Yes, that's what I mean."

"First of all, I thought Nick would be here when we got back. Can you check in with him?"

"I'll try. It might be hard to reach him, depending on where he is."

"Thanks. And maybe touch base with the Murray P.D. on Clifton Morris. And do you want to call the state police to check if they've found Steele?"

"The Trigg County Sheriff's Office is probably keeping track of who's unaccounted for over there. They'd probably know if he's been found."

"Okay, call them," Bill said. "And if you get the run-around, ask Keith or Matt Jackson if they've heard anything. They can check inter-agency files." He took a big bite of his sandwich.

The house was quiet after he left. Campbell used the house phone to call Nick. He answered in muted monosyllables.

"What's up?" Campbell asked.

"I've got a lead, but something's fishy."

"How fishy?"

"Well, the guy we're looking for was living in Murray until the first of June. He gave up his apartment then."

"End of the school year?" Campbell hazarded.

"Maybe. He had been a student at MSU, although his family's in Louisville. And he wasn't done with his degree when he left Murray. Odd that he gave up his digs."

"So you think he wasn't planning to come back to school this fall?"

"I checked with the registrar, and he did enroll for classes at the end of the spring semester, but he hasn't shown up or paid anything since. He's got student loans and a grant waiting to be claimed, but time's running out on those. If he doesn't claim them within a couple of weeks, they'll disappear. And classes have already started. If he's a no-show ..."

"Huh. And you've talked to his family?"

"Yeah. The law firm had already gotten all they could from the family, but it wasn't much. That's why we have the case."

"Right." She rubbed her scalp, thinking. "What was his major?"

"Uh ... theater, I think? Something like that. This would have been his third year."

"Maybe he decided he'd learned enough in the classroom and headed for New York. Or Hollywood."

"Could be," Nick said. "I wonder if I can get anything from the Screen Actors Guild or something similar for stage actors."

"Worth a try. Well, I'm in the office, and Dad's gone to Hazel looking for our missing man from Cadiz. We think he went there to look at a used tractor on Monday."

"Okay, I'll probably come back there to work online."

After closing the call, Campbell sat for a moment to gather her thoughts. Nick didn't always work Saturdays, but if they had a demanding case, they all kept working regardless of the calendar. Nick and her father must feel finding the missing heir was urgent. She took a deep breath and focused on her own assignment before calling the Marshall County Sheriff's Department.

"Still three unaccounted for in Marshall County," the spokesperson told her after she'd identified herself with True Blue Investigations.

"I see. What about other counties? There was a Mr. Crawford Steele in Trigg County, for instance."

After a pause, the man said, "Nope, haven't ticked him off yet."

"Are there still some in Calloway?"

"Two."

"Could you give me their names, please? We've been working on the Clifton Morris case."

"Uh ... I think something came in on Morris. Hold on." Half a minute later, he was back. "Morris is at Lourdes in Paducah."

"Oh." She frowned over the large hospital's name. "He was injured?"

"He's in the cardiac unit, so I'm guessing he had a heart attack. I really don't have any details."

"Thank you, I'll call the hospital." Although she figured that would be like calling a tree stump since she wasn't a relative. Maybe Keith could help her out. A heart attack for a man in his thirties was off the normal paradigm. "Was there another missing person in Calloway? I thought he was the only one."

"Uh ... you're right. All accounted for over your way now."

As she hung up, not truly satisfied, the doorbell rang. She scowled toward the hall door. They kept the front door unlocked in the daytime, and a sign at the front entrance instructed clients to walk in. She got up and hurried to the door. A middle-aged woman stood on the porch, her face taut.

"Is Mr. McBride in?"

"I'm sorry, he's not."

"Oh. I'm Marnie Kellum, and I hoped to see him. The police have taken my husband to Marshall County again. I've phoned our attorney, but Drew wanted me to see Mr. McBride."

"Won't you come in, Mrs. Kellum? I'm Bill's daughter, Campbell, and I work with him. Have a seat, and I'll give Dad a call. He may be back soon. I'll find out for you."

"Thank you."

Campbell led her into the main office and settled her on the sofa near the fireplace.

"Can I get you some coffee or iced tea?"

"Coffee would be wonderful."

"It will be just a minute."

As the beverage brewed, Campbell used her cell phone to contact her father.

"Yeah?" Bill said in her ear.

"Mrs. Kellum's here, Dad. She wants to see you. It seems the police have taken her husband in for questioning again."

Bill sighed. "Okay, I'm just leaving the farm in Hazel. I should be there in twenty to thirty minutes. If she doesn't want to wait, I can go to either her house or the Marshall County P.D. to meet her."

Campbell relayed the information to Mrs. Kellum and asked if she wanted to wait.

"I—yes, I think so."

"That's affirmative, Dad," Campbell said, turning away from the woman. "And FYI, I think our Calloway County missing person is accounted for, but I need to double-check that."

"You mean Clifton Morris?"

"That's the one."

"Okay, I'm on 641, and I'll be there soon."

Campbell took the coffee mug to Mrs. Kellum. "My dad will be here in just a few minutes. Is there anything else I can do for you?"

"Oh, I don't know, dear. Are you an investigator too, or just the secretary?"

"I'm an investigator. I work with my dad, and I'm studying to take the state exam soon, to make it official."

She nodded. "You're familiar with what happened out at our cottage?"

"Yes," Campbell said. "Actually, I was there when the body was found."

"It's such a worry. Drew would never have anything to do with something like that, but the police keep after him."

"They're just trying to get at the truth, Mrs. Kellum. I know sometimes it seems as though they ask the same questions over and over, but they hope you'll remember something that had slipped your mind before."

That and slip up if you're hiding something, she thought, but she kept that tidbit to herself.

The front door opened, and she strode to the hallway, hoping her father was back. Instead, Nick greeted her. He came in drooping, with a backpack slung over his shoulder.

"Hey, Professor. What's up?"

"We have a client in the office," Campbell said quietly. "Mrs. Kellum. She's waiting for Dad, and he's on his way back from Hazel."

"Okay. What do you want me to do?"

"Nothing. I mean, just go ahead with your assignment. You said you had some things to check on the missing heir."

Nick scowled. "Yeah, something's funny there."

"What do you mean?"

"Well, his last known address, the one the family gave the attorney, was in Kirksey, which is just up the road. But apparently he left that apartment earlier than I thought. Right when school got out in May. I haven't found out where he's living now, but I don't think he's left the area."

"Why is that?" she asked.

Nick left out a deep sigh. "One of his friends says he saw him a couple months ago, in Murray. I've got to follow up on every little scrap of information I can find."

"Right."

They walked into the office together, and Mrs. Kellum looked anxiously at the newcomer.

"Hello," Nick said with a tight smile. He went to his desk and set his water bottle and laptop on the surface.

Campbell gave Mrs. Kellum a smile she hoped looked professional and went to her own desk. She and Nick plunged into their work without further conversation. After ten minutes, Campbell got up and offered Mrs. Kellum more coffee. She declined but asked for the restroom.

"Of course." Campbell guided her to it and then fixed herself another cup of coffee.

"So, what's up with her husband?" Nick stage-whispered.

"The police are questioning him again."

"She seems worried," Nick observed.

"I guess I would be too, if the cops kept pulling in someone I was close to." She lifted her chin a little. "Where's this family that's looking for the missing heir? Louisville?"

"Yeah."

"Weird. I mean, why did he come way over here to go to college?"

"Maybe to get away from the family? I don't know. But they haven't heard from the guy for over a year. There was some kind of brouhaha in the family, I think."

"Were his parents paying for his education?"

"No. He worked at one of the car dealerships for a while, but now ... who knows?"

"I thought he was a student."

"He was. But he had a part-time gig with the auto dealership. The boss says he gave notice and left in mid-May."

"So, he'd been full time at the university and part time at the car place. That's a lot."

"Yeah. Maybe he couldn't earn enough part time to pay his tuition, so he quit school to take a full-time job somewhere else and stack up some money."

"I guess that makes sense, if his parents weren't helping him."

Nick shook his head. "His dad's not in the picture. Divorced. Mom's living hand-to-mouth. He was on his own to pay for college."

She frowned. "I'd think he'd want to learn something more profitable than theater."

"All these artistic kids hope to hit it big."

"I suppose. But he's an heir—does he know it?"

"Doubt it, or he probably would have showed up to claim

the inheritance."

"Who died?"

"His grandmother—that is, his father's mother."

"That doesn't add up. The father's not in touch."

"Yeah, but it seems Grandma wanted to give the kid something, even though she hasn't seen him in twenty years, and her own son abandoned his kid."

Campbell scrunched up her nose. "Are they sure the boy's father is alive?"

"Yep, but he wasn't even named in the will. Wasn't happy about it either, I understand."

"Hmm. I wonder if he'll come begging at his son's door—provided you can find him. Is it a large estate?"

"They didn't tell me how much, but I gather it's substantial." At the sound of a vehicle driving in, Nick leaned forward and peered out the window. "Bill's home. He's going into the garage."

"I'll go head him off at the pass." Campbell hurried into the kitchen. Her dad was just coming in through the door to the garage.

"Hey," he said. "Mrs. Kellum in the office?"

"The bathroom. She didn't say much to me, Dad."

"Okay, show her into my office when she's ready. I'll get an update, I'm sure. Oh, and I'll be here tonight, but I'm going out to dinner tomorrow."

It wasn't unheard of—Bill often had lunch with a business contact or a client, and occasionally dinner.

"Nathan and Angela are coming to dinner."

"I meant in the evening. Jackie and I are trying a place in Draffenville."

She watched him stride into the hallway and turn at the doorway to his private office. Realizing her mouth hung open, she closed it firmly.

10

When Mrs. Kellum emerged from the restroom, Campbell met her with a restrained smile.

"My father's back now. Right this way."

After delivering the client, she peeked into the main room. Nick was clicking away on his computer, frowning in concentration. She about-faced and went back to the kitchen, where she took out her phone.

Keith answered his cell promptly, and she blurted, "Keith! Dad's made a date with Jackie Fleming. Dinner tomorrow night."

"All right." He paused, and she didn't say anything, hoping for more. "I hope they have a nice time," Keith said.

"But she's—what if—" She slapped her free hand to her forehead. "This is so bizarre. She's a *suspect*."

"Bill knows that."

"He doesn't date clients."

"Is she a client?"

"Well, no, technically not. The client's wife is in talking to Dad right now. But, Keith—"

"Breathe, Campbell."

She hated that he'd said it, but she complied.

"Better?" he asked a moment later.

"I guess."

"Good. Now, I've got to get going, but I want you to do two things. First, sit down and pray about this."

She sighed. "You're right. I haven't really asked God what He wants for Dad. I guess that's pretty selfish of me. What's the other thing?"

"Wait until your father's free, and then talk to him calmly about it."

She needed five seconds before she could answer that one. "I don't know if I can. Stay calm over it, I mean."

"Then keep praying about it until you can. Then ask him." She heard voices in the background, and Keith called, "Be right there." In a normal tone, he said, "I'm sorry, but I really need to go."

"All right, I understand. Thanks."

She stood in the kitchen for another minute, sucking in deep breaths and thinking. Finally she shut her eyes. *Lord, help me to behave like an adult. And if there's anything I can do to help Dad and support him, show me how. If Jackie is a good thing for him, could You please clue me in? And if she's not … well, I just have no idea what to do, if anything.*

For a moment, she stood in silence, then added, *And please, Lord, help me not to mess things up for Dad or make him feel bad. Help me to be a good daughter.*

She wondered if, on their date, Bill and Jackie would discuss their grown daughters and their relationships with them. She hoped not. Chagrined, she realized she ought to have asked Keith about Clifton Morris instead of blathering on about her father's love life.

After nearly half an hour, Bill's door opened. He came out with Mrs. Kellum, talking to her in upbeat tones.

"We'll stay on it," he said. "I'm sure Mr. Nesmith is doing a good job, and I'll be surprised if Drew isn't home within a few hours."

When he'd seen her out, Campbell jumped to her feet.

"So, what happened, Dad? Why was she here?"

Bill came to the doorway and leaned against the jamb. "Seems old Drew has a bank account that's separate from the couple's joint checking account."

"So? You keep the True Blue finances separate from your personal accounts."

"I do, and so do most other business owners. But Drew doesn't own a business. He works for the county's public works department. The police investigators were looking into his finances and found this other account. There were some transactions between that and his regular account, transferring money back and forth."

"Money laundering?" Nick asked from his desk.

"They're not saying that. At least not yet. But they took him in to give them an accounting of his funds. Mrs. Kellum is upset because she knew nothing about this extra account. She's adamant that Drew wouldn't do anything underhanded."

"But you're not so sure," Campbell said.

Her dad shrugged. "I didn't say that, but I did lay out a few possibilities to her. And I encouraged her to sit down with Drew when he gets home and let him explain it all to her."

He sounded like Keith—talk things out. Practice openness and honesty in your relationships. Campbell was all for that. But what if the other person wasn't?

"If she holds the joint checking account with her husband, how could she not know when he transfers money?" she asked.

"He does the bank statements. Mrs. Kellum doesn't like math. She does carry a checkbook and occasionally writes checks on the joint account. At the end of each month, she gives Drew her check register, and he balances the statement."

"That's convenient," Nick said.

"Yeah, for him." Campbell made a wry face. "I don't like math either, but I do it."

"Because you have to," Nick pointed out. "If you were married, you wouldn't both balance the books."

She sighed. "No, but I'd at least stay aware."

Bill held up both hands. "I can't defend their accounting methods. All I know is, Drew Kellum has a funny way of doing things, and his wife was in the dark."

"And you think he was doing something illegal," Campbell said.

"I'm not saying that, and I certainly didn't say it to his wife. I did assure her that, with the police looking into it, I'm sure all will be explained soon. She and Drew can take it from there."

Nick scowled. "I just hope he can pay us. They might freeze his accounts."

"Well, we have the retainer." Bill shrugged. "If we don't get an explanation within a couple of days, I'll go see Hayden Nesmith."

"But he can't tell you private stuff." Campbell looked to her father to confirm that.

"No, he can't, unless Drew okays it. Since Drew is our client and Hayden's client, we can probably persuade him to keep us both in the loop. And ... there's one other thing Mrs. Kellum told me."

"What?" Nick asked.

"Her brother has a police record. He lives in Madisonville, but she felt it was significant enough to tell, and I'm glad she did. He's a felon with a prison record for theft and half a dozen other charges, and he has a reason to visit this area."

"An excuse, you mean," Nick said.

Campbell leaned her head to one side. "Did we check on missing persons in Madisonville?"

"No, the tornado didn't go there. But I'll be checking up on him this morning. I want to make sure he's still alive, for one thing."

"Didn't Mr. Kellum view the body? Surely he'd recognize his bother-in-law."

"You'd think so, but I want to be certain. And if he is where he's supposed to be, I'll do a complete background on him anyway and try to find out if he was over this way around the time of the storm. You two keep on with what you've been doing."

She nodded and then eyed him keenly. "What did you find out about the tractor guy?"

"He did go to Hazel and look at the John Deere late Monday afternoon. He said he wanted it, but it was too late to go to the bank. He gave the owner two hundred dollars in cash and said he'd come back the next day. But he never showed."

"Because of the tornado," Campbell said.

Bill shrugged. "The owner figured his power was out and he couldn't do the banking yet. He'd tried to call with no result. But after three or four days, he figured Steele had found a better deal and wasn't coming back."

"So, if he left Hazel at five or five thirty, he should have reached home before the tornado struck."

"Yes, he should have. I figure he made at least one other stop on his way home."

Campbell nodded. "But where? And he did give him two hundred. Seems odd that he didn't at least touch base with the seller."

"Everything about this case seems odd," her dad replied.

"Whatever," Nick muttered. "Look, Bill, can I talk to you for a couple minutes about this missing heir?"

"Sure."

Nick got up, lifting his laptop off the desk, and the two of them went into Bill's private office. Frustrated, Campbell turned back to her own computer, determined to find at least one useful thing before she quit for the day.

———

Sunday felt almost normal to Keith. He slept until eight, showered, ate, and went to church. His parents were already there.

"Are you going to the McBrides' with us for dinner?" his mom asked as he settled into the pew beside her.

"Planning on it."

Bill and Campbell attended another church in town, a couple of miles away. Just about everyone in Murray went to church somewhere, and there were plenty of congregations to choose from. Keith had considered switching to Campbell's church, but that would be awkward if they broke up. He'd decided to wait and see, though things looked promising.

Campbell understood him. Sometimes he felt as if she could read his mind. And he was beginning to feel as if he knew her well—her moods, her fears, her aspirations, and her passions—sometimes better than she did. He smiled, thinking of her uneasiness where her father's romantic life was concerned. She'd lived apart from Bill too long, that was all.

Soon she would realize her father was an excellent judge of character. Bill McBride was about the last man on earth he'd expect to fall for a gold digger or a con artist. Not that Bill had much of a stash for an underhanded woman to covet. And no matter what other relationships he formed, he would always love his daughter fiercely.

The music director took his place before the choir, and Keith forced his attention back to the service. He'd get some time with Campbell later, and Bill could take care of himself.

———

Campbell's culinary efforts were well received, and she could feel the tension seeping out of her muscles. Angela and Nathan were perfect guests. They were appreciative without laying it on too thick, and they always brought interesting topics to the conversation.

When Keith asked Bill about his current case, his mother caught her breath with a slight frown.

"We're digging away at it," Bill said. "Mrs. Kellum was quite upset yesterday, but I managed to calm her down. I'm sure you know about her husband's secret bank account."

"I sure do." Keith shook his head, frowning. "He told the investigating officer he was socking a little away for their retirement. He wanted to surprise Marnie, and he was afraid that if she knew about it ahead of time, she'd spend it. Apparently she's always longed for a trip to Europe."

"Yeah, she told me. I'm not sure I buy Mr. Kellum's story a hundred percent, but it could be true. Anyway, Campbell and I are doing a check on her brother—"

"The one with the drug record?" Keith asked.

"That's right. Seems he was busted again the day before the tornado. I'm trying to find out if they kept him in custody."

Angela drew the line. She sat up straight, her shoulders rigid. "Really, boys, do you have to talk business at the table?"

Campbell held back a laugh. Talking shop didn't bother

her, but she could understand Angela not wanting corpses and felons to be discussed while she ate her dinner.

"Well, I've been saving up for something special too," Nathan said with a bright smile.

Angela eyed him doubtfully. "You have?"

"Yes. I plan to take you shopping in Paducah later this week."

"I didn't think we had any extra money, what with the house repairs and all."

Nathan grinned. "As soon as we get that insurance check, we're going. Your birthday's next week, and I want you to buy yourself whatever duds you want for fall."

"That's really nice," Campbell said, patting Nathan's arm. "You're an inspiration, thinking of your wife in the middle of all these challenges."

Keith also seemed willing to turn away from the morbid topics and join in giving his mom more pleasant things to think about.

"I already have your present. Got it a month ago."

Angela blinked at him. "What is it?"

"I'm not going to tell you. You'll have to wait until your birthday."

She put a hand to her heart. "Oh, you're cruel."

"What's on your wish list?" Campbell asked her.

"Not a session with a psychic, I'll wager," Bill said with a sly smile.

"You've got that right!" Angela looked toward the wall, and her eyes lost focus. "I guess a new bedspread and maybe a new dresser. Our bedroom took a hard hit from the tornado."

"You get anything you want," Nathan said. "Just don't start redecorating until the roof is tight again."

Bill helped himself to more of Campbell's pot roast. "I

think they should start naming tornadoes, like they do hurricanes."

"There are so many of them," Angela said in protest.

"I know. That would help us keep 'em straight."

"What would you name this one, Dad?" Campbell asked.

"Hmm, something tough. Maybe Tornado Bogie."

She laughed. "Not Cyclone Bill?"

———

In the restaurant that evening, Bill lowered the menu and smiled at Jackie across the table. "What do you think?"

"The seafood looks good. I think I'll try the crab cakes and the salad bar."

"Sounds good." He laid the menus on the edge of the table, and their server materialized almost at once to take their order. When the waitress had gone, he reached for his coffee cup, took a sip, and said, "How is everything going, Jackie?"

"As well as can be expected, I guess." She sounded uncertain, a little adrift.

"Not as well as you'd hoped?"

She let out a heavy sigh. "Bill, I can't lie to you. Everything's been chaotic. I can't wait to be done in Bowling Green and settle in over here."

"Away from ..." He eyed her keenly.

Her lips quirked into a bitter smile. "Can't fool you, can I? You were always a perceptive guy. I should have come to you for help a couple of months ago."

"What happened then?"

She hesitated, took a sip of her sweet tea, and set the glass down with a clunk. "I like you, Bill."

"I like you too." He tried not to react to the non sequitur. Usually such statements were followed by a "but."

She gazed into his eyes for several seconds, as if trying to decipher him and decide how much to say.

"Look, Jackie, you don't have to tell me anything you don't want to."

"That's just it. I want to. In some ways, I feel like I have to. I can't start a relationship with someone without clearing the air first."

"Clear away."

She puffed out a breath. "Okay, here goes. I had a lot of ... problems ... with my ex."

"You mean Phil? I thought he died several years ago."

"He did. Phil wasn't the problem. It was the man who came along after Phil who gave me grief."

"Okay." Bill resorted to his coffee once more as a distraction while he thought that through.

"I started dating this man—Sidney Galt is his name. We met at an art opening. I'd gone to Louisville to spend a long weekend with an old girlfriend of mine, and she wanted to take in this museum opening. Very posh."

Bill nodded.

"Sid introduced himself to me and spouted a lot of stuff that sounded very intelligent and insightful at the time." She smiled ruefully. "Maybe it was the wine. I don't drink often, but it was part of the atmosphere, you know? Anyway, he seemed like a charming, sophisticated man. And I admit, I was lonely."

"Understandable." Bill had felt occasional moments of oppressive loneliness. His solitary life after Emily's death had changed him. He'd gone through times when it seemed he was absolutely abandoned. That was one reason he'd quit his job and moved to Murray. He wanted a fresh start, where people he met wouldn't think of him as "poor Bill, widower." He met Jackie's gaze. "I went though some of that myself."

"When Emily died?"

"Yeah. I moved over here, and a month later I was sure I'd made a mistake. But gradually ... I don't know. I made friends. I got busy with my clients. And then I hired Nick Emerson. That boy was a handful, I'm telling you. But there were times over the last three years when, if he hadn't been there, I'd have gone nuts. As it is, he'll probably drive me nuts."

They both laughed.

"But now," Bill said, "Campbell's moved home. Things are going really well. She likes working with me, and I feel as if I've got my family back."

"Yes. I thought if I moved closer to Lucy and Garrett, I might have some of that too. She just found out she's pregnant, and I'll be a grandmother next spring." Jackie smiled, perhaps the most lovely and genuine smile he'd ever seen on her face.

"Is she your only child?" Bill asked.

Jackie's face darkened. "No, Phil and I had three. Thank God, Melissa moved to California."

"Why do you say that?"

"Oh, I miss her and all that. But it spared her from the debacle I got into this summer."

The waitress came with their food, effectively squelching the conversation for a while. After Bill had eaten halfway through his dinner and been assured by Jackie that hers was delicious, he wended back to the topic.

"You started to tell me about Sid, the art connoisseur."

She rolled her eyes and wiped her lips with her napkin. "Right. Sid. He gave me a real rush, and I was flattered and probably a little giddy. Phil had been dead more than seven years, and it was thrilling to have a handsome man so obviously interested in me."

Was that how he felt when Jackie appeared at the house

next door, beautiful, classy, someone he categorized as nearly Emily's equal?

"So, anyway, one day he says, 'Let's get married.' I was shocked. I mean, it was too soon. I knew that. I know it even better now." Her lips twisted. "But ... I thought about it, for like, two days, and then I said, 'Okay, let's.' My son, Michael, was horrified when I told him."

"He didn't like Sid?"

"He was cagey toward him. He thought I'd been bowled over by a smooth talker and should take more time. And there was a little bit of a feeling that, in his eyes, I was dishonoring his father. Lucy was more sympathetic. She thought Sid was a nice guy. She told me, 'Mom, he obviously makes you happy. If this is what you want, go for it.' So I did."

Bill stared at her. "You got married."

"Yes. June twenty-ninth."

"But your name's still Fleming."

"I used his name for about a month. I was Jackie Galt. All my friends were so happy for me." Her mouth twisted. "Until they weren't."

Reaching across the table, Bill took her hand. "What happened?"

"I found out I wasn't really married."

"Oh." That was like ice water in the face, but Bill didn't want to pull his hand away as if he were disgusted.

"Yeah. I learned Sid had two ex-wives already, only one of them wasn't actually an ex. They'd never finalized their divorce."

"Was it a mix-up?"

"I hoped it was. But no, Sid knew he was committing bigamy."

He sat back, carefully releasing her hand. "How did you find out?"

"A friend of a friend. Someone told me about his wife, Alanna. I said, 'You mean his ex-wife, right?' and this person said, 'Is she? She's still wearing the ring.' Well, as you can imagine, I marched home to pin Sid down about that. I demanded to see the divorce papers, and he couldn't produce them. Finally he admitted we'd jumped the gun. Alanna didn't want a divorce and was dragging it out forever. According to him, she wanted to take him for everything he had."

"She may succeed after that stunt."

Jackie grabbed her iced tea and gulped what remained in the glass. The waitress appeared to refill it and Bill's coffee.

"I told you I have an appointment tomorrow," Jackie said. "It's with Pastor Flynn and his wife. I knew I needed to talk to somebody about all this."

Bill sat back in his chair. "That's a good choice. Waldo and Nancy are terrific. And listen, if I can help you with anything ..."

She let out a puff of a laugh. "Be careful what you ask, Bill. Sid is giving me a hard time over this. He's the big reason I'm moving. The embarrassment is bad enough, but ... well, there are other complications. Financial ones."

"I see."

For a moment she gazed at him, assessing him. "I believe you do. You probably see this stuff all the time."

"Not all the time, but often enough. You've seen a lawyer, I take it."

"Yes. I had one in Bowling Green for the marriage thing, but I wanted someone over here for the money matters, so I don't have to keep running back and forth."

"Probably a good idea. And if you need investigative services, True Blue is discreet."

"Thanks. Just talking to you is a relief. I didn't like

renewing our friendship without you knowing. It didn't seem fair, and I was nervous about how you'd take it."

"You don't have to be nervous with me."

A weary smile crossed her face. "I think that's true, and I'm so grateful. Thanks for listening."

"Anytime." He looked at their plates. "How about dessert?"

"Oh, I don't know."

"Tell you what, let's get out of here and get some ice cream cones. There's a park just up the road. We can eat them there and take a little stroll. Get some fresh air."

"Sounds good."

Bill grinned and signaled for the check.

11

Monday morning began peacefully enough, with Campbell following leads online for their various cases while her father tried to link Crawford Steele, the tractor buyer, to the unidentified body in the Marshall County coroner's morgue.

Nick had been tapping away on his keyboard, but he gave a little gasp of surprise and jerked his head up, gazing across the room at Campbell. "I think this guy is in Nashville."

"Who, your missing heir?"

"Yeah. He was always into music, and I just found a social media account with a picture that looks like him. Sort of. With longer hair and a beard, and he looks as though he's dropped twenty or thirty pounds since the latest photo we had, but ... yeah." He squinted at his laptop screen.

Campbell got up and walked over to his desk. Leaning in over his shoulder, she saw a young man picking at his guitar, his mouth wide open in song. His eyes were nearly shut as he howled at the moon—or the upper balcony. The picture gave every indication that he was in the midst of a concert. The lights glared, and behind him another young man sat at a drum kit with his sticks in action.

"Show me the other picture," she said.

With just a few clicks, Nick brought up what looked like a class photo, side by side with the musician's picture. She studied them, trying to decide whether the guitarist with the beard could possibly be the clean-cut student from several years later.

"Call me skeptical. How long ago was the first picture?"

"Three or four years. Hold on, there's a snapshot of him that's a little bit newer, but not as clear."

He brought up another photo. This time the young man leaned over the hood of a vintage Mustang, going at the windshield with a squeegee. The hair was a little longer than in the school picture, but she could tell it was the same kid.

"Put that one with the music picture."

Nick complied, and she looked back and forth between the two photos.

"I don't know. There are similarities, but all that facial hair and the expression make it really hard to tell. And you're right, he's thinner."

"Maybe he hasn't been eating well since he joined the band. Blaze Collins. I'm going to find out everything I can about this guitar player. I think it's him. And if he's in a band and getting some gigs in Nashville, I ought to be able to find out something definitive."

"Blaze Collins?"

"Yup, that's what this caption said."

"That wasn't his name before, though."

"No. I think he's changed it. At least, he's started using a stage name. He used to be Barry Capps."

"Hmm. Same initials."

Nick chortled. "Exactly. I'm digging into the band,

especially the bass guitarist." He looked up at her, his eyes gleaming. "Maybe Bill will stand me for a trip to Nashville."

"That's a day trip," she said, "not a stay-overnight-at-the Gaylord."

"Well, it's worth a try. I'll do my research first and ask him when I've got something to convince him it's a good investment—and pick a modest hotel."

"I still say it's a day trip. It's only a hundred miles, you know."

"It's more than that."

"Not much. Two hours and you're there."

"Why don't you go with me?"

"Why would I want to?" A road trip with Nick was about the last thing she wanted to do right now.

"Aw, Nashville's a lot of fun. When was the last time you were there?"

"Oh, let's see." Campbell tapped her chin and looked up at the ceiling. "I went over to the airport three or four years ago."

Nick barked a derisive laugh. "You gotta *do* stuff there."

"I don't think I can afford to. Besides, you don't even know you're going yet."

"Yeah, well, buzz off and I'll find a reason."

She shook her head and ambled back to her desk, but she was smiling.

A few minutes later, her dad looked in on them.

"So, Nick, what have you got on the Capps case?"

"Oh, about that." Nick jumped up. "I'm pretty sure he's landed in Nashville. Now, I was thinking ..."

He followed Bill out into the hallway, and the door to the smaller office closed mercifully as he rattled off the facts he'd found on the musician Blaze Collins and why he was convinced the young man was Barry Capps.

Less than five minutes later, her dad was back, striding into the main office. "Campbell! They've found Crawford Steele."

"Where?"

"In the woods, in his smashed pickup. After he looked at the tractor in Hazel, it seems he stopped for dinner and a few drinks in Murray. The bar shut down when the tornado warning came through, and he headed for home."

"He should have found a shelter."

Her dad nodded grimly. "Apparently he got across the Land Between the Lakes, and then the twister picked up his truck and dropped it a quarter mile off the road, on the other side of Lake Barkley. Less than ten miles from his home, in fact."

"That was a week ago. I take it he didn't survive?"

"No. He was still strapped in when they found him. They think he died almost instantly. One of the clean-up crews found him this morning."

She sighed. "At least we know he wasn't the man in the cottage. Is someone calling his friend, Justin?"

"The Marshall County Sheriff's Office already spoke to him. He was able to give them some information about Steele's family, and they hope to notify the next of kin today."

She frowned, trying to pull out what little they'd learned about the man. "He was divorced."

"Yes, and he had two kids. They're likely to inherit the farm, but they're minors."

Campbell shook her head. Would the mother move her kids back to the farm they'd left several years earlier, or would they sell it? No matter, so far as True Blue Investigations was concerned. That part of their case was a dead end.

"We're no closer to learning who that poor man was than we were on Wednesday."

Bill huffed out a breath. "Too true. Look, what do you think about this musician Nick dug up? Do you think it's really the missing heir, or is Nick just looking for a joy ride to Nashville?"

"I don't know, Dad. He had similarities to Barry Capps, but I couldn't really tell."

"Okay. I'll tell Nick to get some more background on the singer before I let him go over there."

"Yeah. Maybe he could find Blaze Collins's agent or the band's manager. Someone like that."

"Good thinking. I'll tell him." Bill wheeled and headed back across the hall.

Nick came out a few minutes later, looking glum. Campbell said nothing as he returned to his desk and bent over the keyboard, frowning in concentration.

At noon, her dad came out of his hidey hole again. "Thought I'd get lunch for everybody. What do y'all want?"

"Is August Moon open?" Campbell asked.

"I'm not sure. Why don't you give them a call? If you place the order, I'll go pick it up."

In no time flat, she established that their favorite Chinese restaurant was, indeed, open and serving their full buffet menu. They each chose a couple of dishes, and she added fried rice and a couple of appetizers.

"Great! Back in half an hour." Bill tossed his car keys in the air and caught them as he headed out.

"Wasn't last night his big date?" Nick asked after the garage door closed.

"Uh-huh."

"How'd it go?"

"He didn't say."

Nick's dark eyebrows morphed together. "You didn't ask?"

"I was asleep when he came home, and no, I didn't ask. I figure if there's something he wants me to know, he'll tell me."

Nick shook his head.

No way would she tell him how badly she'd wanted to ask. As far as Nick was concerned, she couldn't care less about her father's love life. Somehow, she didn't think she was fooling him. This morning, it had almost seemed as though her dad was avoiding personal conversation. She lowered her head and forced herself to get on with her work. Her stomach rumbled, and she hoped he returned soon with their lunch.

"Eureka!"

Nick's shout jerked Campbell from the notes she was studying in the Kellum file.

"What?"

"They're playing in Paducah. How did I miss that before?"

She frowned at him. "Either explain yourself or be quiet. I'm working."

"Blaze Collins's band is playing in Paducah this weekend."

"I guess you still think he's the man you're looking for?"

"More than ever." Nick brushed his dark hair back off his forehead. "I found a Facebook page for the band, and there are a ton of pictures. It's him. You wanna go to the concert?"

She opened her mouth to give him a flat refusal but heard herself say, "How much are the tickets?"

"Looking now."

Nick went into silent mode, but the moment Bill's car rolled into the driveway and the garage door creaked up, he hopped up and charged into the hallway. Campbell could hear his excited voice as he unloaded his find on her father in the kitchen, but she couldn't make out his words. She pulled in a deep breath and picked up a legal summary she wanted to read before her exam.

"Guess what?"

She looked up.

Nick stood in the doorway, fanning out a sheaf of twenty-dollar bills. "The boss sprang for two tickets. You and me, Friday night."

"Oh, Friday?"

Nick scowled. "Don't tell me you've got a standing Friday night thing with Keith."

"No, not every Friday. It depends on his work schedule."

"Well, tell him this week you're going to Paducah with me, and it's business."

She almost laughed. She could tell him Keith was on the swing shift all this week, but why make things easier for him? Of course, Nick had a long list of girls he could call for a date if she backed out now, but for some reason it was important to him that she was the one in the extra seat.

"Bill says let's eat in the dining room," Nick added.

The spicy, sweet scents hit her as she entered the room. Her dad had set out an array of take-out boxes, along with plates, chopsticks, forks, and glasses of iced tea.

"Wow, Dad, quite a spread." She smiled at him.

"You're the one who ordered it." He didn't look unhappy, though, as he claimed his usual chair at the head of the table.

After they'd eaten enough to stifle their hunger, Bill paused with a strip of beef in his chopsticks. "I called the police station while I waited for the order. Matt Jackson told me the autopsy is under way."

"The cottage guy?" Nick asked.

"That's right. They should get a preliminary report by this evening. Matt said to call him or Keith. Sounds like Keith is on the evening shift."

"I hope they can tell us who he is," Campbell said.

"Was," Nick noted.

She nodded soberly. "I keep thinking he has to be from around here."

"Not necessarily." Bill peered into one of the containers. "Anyone want more sweet and sour pork?"

Nick shook his head, and Campbell said, "Go ahead." While her dad scooped out the remainder of the dish onto his plate, she pulled in a deep breath and said, without looking Nick's way, "So, is Jackie moved yet?"

"They're closing Friday, and she's moving in Saturday. Thought I'd go and lend a hand, if we're not too busy."

"So ... she's staying with her daughter until then?"

"She's going back to Bowling Green tomorrow and coming back here on Friday for the closing. She said she still had a lot of loose ends to tie up."

Campbell took another bite.

"I'm surprised she came back this weekend," Nick said with his most innocent air.

"Well, she has a meeting here in town tomorrow. I'm meeting her and Lucy for lunch afterward."

"Lucy?" Nick asked.

"Jackie's daughter."

"Ah." Nick attacked his lemon chicken, dropped a piece, and abandoned his chopsticks for a fork.

———

That evening, Campbell settled down at the desk in her bedroom with books, folders of print-outs, and a notebook. She managed to focus on the job at hand—studying. All through school and her brief teaching career, she'd been able to zone in when she needed to master a subject, and now was no exception. She shut out concerns about the tornado victims, the corpse, and the Fleming family and concentrated on what a private investigator could and could not do.

And her dad? He hadn't gone out that evening. She could

hear muffled sounds from the television set in the sitting room, and once she heard her father's unmistakable tones and assumed he was talking on the phone.

She pushed aside curiosity and focused on her notes. Finally, when she'd been at it almost two hours, her cell rang.

"Keith, hey."

"Hi. What are you up to tonight?" he asked.

"Studying."

"Oh, right. When's the exam?"

"Thursday morning."

"Coming right up. You'll do great."

She closed her eyes for a second. Keith could always calm her and make her feel more than competent.

"The autopsy prelim is in," he said. "Thought you and Bill would want to know."

"We do. Thanks. Anything useful?"

"Our lab is running the fingerprints now. We hope to have an I.D. before morning."

"Cause of death?"

"There's some head trauma and some bruising. They weren't positive yet, but tentatively it's asphyxiation."

"He was strangled?"

"Or at least denied oxygen. We'll know more when we get the final report, but there weren't any gunshot or stab wounds."

"Okay, thanks. I'll tell Dad."

"Listen, I think I can get Friday off. Are you free?"

Campbell's heart sank. "I meant to tell you, I'll be on the job that night. Nick is doing a missing persons search, and he thinks he's located the guy in a band. He's taking me to a concert they're playing in Paducah that night. Dad paid for the tickets. It's not—"

"No problem," Keith said. "Sounds like an interesting case.

Do I dare ask about Saturday? I might be able to get that day off instead."

"I'd love to do something with you on Saturday."

"Great. How about lunch out, followed by a hike at LBL?"

"Won't you be helping your dad?"

"I've been helping him mornings, and his roofers are coming Thursday. I expect they'll need a few days. We'll finish up inside next week, after the roofing crew's done."

They settled particulars for their outing on Saturday, and Campbell went down the hall to tell her dad about the autopsy report. The TV was muted, and he was talking on his cell. He closed his call almost immediately when she came in.

"Jackie," he said with a little smile.

"Oh? How is she?"

"Good. She's heading back to Bowling Green tomorrow. She has a meeting in the morning, then we're going to have lunch together, and then she'll head out."

"Okay." She watched his face closely but couldn't detect anything other than satisfaction. "Keith called, and the preliminary autopsy report came in." She sat down and plunged into the details. "I wish they had something more definite," she concluded.

Her father nodded. "You, me, the police, and the Kellums. Well, we'll just have to take what we've got and work with that."

12

On Tuesday morning, Bill sat down with his two investigators.

"I'm going into overdrive to ferret out anything I can about Mr. and Mrs. Kellum."

"Don't you believe they're innocent?" Nick asked.

"I surely hope so, but you know there are some gaps in Drew's alibi, and Marnie's brother is a powder keg."

"Did you find out if they held him in jail through the night of the tornado?" The man had been a concern of Bill's since his private session with Mrs. Kellum on Saturday, but he'd handled the research himself.

Bill sighed. "It looks like they held him two nights, and he was supposed to be arraigned Monday. But because of the tornado and its effects, court was closed Monday. The officer I spoke to thought the arraignment took place later in the week, but he wasn't certain."

"Couldn't he check their records?" Nick asked.

"You'd think so. He told me he wasn't sure and to call back later."

Campbell pushed back her hair. "I thought the tornado didn't strike in Madisonville."

"I thought so too," Bill said. "I guess the power outage could have reached that far. Anyway, I'll call back in an hour and check on it."

"Well, even if they only held him one night, there's no way he was involved with putting that body in the rubble." She frowned questioningly at her father.

"That's the way it looks."

Campbell hoped they wouldn't have to drive over to Madisonville. It would be an all-day assignment.

"At least we know he's not the dead man, but we haven't absolutely ruled him out as the killer." Bill made a face. "I hope I don't end up having to tell the client his wife's brother is the one who put a body in his cottage."

"How could that be?" Campbell asked.

"We have a fairly narrow window on when the body was dumped, but not so tight on when he was killed."

"You think it's possible he stashed the body in Aurora and then drove back to Madisonville and got arrested."

Bill ran a hand through his brown hair. "Probably not. But it's always the detail you didn't check that stabs you in the back."

Campbell finished her mundane work and did a little checking herself on Mrs. Kellum's brother, Ron Weston. She read her father's notes in the Kellum file. To her, it sounded as if he was in the clear for the murder and hiding the body. Not so clear on the drug charge. She probably wouldn't find anything he hadn't already discovered.

Only two days until her exam. Maybe she'd better hit the books again. Still, she hated to study on company time. That didn't seem right, even if it was sort of a business venture.

Bill came out of his office at eleven thirty and paused in their doorway. "I'm heading out to meet Jackie and Lucy. Call me if anything urgent comes up."

"Okay." Campbell knew her dad's disdain for people who talked on their phones in restaurants. But business was business.

"See you later," Nick called. As soon as he was gone and they heard his car's engine start, he looked over at Campbell. "Think it's a love match?"

She clenched her teeth and ignored him.

A minute later, he said, "She is a pretty lady."

Campbell huffed out a breath and fixed him with a glare. "Would you stop?"

"It really bothers you, doesn't it?"

"I won't stoop to answer that. What my dad does is none of your business."

"Sure, it's my business."

Rolling her eyes, she shoved her chair back and stalked into the hall. In the bathroom, she stared at her crimson face in despair. Someday, Nick was going to push her too far. She splashed cold water on her face, wiped it with a hand towel and put out a fresh one for visitors.

As she approached the main office, she heard Nick's voice.

"Nah, he just went out. Lunch with the classy Mrs. Fleming and her daughter." He wiggled his eyebrows, even though the caller couldn't see him. "Meeting the family. Over to Martha's Restaurant."

"Who's that?" Campbell stepped forward with her claws out.

"Eh, Campbell just walked in. Hold on, I'll switch you over."

"What's going on?"

"It's Keith."

She strode to her desk and pushed the blinking button. "Hey. Did you want to talk to Dad? He's out."

"So Nick told me. I wanted to come over and talk to you all in person, but I can't leave the station right now."

"I thought you were on the evening shift."

"We got the fingerprint results on the corpse, and they called me in."

Her pulse rioted. "Who is it?"

He hesitated. "Can you come to the station? It's one of those things I hate to give out over the phone."

"But it's okay for you to tell us?"

"Well, the chief's giving a press conference in thirty minutes. I can sneak you in there."

"You wouldn't get in trouble?"

"No, it'll be fine. But I might catch some flak if I tell a civilian before then."

"I'll be right over." She hung up.

"Well?" Nick drilled holes in her with his dark eyes.

"I have to go to the police station."

He frowned. "Guess I'm the odd man out. What do I tell Bill?"

"Nothing yet. Keith hasn't told me anything either. I have to find out when everybody else does—they're holding a press conference."

"They've I.D.'d the body," Nick guessed.

"Maybe. I'll tell you when I come back. You stay here near the phone."

He opened his mouth and closed it. He wanted to go, she could feel it. Keith had passed over him for Campbell. That shouldn't surprise Nick. And if her father were here, he'd be the one to go. But knowing he'd have been next in line if Campbell hadn't joined the team and started dating Keith must be galling for Nick.

"Look, I'll keep you in the loop," she said.

"Sure, sure."

As she headed her Fusion for the police station, she wondered how she'd sit through the concert with Nick on Friday night. That was assuming she lived through the exam on Thursday. If she flunked it, no way would she go out the next night. Why hadn't she considered that before she accepted the invitation? Of course, she probably wouldn't get the test results for at least a week.

Parking spaces were hard to come by at the police station, and she parked down the block and sent Keith a text saying she was outside. He came out the door and looked around, spotted her, and waved her in.

"They're in the conference room," he said. "I told the sergeant you were coming, and he okayed it."

Campbell breathed a little easier. Detective Sergeant Vickers was aware of the assists True Blue had given his squad in the past, and he and Bill respected each other. She'd only met him once, though.

"I appreciate that," she murmured as they approached the open door.

Voices hummed, and she was surprised to see a dozen people gathered around the table and a camera crew from WPSD in Paducah setting up in a corner. The only chairs available were lined up against the wall, and Keith flicked a hand toward an empty one. Campbell slid into it, beside a woman who had a reporter's slim notebook on her lap.

"Hi." Campbell gave her a tentative smile.

"Hi. I'm Payton Goodale, with the *Murray Ledger and Times.*"

"Campbell McBride." She almost added "True Blue

Investigations," but bit it off. She didn't want the local reporter to focus on her and her reasons for attending the event.

"Thank you all for coming." Detective Sergeant Vickers nodded at the group. "We're here to discuss the body that was found last week in the debris from a ruined lakeside house in Aurora. The Kentucky State Police are handling that case, assisted by the Marshall County Sheriff's Department, but they decided to have this press conference here because the victim has been identified, and he was a resident of Calloway County."

A murmur went through the room, and most of the reporters scribbled notes. Campbell looked over her shoulder. Keith stood near the doorway, leaning against the wall.

"I'd like to introduce to you State Police Detective Roland," Vickers said.

A man in a suit took his place behind the lectern at the end of the table. "Good morning. I know you and your readers and viewers have waited for the last week to learn the identity of the man whose body was found in the tornado debris in Aurora. As you know, several area residents were killed in the storm. Yesterday we announced the recovery of remains in Trigg County, those of Crawford Steele."

Campbell clenched her teeth. Would he just get on with it? She was sorry about Mr. Steele, but that was yesterday's news.

"The victim we're discussing today was found under a pile of debris near the west shore of Kentucky Lake, where a cottage had stood. We were able to identify him through his fingerprints, and the family has been notified," Roland said. "The victim was Weylan Osgood, a resident of Murray. We have received a preliminary autopsy report, but that was inconclusive as to the cause of death. We should have more information for you in a few days. Thank you." He nodded firmly.

"That's it?" Payton scowled as Campbell scribbled the name in her notebook.

Several hands shot up, and at least three people called out questions.

"I'm sorry, that's all I have for you at this time. We'll cooperate with the Murray Police now, as well as the Marshall County Sheriff, on this investigation." Roland strode toward the door.

"Was the man murdered?" a young man shouted after him, but Roland didn't pause.

"Hardly worth coming out for," Payton muttered. "I feel sorry for the crew from Paducah."

Campbell stuffed her notebook and pen in her purse and headed for the door. She wasn't complaining. It was a lot more than they'd had that morning. She and her father and Nick could pile up a lot of information on Osgood in the next few hours.

Keith had left his post, but she found him in the hallway.

"That wasn't much, but it's a help," she said.

"Yeah. We're already working on it. We need to find out who this guy was—I mean, what he was up to—and why nobody noticed he was missing for the last week."

"That's a good question. Do you know anything about him so far?"

Keith pulled her into a small, windowless room and said softly, "Not a lot. I can let you and Bill in on anything we find, but I'd better come by your office later."

She smiled. "So, you just wanted to see me this morning, or what?"

"Well, that too." He shrugged sheepishly. "No, I meant what I said about passing data over the phone. Sgt. Vickers is okay with it, but other people might not be."

"Gotcha. But a lot of people saw me in there."

"I think we're good."

"I didn't tell the woman I sat next to that I was with True Blue. She was from the *Murray Ledger*, and I didn't want her pumping me for specifics on why I was there."

"Probably for the best. She's a real go-getter. Ferrets out every little thing. I need to get back to my desk, but I'll talk to you later."

"All right. Thanks again."

She left the building and drove the few blocks from Fifth Street to Eighth and then onto Willow. She was disappointed to find her dad's car wasn't in his slot in the garage. Should she call him? She knew what he'd say. *You and Nick get to work on it. Find out everything you can about that guy.* With a sigh, she went in through the kitchen to bring Nick up to speed.

"That's why I asked Lucy to join us," Jackie said, giving her daughter and Bill a tight smile. "I know I get riled up with I talk about this mess, and I wanted someone here who would keep me steady. Lucy knows everything."

"Well, I'm mad at him too, but I'm distanced one step from the fiasco." Lucy huffed out a breath. "Mr. McBride—Bill—if you can do anything to help Mom, we'd all appreciate it."

"At this point, I'm not sure I can." Bill pushed away his plate and took out a pocket notebook. "Just tell me everything, from the beginning. Jackie, you told me how you met Sid. I need to know every red flag, every little snippet that made you uneasy, and every clue that told you toward the end that something wasn't right." He leveled his gaze at Lucy. "You too."

"I was just happy for Mom at first." Lucy's face skewed.

"She hadn't been so upbeat—so *alive*—since Dad died. And Sid seemed like a terrific guy at first."

Bill nodded. "What was the very first thing that told you maybe he wasn't as terrific as you thought?"

Lucy went pensive, gazing at her mom, who kept quiet. Her resemblance to Jackie struck Bill. Jackie was never as pretty as Emily, but she had something special. Neither she nor Lucy would win a beauty pageant, but then, they probably wouldn't be interested in pageants. Both had bright, intelligent, dark eyes and strong facial structures that made them stand out. Interesting faces.

"I guess it was when Mom told me he'd maxed out her credit cards."

That'd do it. Bill made a note, figuring this was the financial problem Jackie had alluded to on Sunday.

"She'd told me about a couple of things he'd spent a lot of money on."

"But I thought it was *his* money." Jackie gave a little moan. "I really thought I loved him." Tears shimmered in her eyes. "He was so good to me."

Lucy patted her arm. "I thought so too, Mom."

"Now I just feel stupid."

"Aw." Her daughter pulled her into a hug.

Bill stared blankly down at his notebook.

"It's not your fault," Lucy murmured.

But wasn't it? Jackie had let her defenses down. She'd overlooked important signs of trouble on purpose.

Now Bill felt guilty. If Sid Galt had committed a crime, he shouldn't be blaming the victim. It sounded as though the guy had taken advantage of Jackie, and perhaps other women. He could be a con man, a serial fraudster. He'd probably left a trail of heartbroken, bankrupt women behind him. But this time he'd gone so far as to marry his mark, when he had no legal right to do so.

"Okay, you said you have a lawyer." He looked at the two women.

Jackie nodded. "In Bowling Green." She told him which lawyer she'd employed, and Bill recognized the name but had no associations, good or bad, with the man's firm. "But it might be best to engage one over here now, so I don't have to keep running back and forth. Besides, I'm not sure my attorney did everything he could have for me. He's sort of stalling, telling me he's not sure they can do anything more."

"Well, bigamy is still a crime in this state."

"And Sid has no right to your money," Lucy said staunchly.

Bill hated to dispute that, but he had to. "Actually, since your mother voluntarily put his name on her accounts ..."

Jackie nodded grimly. "That's what they're telling me. Yes, he married me under false pretenses, but I didn't have to accept him into my finances that I'd accumulated before I met him. I could have kept them separate."

"Why didn't you?" Bill asked. "Was that your idea or his?"

"Hmm. One day before we were married, we were at the grocery store. He'd been kind of splitting the bills with me, but he said he'd forgotten his wallet that day. So I used my debit card. Then we stopped for gas, and I had to use it again. I said, 'You know, since we're going to be married soon anyway, it would be easier to just put your name on my account and my name on yours.' And we did."

"Did you do it that day?"

"We did mine, but Sid's accounts were at a different bank. It was nearly closing time when we left my bank, so we agreed we'd do his another day. Then came the weekend and the ceremony and ..."

"You never gained access to his accounts," Bill guessed.

"Yeah. I figured we'd get to it. But then other things happened. Little things came up on the honeymoon, and I ended up using my credit for the hotel and some other stuff. He said we'd sort it out when we got home."

"But you didn't."

Jackie pressed her lips together. "We didn't. Debits started multiplying on my checking account, and then my credit card statement arrived. I hadn't added Sid to that account yet, but there were charges I didn't recognize. I thought at first someone had hacked my account, but when I showed him the statement, he admitted he'd used my card to order some stuff online and by phone."

"He got in your purse and stole your card?" Lucy's eyebrows shot up like an erupting volcano.

"I guess so."

Bill made a few notes while the waitress refilled their coffee cups. "So, what was the first inkling that you weren't legally married?"

"I ... I saw a letter he'd received that was addressed to Mr. and Mrs. Sidney Galt. He'd already opened it and left it on his dresser. I figured it was for me, too, so I looked inside. It said, 'Dear Sidney and Alanna.' My heart just stopped for a minute. Then I told myself, well, that's his ex. They just don't know she's not Mrs. Galt now. He needs to notify them."

"Did you mention it to Sid?" Bill asked.

She shook her head. "I was too embarrassed. I'd have to tell him I'd peeked, and he might think I was snooping."

"Did he accuse you of snooping before?"

Jackie pulled in a shaky breath. "Kind of. I asked if he still kept up with his ex-wife once, and he got upset—asked me why it was any of my business. So I ... I tried not to do that sort of thing again. But that letter ... I honestly thought it was to both of us."

"What was it about?"

"It was a past-due notice on something they'd bought last winter. Only Sid had told me he'd been divorced a couple of years."

"So, his ex-wife's name still seemed to be on his financial accounts."

"It sure looked that way, but I didn't want to rock the boat, so I kept quiet. I figured he'd sort it out."

Lucy frowned at her mother. "Did it occur to you then that maybe it was a good thing he *hadn't* put you on his bank accounts?"

"Yeah. And it made me think hard about him using my credit card." She looked at Lucy. "I told you about it then."

"You did tell me you were uneasy about the credit card thing. You didn't tell me he'd got it out of your purse without you knowing about it. Or about the ex-wife. Or, maybe I should say the real wife."

Jackie heaved out a big sigh, and a tear ran down her cheek. She grabbed her napkin and wiped it away. "I was so naïve."

"I hope he's not still using your credit cards," Bill said.

"No, I canceled everything after I found out the marriage was a sham. Now I'm trying to rebuild my credit, but it's going to take some time."

Bill glanced around at the crowded restaurant. "Okay, I'm going to need some more information about Sid—as much as you can give me. Maybe it would be better to do this at my office."

"Yes, Mom." Lucy patted her mother's back. "Let's go someplace more private, at least." She looked over at Bill. "Our apartment's quiet. Garrett's at work. You could come there to talk."

"Okay." Bill thought it would be easier that way—he wouldn't have to explain everything to Campbell. He wasn't sure he was ready to do that, considering her ambivalence toward Jackie. "Let's go."

Jackie pulled a tissue from her purse and swabbed her damp cheeks. She nodded, and Lucy pushed back her chair.

"Come on, Mom. I'm driving." She gave Bill the address.

Bill quickly signed off on the tab and followed them to the parking lot.

When he reached them beside Lucy's car, Jackie's face was white, and she was shaking.

"Everything okay?" Bill asked.

"She thought she saw Sid," Lucy said.

"Where?"

Jackie pointed to the parking lot exit. "There. It was the same color and model car he drives, and I'm sure it was him."

"Did you see him?" Bill asked Lucy.

She clenched her teeth. "I'm sure it was a man driving, but I really didn't get a good look."

"So, you couldn't swear it was Sid Galt?"

"Afraid not." Lucy glanced sheepishly at Jackie. "Sorry, Mom. I should have gone for the license number, instead of trying to see his face—which I couldn't. If he'd turned toward downtown … But he didn't. He headed north."

Bill looked along Route 641 in the direction she'd indicated. "Well, there's not much we can do now. But if you're sure it was him …"

Jackie's bleak eyes met his. "I … I'm not positive. I thought I saw him once a few days ago, when I was going to meet the real estate agent, but I'd about decided I was imagining things."

"That's twice." Lucy eyed Bill anxiously.

"But there are a lot of white Trailblazers," Jackie admitted. "I'm sorry, Bill."

"Don't apologize. If you don't mind, I think I'll alert a

buddy of mine at the police station. You don't know his plate number, do you?"

"No, sorry. He wanted to get a vanity plate, but he hadn't got around to it before things blew up."

"Okay, let's get you out of here."

13

Wednesday passed in a blur for Campbell. Her father excused her from work so she could study for her exam. When she emerged from her room at one o'clock to rifle the refrigerator for sandwich makings, her dad came into the kitchen.

"How's it going?" he asked.

"Okay. Do you think most of the questions will be on legal stuff?"

"As I remember, there are quite a few on practical skills too. Maybe Nick could tell you—he took it more recently than I did."

Scratch that. Campbell slapped mayonnaise onto a slice of bread and added shaved ham and lettuce leaves.

"What have you been up to?" she asked, more to be polite than to get information.

"Reading up on Weylan Osgood. He was employed at Murray State."

"Oh?" That mildly interested her. "Was he a professor?"

"No, it seems he was on maintenance and grounds. Had a small house off Route 121."

"And nobody missed him?"

"His boss thought at first he was just taking some time off, but after a week or so, he figured he'd moved on to another job and didn't have the decency to tell him. They've already hired his replacement."

"What about his family?"

"They're in Indiana. He lived alone."

"I guess the police have been to his house already?"

"Yeah. Keith said he got to read the full report and inventory from the state police search."

She put the lid on her sandwich. "I'm guessing they didn't find anything, or you'd have said so."

"Well, it was kind of odd." Her dad pulled out a chair and sat down at the table. "It looked like he'd had company. They've taken some prints. Keith said it appeared as though some things in the house had been wiped clean, but not everything."

"Just the things the guest touched?"

"We'll have to find out, eh?"

"Was there anything that connects him to the Kellums?"

"No, nothing. And of course, they've talked to the Kellums again, to see if they could think of any time they'd met the guy."

"Hmm."

Bill got up and headed for the coffeemaker. Campbell wondered how many cups he'd already drunk.

"One other odd thing," he said as he stirred in creamer. "Seems Osgood had a tornado shelter set up in his cellar, similar to what we have. Sleeping bag, nonperishable food, weather radio, flashlight, and so on."

That in itself wasn't odd—everyone in Tornado Alley had a

designated shelter. Campbell paused with her plate in her hand and gazed at him. "Do they think he was down there during the tornado warning, not out at the cottage?"

"They do. And he wasn't alone in the basement."

"Who was with him?"

"They have no idea, and no one's come forward."

She hesitated. "A girlfriend, do you think?"

"I don't know. They didn't find anything feminine. But the basement was a mess."

"Lots of clutter?"

"No, not that kind of mess. According to Keith, it looked like there'd been a scuffle. Stuff was tossed around and knocked over, even though his place wasn't in the path of the tornado. And there was a little blood."

She stared at him. "Was it Osgood's?"

"They haven't got the test results yet. Keith's going to ask Detective Roland if he can take a look in there."

"Good." She wondered why Keith hadn't called her and told her all this, but she thought she knew. She'd informed him that she'd be incommunicado today, while she crammed for the exam.

Even so, he called her cell just before three o'clock.

"Hi." She pushed aside the book she'd been poring over. "Dad told me about Osgood's house."

"Yeah, weird thing. They're pretty sure he had someone with him in the shelter downstairs. Detective Roland says I can go over there this afternoon, and the sarge okayed it before I go in for my shift. I'm headed there now. But I wanted to touch base and tell you I'm praying for you."

She swallowed hard as tears threatened. "Thanks."

"Nervous?"

"Yeah, big time. But don't tell Dad I said that, and especially don't tell Nick."

Keith chuckled. "I won't. Hey, don't stress too much over this, you hear? I know you're going to do well, but if not, you can take it again, right?"

"Yeah. But I don't want to have to go through it again, and it would be months and months ... and Nick wouldn't let me hear the end of it."

"I won't make a big deal of it if that happens. In fact, I'll take you out for ice cream either way. How's that?"

"Sounds good." She caught a glimpse of herself in the mirror over her dresser. She was smiling.

"What time do you have to be over at the university?" Keith asked.

"Eight thirty."

"I'll be up. I could drive you over."

"No, thanks. I'd rather take myself."

"Okay. But I'll be thinking of you. Now I've got to get going."

As she laid down the phone, a soft tap came at her door. "Soup?"

"Yeah, Dad?"

He opened the door a crack. "I brought you a glass of tea."

"Thanks." She got up and stretched before she took the glass from him.

"Lucy Holm just called me," her father said. "She thinks somebody's watching her apartment unit."

"Someone's watching her? Or her mother?"

"I'm guessing Jackie—she thought she saw her ex tailing her before."

"I thought she went back to Bowling Green," Campbell said.

"She did, but she's coming back Friday to close on her new house. Lucy's alone. Her husband's at work, so I'm going over there."

"Okay."

"I'll take Nick with me. You'll have to answer the phone if it rings."

"No problem."

He was already halfway down the stairs. Campbell watched out the window as her dad drove out of the garage with Nick riding shotgun. She took a long drink of tea and turned back to her books.

————

Bill spotted the car right away. The gray Impala Lucy had described was parked, across the street and half a block from Lucy's building, and a man sat in the driver's seat drinking coffee. Pulling in behind a minivan, Bill glanced at the apartment door with the number she'd given him. The complex's one-story units were built in rows of four. The Venetian blinds were closed on the front of Lucy's. He gave her a quick call.

"It's Bill. I'm outside."

"Thank you! Do you see him?"

"I do. Just sit tight and stay away from the windows."

"Got it."

Lucy clicked off, and Bill checked the shoulder holster under his jacket. He didn't expect to need the gun, but if this was Jackie's ex, no telling what tricks he'd pull. He looked over at Nick.

"I'm going to stroll down there and beyond, to see what I see."

Nick nodded. "What do you want me to do?"

"You can come along if you want to."

"Just so you know, I'm packing—my ankle holster."

"Right." Bill had been a bit uneasy when Nick started

carrying, but his young protégé had never fired the pistol at a human being, and it had come in handy once or twice.

Bill locked the car, then he and Nick sauntered down the sidewalk, away from Lucy's unit but right past the Impala. The man inside eyed them warily then looked away and took a sip from his travel mug.

So, he'd brought the coffee with him, expecting to sit for a while.

"Is that Galt?" Nick asked.

"I don't think so." Bill had studied photos of Sid Galt online after Jackie told him about her ersatz marriage to the man. They kept walking to the end of the block, with Nick keeping pace beside him. Bill checked to be sure the driver couldn't see them.

"Okay, I'm going to talk to him. You come up on the passenger side."

"Got it."

Bill edged back toward the watcher, one vehicle at a time. One car back from the Impala, he waited for a pickup to pass then stepped into the street. He strode quickly up from behind the gray car and knocked on the driver's window.

The man jerked his head around and gaped at him. Definitely not Galt. Bill gestured for him to open the window. It slid downward about three inches.

"May I ask who you are and what you're doing?"

The man's eyes widened. "I could ask you the same thing."

"I'm Bill McBride. Who are you?"

His face reddening, the man said, "I really don't see that that's any of your business."

"Maybe not, but I can have the cops here in two minutes flat."

The fellow hesitated then said, "My name's Stephen Maguire, and I have a right to be here."

"Probably so."

Nick eased up to the passenger side window, and Bill nodded at him over the top of the car. Nick pulled out his phone and did some quick tapping and swiping.

"Why are you watching the Holms' place?" Bill asked.

"Who says I am?" Maguire's gaze hardened.

"He's a P.I. out of Clarksville," Nick said.

Maguire whipped around toward the passenger side. Nick bent down and waved at him through the window.

"My assistant," Bill said.

Maguire's lips twitched as he swore and turned back toward Bill. "Who did you say you are?"

Bill smiled. "As I said, I'm Bill McBride, and I'm a P.I. here in Murray. If you roll down the window, I'll shake your hand."

Instead of complying, Maguire eyed him with distrust. "I've heard of you."

"Have you? I've never heard of you. How long you been practicing in Clarksville?"

"About a year."

Bill nodded, guessing this guy was new at the game. Either that, or he'd been run out of some other town. "So, who hired you?"

Maguire clenched his teeth. "You know I can't reveal my client's name."

"That's okay. I think I know the answer." Bill held his gaze. "Look, Lucy Holm is a sweet young woman with no reason for anyone to stake out her apartment. It's got to be her mother you're after, and the most likely person to pay you to do it is Sid Galt."

Maguire closed his eyes for a moment then glared at Bill. "If you're in this business, you know I have a right to be here. You're harassing me. Now, why is that? Is someone paying you to watch Jackie too?"

Bill smiled, hearing the confirmation he wanted. "No, no, not at all. But I can tell you right now, Jackie's out of town. You could sit here all night, and you wouldn't see her."

Maguire's whole face drooped.

"Have a good ride back to Clarksville." Bill started to leave but turned back. "Oh, and good luck getting Sid Galt to pay you what he owes you. I hear he's in financial limbo." He gave Nick a nod and strode back to his car.

14

At twelve thirty on Thursday, Campbell emerged from the university's testing center and plodded to her car. She removed the temporary parking permit from her rear-view mirror and headed slowly home, dreading what awaited. Her dad and Nick—even Rita, since it was her day to come in and clean and cook for them—would ask her how she did, and she didn't know if she could stand that. Maybe if she got them all together one time and said, "I flunked, okay?" they would leave her alone.

I might as well face it. I'm worthless as a P.I. Time to start applying for jobs again.

Of course, it was too late to apply for jobs in education. The school year had begun less than a month ago. Maybe she could flip burgers or wait tables or restock shelves.

She pulled into the driveway of the Victorian house but didn't advance to the garage. She hadn't decided yet whether to go out again, somewhere away from the house, or to barricade herself in her bedroom.

Creeping in through the kitchen door, she hoped she could avoid Nick and her dad.

"Hey, Professor! How'd it go?"

No such luck.

She paused at the bottom of the stairway and turned. Nick stood in the office doorway, smirking at her. Okay, other people might see that as a friendly smile, but it sure felt like a smirk right now.

"Not great." She headed up the stairs.

"Wait," Nick called. "Rita's got a special lunch ready. She's been holding it until you got back."

"Not in the mood to celebrate, Nick." Campbell made sure her bedroom door closed loudly enough that he'd hear it as a finale to the conversation, but not so loud her father would construe it as a spoiled child's slam.

Flopping on the bed, she let a few tears come. A couple of minutes' indulgence later, she reached for a tissue and sat up to wipe her eyes. She still wasn't ready to go downstairs and accept condolences from Nick and her dad, let alone rave over Rita's latest culinary creation.

She wished she was still in Iowa, but that thought was fruitless. Her old teaching job was gone. Staying here as an object of pity was not an option. She could act as a receptionist, or she could even take over Rita's duties. But that would put Rita out of a job, and anyway, Campbell wasn't much of a cook.

Maine was looking pretty good, or Seattle, even. Someplace as far away as she could get without a passport. Dad would miss her, but not for long. He had Jackie now.

Her lips twisted at that bitter thought. She couldn't call their relationship a romance yet, but what would she do if it blossomed? Could she carry on working with her dad if it did —or if he got married again? Could she keep living in the same house with him if she gained a stepmother? She shivered. After her mom died, she'd left her dad alone for years, but somehow she wasn't ready to do that again. Not now, after they'd formed a close bond once more.

A quiet tap came on her door.

"Honey?"

She hesitated. How long since her father had called her that? He was offering the sympathy she dreaded.

"Keith's here. He's got some news, and we'd like it if you came down to eat with us."

Slowly, she stood and walked to the door. She opened it a crack. "I'll be down in a minute."

"Okay."

He turned and left her, just like that. No comments on her blotchy face or the dull eyes that studied her from the beveled mirror above her dresser. She hurried to the bathroom to make herself presentable.

Unable to completely rid her cheeks of an unbecoming flush, she trudged down the stairs and into the dining room.

Keith was already seated, with Nick and Bill, at the table, but he rose as she entered.

"Hi."

"Hi." She slid into the seat next to him, avoiding a direct look at his sympathetic face.

After Bill asked the blessing, Rita brought in the hot dishes —Campbell's favorite lasagna, along with fresh yeast rolls and a salad of mixed greens. The men chattered a little as they ate, and Campbell gradually relaxed.

When Rita took away Bill's plate and refilled his coffee, he looked over at Keith. "Okay, let's have it. You said there was something new."

"Yeah. The information your office mined yesterday was a big help."

"You can thank these two," Bill said, nodding at Nick and Campbell.

Undeserved on her part, Campbell thought. She'd spent all day studying. Dad was being overly generous.

Keith smiled. "And we do thank you. Of course, we had to confirm everything, but it seems you're right about the leads you found. We've been in touch with Osgood's widowed mother in Indiana, and I've also spoken to a brother up there. Our officers have also talked to his boss at MSU and a couple of coworkers."

"Did you find anything new at his house?" Bill asked.

"As a matter of fact, I found some cash inside a hollowed-out book in his living room bookcase."

"The CSIs missed it?" Bill frowned.

"Apparently. I alerted them, and they're back over there now, being more thorough."

Campbell spoke up for the first time. "Dad said they think someone was with Osgood in the house the night of the tornado."

"Yes, and we've located a witness who saw him with another man earlier that day."

"Who was it?" Nick asked.

"We don't know yet, but we're working on it. They ate lunch together, and we're hoping to get a credit card ID. We've got a sketchy description of his vehicle, but nothing solid yet. Now, if the lab can find a few fingerprints that aren't Osgood's, or if the blood downstairs isn't his ... The M.E. thinks now that it was the head wound that killed Osgood. Well, like I said, we're working on it."

"How about the cash?" Bill asked.

"We'll check for prints, but we expect any we find on it to be Osgood's since it was hidden away."

"How much was it?" Nick asked.

"About fifteen hundred. Not huge, but enough to make it worth trying to trace."

As Keith spoke, Rita came in with bowls of ice cream and a plate of macaroons, another of Campbell's favorites.

"These look great, Rita," she said as she helped herself to one. "Thanks for going to so much trouble."

"No problem." She patted Campbell's shoulder. "Anyone for more coffee or sweet tea? Campbell, more ice water?"

"Yes, please." Campbell had been trying to cut down on her sugar intake, and she'd decided juices and sweet tea were commodities that made it all too easy to drink calories and sugar. She still indulged, but more moderately than in the past. Bill followed her lead, but he was still guzzling several cups of coffee every day.

As Rita left the room, Bill said, "What's next, Keith?"

"We'll be digging into Osgood's finances, you can bet on that. And also poking into his associates. We're talking to anyone we can find who knew him. He'd only been in Murray two or three years, so he doesn't have a lot of old friends here. But we're interviewing everyone we can find. And we'll be working with the state police more closely now, knowing the victim lived in our town."

"His finances," Campbell said, finally more interested in something other than her test results. "Did you find something that made you suspicious, other than the hidden cash?"

"Actually, yes. His pay goes into his bank account every week by direct deposit, but there are some other deposits he made himself that we want explained."

"Big ones?" Bill asked.

"Three thousand last spring and another five thousand this fall, both in cash. We're trying to find out if he sold something —say, a used vehicle—or if those amounts were payment for something else."

Bill nodded pensively. "The fact that his body was found in Marshall County ..."

"Yeah. I'm convinced he was killed here in Calloway."

"But would the state police hand the case back to you?"

"I doubt it. But we'll make sure we set the pace on this end, and we're rarin' to go." Keith ate the last of his ice cream and set his spoon in his empty dish. "And speaking of that, I'd better get going. We'll find out who did this."

"I'm sure you will," Bill said. "I'll tell the Kellums you're making progress, but I won't reveal the details to them."

Campbell rose and walked to the front door with Keith. At the end of the hall, he faced her and touched her arm.

"How are you holding up?"

"I'm afraid I lost a little of my bravado today." She straightened her shoulders. "I need to get my focus off myself and onto other people."

He smiled, and her stomach quirked. Keith was always there for her.

"May I kiss you?" he asked.

And always the gentleman.

"I think that may be just what I need," she whispered.

He hauled her in close and bent to meet her lips. She edged away after a moment, then nestled into his embrace. He held her tight with her head over his heart.

"Thank you," she whispered. "For everything."

"No matter what happens with the test, you'll be okay. And you'll still have me." He gave her a little squeeze.

"That's reassuring."

"I'm not going anywhere."

She sighed in contentment and let go of the anxiety.

———

Minutes after Keith left her, Nick was out the door on an insurance case, and Bill left with his briefcase, headed to confer with his legal friend, Barry McGann, who sent a lot of work their way. Campbell huffed out a big breath and trudged to the kitchen. The dishwasher was running. Rita looked up from the pan she was scrubbing at the sink.

"Let me help you," Campbell said.

"You don't have to." Rita smiled and kept scrubbing.

"I know."

"Well then, can you check on the cookies in the oven?"

Campbell grabbed a potholder from the counter and opened the oven door. A blast of heat and sweet cinnamon hit her. She eyed the tray of cookies critically. "Not brown yet."

"Thanks." Rita turned on the water to rinse out the pan.

Shutting the oven, Campbell noticed that the timer still had five minutes on it. Rita had given her busy work.

"What else can I—" The wall phone rang. They exchanged a glance, and Campbell reached for the receiver. "True Blue Investigations."

"Campbell? This is Nathan Fuller."

She smiled, hearing Keith's dad's voice. "Hi, Nathan."

"Is Bill home? The volunteer crew is cleaning up the rest of the debris from that cottage—you know the one I mean."

"I sure do."

"I thought Bill would want to know," Nathan said.

"He's not here right now. In fact, he just left for an appointment. I'll tell him, though."

"Thanks. I don't like to call Keith unless it's an emergency."

"I understand." Should she tell him his son was here for lunch and was probably just getting back to his desk? Or maybe ... Campbell raised her chin. "Say, Nathan? Would it be okay if I came out?"

"Sure. There's a sheriff's deputy here keeping an eye on

things. The more the merrier."

She chuckled. "They probably won't find anything the police didn't."

"You never know."

"Right. Thanks." She signed off and turned to Rita, who was watching her unabashed.

"Keith's father," Campbell said. "I'm going to run out to their place. Would you mind answering the house phone if it rings, until I get back or Dad does?"

"Sure," Rita said. "I'll take a message if anyone calls."

Campbell grabbed her purse and hurried to her car, which still sat in the driveway. She shouldn't have left it where other people had to drive around it. Even that small act was selfish. She started the engine and decided she'd better let her father know where she was going. That was one thing he'd pounded into her after she had a close call a couple of months earlier. She started to tap his contact icon, but after a moment's thought she scrolled down to Nick's.

"Yo, Professor. What's brewin'?"

"Nick, Dad's gone to Dunn & McGann, and I didn't like to disturb him." She pulled in a deep breath. "Can you please tell him I'm headed out to Kentucky Lake? Keith's dad called and said the cleanup crew is finishing off at the cottage where the body was found."

"A-OK."

"Thanks." She closed the connection and stuck her phone in the dashboard holder.

———

"Hi!" Nathan grinned and squeezed Campbell's hand for a moment, then released it.

"How's it going?" She turned to stand beside him,

watching a front-end loader lift a bucket full of debris from the site of the Kellums' cottage and swing it over a waiting dump truck's bed.

"Good. They'll be done with this one soon. After they haul away all the rubble from the Kellums' cottage, they'll start on the Laffertys', right there." Nathan pointed to the pile of rubble that was closer to his own home.

"That's the one that was for sale before the storm, right?"

"Yeah."

A sheriff's deputy sporting the Marshall County insignia stood at the edge of the lot, gazing at the front-end loader clearing debris.

"Do you know Deputy Sandberg?" Nathan asked.

"I don't think so." Campbell followed Nathan as he led her across the nearer lot, skirting the heap of broken building materials.

"Hey, Archie," Nathan called as they approached, and the deputy turned.

"This is my friend, Campbell," Nathan said. "She came out to watch the fun."

She noted that he didn't give her last name or mention that she was Keith's girl or that she worked for True Blue. Maybe he figured Sandberg knew her father, at least by reputation, and didn't want to plant any assumptions.

The deputy nodded at her. "We're just here as a formality, since this is where the remains were found."

"Probably a good idea," Campbell said. She was glad to be included, but the outing seemed anticlimactic. The chance of finding more evidence today was slim. Nick and her father were no doubt having a much more exciting afternoon.

"Just stay back from all the debris and the vehicles." Sandberg flicked a glance at Nathan. "I suppose you know the people who owned these houses."

"Slightly," Nathan said. "We knew the Laffertys better than the Kellums. Well, their place was right next to ours. But they had planned to sell it."

"So I've heard."

"Tough break for them." Nathan shook his head.

They watched the loader for a few minutes in silence as it scooped a load from the cottage site and transferred it into the bed of the dump truck with a clatter. The throb of its engine made conversation a chore. Chunks of building materials mingled with bits of furniture, occasional dishes, a broken picture frame, and a mangled book. Dust hovered over the truck after each bucketload was dumped.

The wind blew across the surface of Lake Kentucky, whipping up waves. Campbell shivered and zipped up the front of her sweatshirt.

Eventually the loader paused while the operator had a few words with the truck driver.

Campbell smiled at Nathan. "So, how are the repairs on your place coming?"

"Slow, because it's hard to get the supplies I need right now. Everybody wants lumber and paint and all that. But it is coming along."

"Take it slow but steady," she said.

"Right. You want some pop?"

"Oh, you don't have to—"

"I'm going to go get myself a Coke. Want one? Angela's got diet."

"Okay, if you're getting one anyway. Is Angela home?"

"Nah, she went to her women's group today." Nathan shot a look toward the deputy, but he was talking to one of the men in hard hats. "I'll be right back." Nathan wheeled and headed toward his house.

As the loader moved toward the pile again, Campbell

turned her attention back to the workers. There wasn't much left of the Kellums' cottage now for the cleanup crew. Two men jumped down into the slight depression that had been under the building and started throwing the boards and other junk that remained into the machine's bucket.

Sandberg strolled her way. "They'll start on the other place next."

Campbell walked slowly to the edge of the second smashed cottage, about fifty yards from the Fullers'. Though a lot of the debris was piled where the house had stood, more had been strewn between the foundation and the lake. Again she marveled at how close the Fullers had come to losing their home. Although the damage was serious, Nathan and Angela had comparatively little to worry about.

The dump truck lumbered out the dirt road, and the workers took a break. Some visited their vehicles and returned to the site with beverages and snacks.

Nathan came from his house carrying two bottles of Coca-Cola and handed one to her.

"Thanks." Campbell opened it and took a deep swig.

"I s'pose this is boring for you," Nathan said, "but I told the Laffertys I'd keep an eye out for anything salvageable they could use."

"I'm surprised they're not out here themselves."

He shrugged. "Work. Life must go on, you know?"

Campbell nodded and looked around. A wide swath of downed trees disfigured the woods that had been a quiet sanctuary. Chips and sawdust lay in the gravel road, where earlier crews had cleared the way for vehicles. The point beyond the Kellums' cottage lot jutted into the lake, and it was stripped of trees and brush. She couldn't see beyond it.

"Are the houses on the other side of the point wrecked too?"

Nathan shook his head. "Hardly at all. I think it crossed here and touched down again on the other side of the lake."

"But—all the way across the Land Between the Lakes? We saw damage over in Cadiz the other day."

"Yeah. It was an odd one." He shrugged. "I guess they're all odd. There's no typical twister, you know?"

A different dump truck rolled up, and the loader operator went over to talk to the driver. While the truck was being positioned for him to fill it, he started the loader and drove it over to the Laffertys' lot. The volunteers began gathering scattered debris that had flown outside the cottage site.

"There weren't many personal belongings in there," Nathan said, frowning at where the house had stood.

Campbell tried to remember how it had looked, but she couldn't picture it. "They had it mostly cleared out to sell it." Her mind had been focused on Keith and his parents in the few times she'd visited before the tornado.

"I think they left a few pieces of furniture, but certainly nothing valuable," Nathan said.

"They had a cellar, though, right? The Kellums didn't."

"Yes, it was a walk-in cellar with a couple big windows on the lake side."

The loader scooped up several loads of debris and deposited them in the truck. When they'd mostly cleared one end of the cellar hole, two gloved workers jumped down in it and began tossing small pieces the bucket had left behind onto the larger pile. Most of it was wood, but in the bottom of the hole she could see fragments of metal and broken glass.

One of the workers tossed some bits on the heap then reached for a piece of dull metal. When he picked it up and scrutinized it for a moment, Campbell realized it was a wrench. He walked to the edge of the hole and tossed it up on the rim.

When he turned back to his task, Campbell edged over a few yards to the spot where he'd put it. She frowned down at the tool, then looked up to spot Nathan, but he'd headed the other way, watching the other volunteer. She stooped and reached her hand toward the wrench.

"Careful." She looked up and found the worker who'd placed it there eyeing her with critical brown eyes. "You don't want to fall in here."

"Right. I ... thought maybe Mr. Fuller would want to save this for the owners."

"Probably the salvage company will get it to them." The man eyed her keenly.

Campbell took two steps back and looked toward the loader.

The worker returned to the job, and she gulped in air. When his back was fully turned, she took the necessary two steps and stooped to pick up the foot-long wrench. Had he really tossed that aside as salvage for the Laffertys? Or for himself? She whirled and hurried away.

"Hey, Nathan," she called.

He turned her way and met her halfway around the edge of the site.

"Better step back a little, Campbell."

She held up her find. "One of the men just threw this out of the cellar hole."

Nathan frowned at it. "What was that doing in there? That was a finished basement. Red didn't keep tools ..."

"Nathan," Campbell said, a bit louder, turning so that her body shielded the view of the wrench from the workers. "That looks like blood."

15

Nathan squinted at the wrench, and Campbell watched his face. A dark brown stain smeared the larger end. The dried material definitely looked like blood to her.

Nathan's curious gaze turned to a wary frown. "We'd better call Keith."

"What about the deputy?" Campbell looked toward the uniformed officer, who stood on the far side of the cellar hole, watching the loader.

Eyeing her uneasily, Nathan said, "What do you think?"

It took Campbell only a moment to decide. "Call Keith. I'll take it over to your house."

Nathan pulled out his phone. Careful not to make any additional fingerprints on the wrench, Campbell held it down along her pant leg and walked quickly around the wreckage and toward the Fuller home. She reached the haven of the screened porch and looked back to see Nathan speaking to the volunteer worker.

A minute later, he reached the steps and said, "Keith's

coming right out. He said to lay it down and don't let anyone else touch it."

Nathan and Angela had a table on the porch, where they often ate lunch. Campbell set the wrench on top of it.

"That guy in the hole asked me where it went," Nathan said, shutting the screen door behind him.

"What'd you tell him?"

"That the police needed to see it. I think he was going to keep it for himself."

"He didn't notice the blood then?" Campbell looked down at the obvious stain.

"I'm not sure, but he didn't mention it."

She shook her head. "These workers are supposed to be helping people, not stealing stuff they find in the wreckage."

"I know."

"Maybe he *did* notice it." She frowned.

Nathan set his Coke bottle down on the corner of the table. "Where's your bottle?"

"I—I set it down out there when I picked up the wrench. I'm sorry."

"Don't worry about it. I'll get it later, if they haven't tossed it in the truck."

They stood in silence for a moment.

"You know this is a long shot," Campbell said. "The body was in the Kellums' cellar hole. If this was—you know—the weapon, why would it be in the Lafferty's place?"

"I have no idea, but I think we should get it checked out, don't you?"

"Absolutely." She scrunched up her face, thinking. "The medical examiner should be able to tell if it was the murder weapon."

"Keith told me the cause of death was blunt force trauma. Head wound."

"Yeah." She swallowed hard, remembering the day they'd discovered Weylan Osgood's body. He hadn't had a name then. He was just ... a corpse. Did she think of murder victims as nameless objects? Maybe she'd read too many mystery novels.

Nathan locked the porch's outside door and brought more colas.

"Oh, no thanks," Campbell said.

They sat together at the table, keeping guard over the wrench. Nathan took only occasional sips of his drink. Campbell thought it was something to do with his hands while they waited.

"So, what's Bill up to today?" he asked after a while.

"Oh, he had to meet with an attorney that we do a lot of work for." She considered telling him the information Keith had given them at lunch, but she wasn't sure how much to reveal. They generally kept mum about their cases. If Keith wanted his dad to know, he'd tell him.

Nathan nodded. "Bill's a good guy." He leaned back in his chair and waved a hand toward the choppy lake. "I gotta get him out here to go fishing. But not until things calm down, I guess."

"It's windy today."

"Yeah, it's supposed to rain later."

Campbell frowned at the color of the water. "It looks—I don't know—muddy."

"The twister put a lot of trash in the lake, and it's still recovering. The National Guard is going to try to haul out the worst of it. The river current will have to take care of the rest, I guess." Nathan sighed. Kentucky Lake, like Lake Barkley, was an artificially widened stretch of river.

Restless, he hopped up and strolled inside the house and through the rooms to the door facing the road and back again.

"No sign of him yet." He peered out through one of the

screened windows, toward where the crew still plugged away on the Laffertys' lot. "Keith said you took your private investigator's exam today." He swung around. "How'd you do?"

"I don't know yet. But ... maybe not so well."

Nathan made a face. "Sorry to hear that. I shouldn't have asked."

"No, it's okay." She dredged up a smile. "If it doesn't work out, I'll do something else."

He walked around the table and resumed his seat. "I thought you were doing pretty good at the job. And Angela, well, she thinks you're the best P.I. in western Kentucky."

"I think she's a little prejudiced, since she helped me on that case last month."

"Maybe so." Nathan picked up his Coke bottle and took a swig.

Campbell excused herself to use the restroom. When she returned, Nathan was giving his son a mile-a-minute account of their find. Keith hunched over the table, eyeing the wrench closely without touching it, but when she entered the room, he straightened and gave her a big smile.

"Can't quit nosing out evidence, can you?"

"It was practically thrown at me."

He chuckled. "Dad told me how the guy tossed it up out of the cellar hole."

Nathan said staunchly, "I'm telling you, Red had that house pretty much stripped. There were no tools lying around in the cellar. And even before the twister hit, that was a finished basement. They had a big screen TV down there, and a couch and a Ping-Pong table. And there was an extra bedroom and bath down there too. Not a tool shed. And they took out the TV and all the furniture when they put the place on the market."

"Okay, Dad. I guess the next thing is to go see Mr. Lafferty and ask him if the Crescent wrench belongs to him."

"You're not sending it right to the police lab?" Nathan's lips sagged.

"Well, it looks like blood, but we can't be sure without tests, and even if it is, we'd have to have it matched to Weylan Osgood's blood to do us any good in this case. Before we go through all that, we need to make sure the property owner doesn't have a simple explanation that rules it out as a murder weapon."

"I get your drift." Nathan seemed a little deflated.

Campbell said quickly, "Is there anything else we can do, Keith?"

"I'll need you both to make statements later at the station. But let's hear what Red has to say first."

Nathan nodded soberly. "Whatever you say, son."

"Can we give you a bottle of pop before you go?" Campbell asked. "Or coffee?"

Keith's face brightened. "I could use a cup of coffee." He glanced at his watch. "A quick one."

"I'll get it." Nathan headed for the kitchen.

Keith focused on Campbell's face. "Did you see exactly where the wrench came from?"

"Not really. The loader had taken out a big bucketful of debris, and small stuff fell off. When it was out of the way, heading for the dump truck with the load, the two guys out there jumped down in the cellar hole and started picking up pieces that were too far from the pile for the bucket to get them. If it was wood and stuff like that, they tossed it on the pile for the next load."

"But not metal?"

"I'd seen them set aside a few things over at the Airbnb—the Kellums' place. I thought they were going to give them back to the owners. Now I have to wonder if they were going to keep them."

"What makes you think that?"

She smiled ruefully. "I have to admit, your dad put the idea in my head. They were probably just rescuing a few usable things for the family."

"Tell me about the wrench."

"Well, it was by itself after the loader moved out. I suppose, being heavier than the wood pieces and wall board—that stuff—it sifted down when the pile was disturbed."

"Could be."

Campbell looked into his eyes. "Keith, why would the wrench be in the Laffertys' cottage, when the body was in the Kellums'?"

"Good question."

She frowned, thinking. "I guess I could come up with a scenario."

Keith's smile lit his face. "I just bet you can."

With a playful shove, she said, "Stop it. I bet you can too."

"All right, I can see someone with a body to unload driving out there and choosing the Kellums' place as one that was totaled. A place where, if anyone was in it when the storm hit, they might very well be killed by flying debris. Also, one that wasn't really close to an occupied structure like my folks'. And then ..."

Excitement spiraled up in Campbell. "And then, he went back to his car and realized he hadn't got rid of the wrench yet. So he took it and tossed it into the nearest pile of rubble and then hightailed it out of there."

"Mmm ..." Keith's eyebrows lowered as he considered that. "But it wasn't on top of the pile or we'd have seen it the next day. At least, the cops who examined the scene after the body was found would have spotted it."

"If not them, then your dad or your mom would have over the next few days."

"Right. They're pretty sharp. And Drew Kellum was out here a couple of times too, looking things over. That makes me think whoever put it there at least stuck it under some of the debris before he ran."

Nathan returned with a travel mug marked "Murray Racers" and handed it to Keith. "In case you need to get moving."

"Thanks, Dad."

———

Campbell could hardly wait to get home and tell her father about her discovery. When she entered the kitchen through the garage door, Rita was putting on her sweater, and her purse sat on the pine table.

"Heading out, Rita?" Campbell asked.

"Yes, and supper's in the slow cooker."

"Bless you! Are Dad and Nick home?"

"They just came in. I believe they're having a preprandial beverage."

"Oh?" Campbell arched her eyebrows, surprised that Rita knew the word. "Not an aperitif?"

Rita grinned. "I'm reading a lot of British novels these days, and it's increasing my vocabulary."

Campbell laughed. "That'll do it. Did Dad pay you?"

"Yes, he did." Rita slid the strap of her purse onto her shoulder and patted the bag. "I left a couple of phone messages on your desk. See you next week."

Determining to ask her father if they could afford to have Rita come two days a week instead of one, Campbell went into the hall. Voices emanated from the main office, and she paused in the doorway.

The September afternoon was still warm enough to warrant air conditioning, yet the two men sat in front of the empty fireplace. They'd have to reconsider the seating arrangements—although she supposed that could wait until next summer. It wouldn't be many weeks before a blaze would feel good in here.

"Hey, y'all." She exaggerated her drawl as she stepped into the room, and both men turned their heads her way.

"Well, Soup, how was your adventure?" her dad asked.

"Probably more exciting than yours." She dumped her purse on her desk and headed for the single-serve coffeemaker.

"What happened?" Nick asked.

"No, you guys tell me your tales first." She left her chai tea brewing and went over to sprawl in an armchair near them.

"Barry handed me some more work. Nothing urgent, but it will keep us busy when we're not working on the Kellums' case," Bill said.

And Jackie's, Campbell thought.

"I spent the afternoon watching two different people with insurance claims pending," Nick said. "Both seem to have legit cases. Yawn. Now you go."

Campbell got up and sauntered to the coffeemaker for her tea. "It wasn't much, really, but Nathan and I did have to call Keith." She picked up her cup and turned to face them. "We may have found the murder weapon."

Nick's jaw dropped.

"Well, well, well," her father said, grinning from ear to ear. "Nice work, kiddo."

"It's not definite, but Keith took it away for the lab to analyze."

"What was it?" Nick demanded.

Campbell drew out her tale, deliberately making it more suspenseful as she described the way the cleanup crewman threw the wrench out of the cellar, practically at her feet.

"They'd better put a rush on that at the lab," Bill said.

"Keith was going to take it to Mr. Lafferty first, to see if it was his. If it's not, he said he'd take it to the medical examiner to see whether it was possibly the weapon used on Weylan Osgood."

Bill nodded. "No sense sending it off to the lab if it doesn't match the wounds."

Campbell drained her cup and smiled at them. "Rita told me our supper's ready, and I smell something delicious."

"Pot roast." Nick had obviously been investigating the kitchen.

"I've invited Nick to stay," her father said. "There's plenty, and he's put in a good day's work."

Thursdays were not only Rita's day to work for them, Campbell noted, but also the day Nick took most of his meals here. She went to set the table and found that Rita had already done it.

After they'd eaten and Nick headed home for the night, Campbell and Bill went upstairs to their sitting room. Bill picked up the TV remote.

"You know I'm helping Jackie tomorrow afternoon, right?"

"Oh, tomorrow's her closing, I think?"

"Yeah, she's going to the lawyer's for that at ten, and she'll call me after that. A truck is taking her stuff to the new house around one o'clock, and I'm going to help her unpack."

"Okay. I'll hold the fort here while you're gone. But don't forget, Nick and I have that concert tomorrow night."

"I told him to come in late tomorrow. You should have the morning off too, I guess."

"It's okay. I'm taking Saturday off. Keith and I have plans."

Campbell sat down in one of the recliners. She wasn't big on crime shows, but sometimes her dad's favorite programs raised questions they could discuss afterward—things that might come up in their work. She decided she'd sit through an hour-long show just to have this bit of time with him.

The evening news was just ending, and he clicked to pause it. "So, Soup, I want you to think for a second. What was it about that guy on the cleanup crew that made you think he intended to keep the wrench?"

She could see that he was deeply interested, so she cast her thoughts back to the moment when the wrench appeared. "I guess because he spoke to me when I went over near it. And then he asked Nathan what happened to it after I walked away with it. Nathan told Keith he seemed a little belligerent that we were taking it. But he couldn't very well say, 'That's mine,' could he? Because it wasn't. On the other hand, maybe he thought I was stealing it, not him."

"Could be."

After a moment's thought, she added, "I'd had the thought that he might keep it, but I think Nathan actually said it first."

Bill nodded, his face sober. "Had you ever seen the man before? Maybe on one of the other crews?"

"Not that I remember."

"Did he work for the people who brought the equipment? The loader and the dump truck?"

She frowned. "Maybe. But … I think he was just a volunteer."

"Why do you think that?"

Campbell racked her brain. There was something. There had to be. "Well, the man who was working with him had on coveralls and a cap with a logo. This guy was just wearing jeans and a plain T-shirt. No hat." She met her father's gaze. "I don't know. If they were with the same company, wouldn't they both have worn the same outfit?"

"Not necessarily. And a volunteer might wear coveralls that he normally wore to his job or when he was working on his car at home."

"So, is that a dead end?"

"Maybe. Or maybe I can find out who sent the heavy equipment out there today and ask the supervisor about the crew." He clicked a button on the remote and settled back in his chair.

16

Bill climbed out of his car and looked Jackie's new house over. The small, modern ranch probably had two bedrooms, possibly more, but he doubted it. The lot couldn't be more than a half-acre, but it was pleasantly landscaped. Roses bloomed along the walkway between the drive and the front door. The attached two-car garage met his approval. It would provide a bit of security for a woman living alone.

The garage door was up, and Jackie's car was already inside. She came out the door that led into the house and grinned as she walked out to meet him.

"Well, what do you think?"

"Looks well cared for."

She nodded. "It's small, but I don't want anything huge for just me. Well, me and Miss Pepper." She laughed. "My cat. I left her with a friend. Didn't want to bring her over here until I'm settled and don't have to open the door every two minutes."

"Probably wise."

She led him to the steps. "This goes into the kitchen.

There's a spare room, in case one of the kids comes to visit, but not enough space for any of them to camp out here long."

Bill smiled but didn't comment. One of the best days of his life was the one when Campbell helped him out of a tough spot and then moved in with him. If she left again, he'd have a huge hole in his life.

"Did you eat lunch?" Jackie asked.

"Yeah. How about you?"

"I picked up a couple of burgers and drinks."

"Well then, you should eat."

He followed her inside, where she had set up two folding patio chairs in the empty living room. On the floor near one was a bag from a fast-food restaurant and two large to-go cups.

"I got root beer for you, if you want it." She held out one of the cups.

"I'll force myself," Bill said with a smile.

They sat down and Jackie rather self-consciously opened the bag. "Sure you don't want a cheeseburger? Or some fries?"

"No, thanks. I just ate."

She unwrapped a burger and took a bite.

Bill hoped the truck wasn't late. The situation felt awkward, and he started trying to think of small talk topics.

Jackie swallowed and said, "Lucy told me about that investigator guy. That was a little scary."

"Yeah, she was shook up."

"Thanks so much for going over there."

"No problem," Bill said.

"I just can't believe Sid would hire a P.I. to do surveillance on me. At my daughter's apartment, no less."

Bill studied her face. "I've been thinking about it."

"And?"

"I probably should have asked the guy a few more

questions, but I see three options. One, Sid sent him there. Two, somebody else is keeping an eye on you. Three, someone is watching either Lucy or Garrett."

"No. I can't believe that. Why? Lucy's a sweet little bride, and Garrett—well, he's a standup guy. I don't think he'd be involved in anything shady."

"We do know that Lucy isn't having him watched."

Jackie's eyes widened. "Of course not. Why would she?"

Bill shrugged. "We have to check every angle."

Jackie's mouth took on a grim line. "I can assure you, if she had any reason to need to keep an eye on Garrett, she'd tell me about it."

"Okay, I'll take your word for that. She certainly wouldn't have called me if she'd hired the investigator."

"Right." Jackie sat looking at him for several seconds.

Bill had a feeling he'd taken a misstep. He should have changed direction in the conversation. "Anyway, Maguire didn't deny he was watching for you when I said you were out of town. And he left immediately after, so I really think he was there trying to track you, not either of the kids." He sipped his root beer.

"So, where does that leave us?" Jackie asked.

"It takes us back to Sid, I guess. That is, if you're positive there's no one else who'd want to watch you."

Her face clouded up. "No one."

Did she take just a second too long to answer? Was she holding out on him?

Her lips trembled, and Bill felt like a heel. He had to ask these questions if he wanted to get to the truth, but now she acted as though she didn't think he trusted her. Did he?

He sighed. "Jackie, I don't like having to ask you these things."

"I know."

He couldn't stand that crushed expression on her face. Standing, he held out his arms. "Come here."

She set down her cup and what was left of her burger and came to him, just a little stiffness in her back at first, but then folding softly against him. Her arms slid around his waist, and she clung to him.

Bill gulped. If she burst into tears, he was lost. Tires on the driveway and a peremptory honk of a horn were welcome sounds to his ears.

He eased away from her and glanced out the front window. "Come on. Your stuff is here."

———

"I'll make certain Mr. McBride knows about it. Thank you very much for getting back to us, sir." Campbell hung up the landline and smiled grimly as she wrote a message for her dad.

"What is it?" Nick asked from across the room. He'd come in an hour ago, at three, but Bill still hadn't returned from Jackie's.

"That," Campbell said archly, "was the construction company whose equipment was working demo duty on the cottages near the Fullers' house yesterday." She finished the note with a flourish. "They said some of their employees worked on it, notably the guys driving the loader and the truck. But there were some volunteers helping out too. It took them a while, but they're pretty sure there was at least one volunteer working on the site of the Laffertys' cottage."

"Do they have his name?"

"Afraid not. They asked their drivers, and they said they'd met the guy at the volunteer station in front of the courthouse, but neither of them remembered his name. Since he was a community volunteer, they figured they didn't need to remember."

Nick shook his head. "Too bad you didn't snap a picture."

Campbell's self-confidence sank to a new low. He was right. If she'd thought to do that, someone would have identified the worker by now. Any other investigator would have done it as second nature. *Next time, I'll take a million pictures.*

Right. If there was a next time.

————

Bill carried the five hundredth box into the house, or at least it seemed that way. The two movers were right behind him, wrestling Jackie's clothes washer up a temporary ramp.

"This is it." He plopped the carton marked "Pots and Pans" down on her new kitchen island. "They're coming with the washer."

Jackie bustled out to supervise as they wheeled the machine into the laundry room. She praised their work, offered them coffee—which they declined, signed their paperwork, and saw them to the door. She returned and sank down on a stool by the island, exhaling in a puff.

"We did it."

"Yes, we did." Bill grinned at her, every muscle aching. "I put your bed frame together. If you know where the linens are, I'll help you make it up. That way you can fall into bed when I bring you back from dinner."

"Dinner?"

"I'm starved. Aren't you?"

Jackie shrugged. "I hadn't thought about it, but yeah, I am."

He laughed. "Let's go. I'm buying. You want Sirloin Stockade? Culver's? Wherever you want."

"Anything, but first let me wash my face and run a comb through my hair."

Bill held up both hands in surrender. "If you can find what you need, go ahead. I'll give Campbell a quick call and tell her I won't be home for a couple hours."

They hit the buffet and returned an hour later.

"What now?" Bill asked, pulling up before the house once more. "Make the bed?"

"I'll do it. You should go home and relax."

"Oh, I'm good for another hour or two. You know that when you get up tomorrow morning, it will be a blessing to see that much more unpacked."

She smiled up at him, her dark eyes sparkling. "Bill McBride, *you* are a blessing to me. I don't think I've ever once met up with you when you weren't a help or an encouragement."

To his embarrassment, Bill's face heated. He muttered, "I don't know about that."

"You don't? How about way back, ten years or more ago, when I had a flat on the highway? You drove by, and I didn't even realize it was you, but you turned around and came back. You not only changed my tire, you let me charge my phone in your car while I waited. I hadn't been able to call for help, because my phone's battery was deader than a doornail."

He smiled. "No more than I'd do for any woman." The truth was, he hadn't realized the lady with the flat tire was Emily's friend until he went back to investigate, but he'd never revealed that to her.

"I'm sure that's true." Jackie turned to survey the Mount Everest of cartons piled in her new living room. "Well, if you're determined, pick a box. I see one that says 'Lamp,' and there's one of books, and another that says 'Hall Bath.' That one's probably full of towels."

Bill set to work. Now and then, she called out to him from the master bedroom, where she was busy with the linens and her clothing. He heard hangers sliding on the closet rod as he walked past to deliver the towels to the hall bathroom.

For an hour, he was comfortable, toiling with her but not right next to her. The truth was, if he'd stood across the bed from her, straightening sheets and pillows, that would have been a bit too personal for wherever it was their relationship stood now.

When she emerged at last from her sanctuary, she stood in the living room doorway, smiling with satisfaction.

"Oh, good. You found all the lamps."

"Well, I wasn't sure ..."

She nodded toward one. "That one used to be in Lucy's old room, but I think I'll put it in the spare room now, with my sewing machine. Oh, no, leave it for now," she said hastily, as Bill moved to unplug it.

"All right." He surveyed the etagere holding two shelves of books and various knickknacks. "You'll want to rearrange those things, I'm sure."

"There's time. Just having them out and the boxes broken down is wonderful. If I can get the kitchen sorted out tomorrow, I'll probably go and get Miss Pepper Sunday afternoon." She turned that radiant smile on him. "Let's have a cup of cocoa and call it a night."

He followed her to the kitchen and eased onto one of the stools.

Jackie gasped. "I can't believe you put the table together too. Bill, you're Superman."

He blushed in earnest. "Wasn't much."

"What did you use for tools?"

"My pocketknife has a screwdriver."

She laughed, a rippling melody, so much more of a statement than Emily's quiet chuckles. "Brilliant."

"I expect you have a tool kit somewhere, but I didn't want to ask."

"Smart choice. I don't think it's surfaced yet." She flipped on the radio that sat on the counter and opened a cupboard door. "Oops. I haven't unpacked the kitchen yet." With an apologetic frown, she turned to face him. "Sorry, I have mugs, but I've no idea where the cocoa mix is. Is it too late for coffee? I did set up the coffeemaker earlier."

He remembered, as they'd shared a cup of brew midway through the afternoon. "Oh, that's okay, Jackie. I should be getting home, anyway."

She hesitated, giving the radio announcer time to finish his forecast—no tornadoes in the foreseeable future, but they might get half an inch of rain in the night.

"I'd tell you to stay longer, but I know you're right. It's been a long day for both of us." She stepped toward him. "Bill, I can't thank you enough."

He opened his mouth to frame a gracious reply just as the radio announcer said, "Police have identified the man whose body was found last week in the tornado debris in Marshall County as Weylan Osgood of Murray.

Jackie froze then turned to stare at the radio. "Weylan Osgood?"

"... medical examiner said the cause of death was blunt force trauma. In other news—"

Jackie snapped off the radio.

Bill's pulse was thundering. "You knew Osgood?"

"He—no, not really, but ..." Her brow furrowed, and she swung her chin up slowly, meeting his gaze. "The name's familiar."

Was there something else? Bill couldn't help feeling she knew more.

"That man," she said. "The one outside Lucy's apartment. What if ..."

"What?" If came out sharper than Bill had intended.

"I don't know. Just ... I've thought someone was stalking me, as you know, and I thought it might be Sid. What if it's someone else?"

"Who?"

She looked away, still fretful.

"You have someone in mind?" Bill asked.

She pulled in a breath. "No."

"Well, we know someone put a private investigator on you. People don't do that lightly. It's expensive."

Her gaze slid back to his.

"Jackie, I want to help you. If you know something—if you even suspect something, tell me."

She held out one hand, fingers spread. "I don't. I'm just trying to make sense of it."

.

17

Campbell followed Nick reluctantly to the door to the right of the stage. The concert had outlasted her interest. First off, she wasn't a big fan of country music, and second, she doubted this band would ever win a Grammy. She wished they could head down the road for Murray.

But of course, they couldn't. Not until Nick took his shot with Blaze Collins. She had to admit, the bass guitarist looked a lot like the photos Barry Capps's family had given them. Too bad they didn't have recordings of his singing. She could have told Nick within three bars if this was his man.

The auditorium emptied slowly, and they were fighting the tide. Finally they got in line behind several other fans. A few were allowed through, but most were turned away.

It took five minutes of fast talking on Nick's part and three phone calls backstage by the guard before he finally let them in, guided by a young woman whose torn jeans contrasted with her glittery eye shadow. Backstage was hectic, with roadies already dismantling and removing the band's gear and theater employees starting to clean.

After winding through a warren of passageways and storage spaces, they reached a hallway with a row of dressing rooms. Another muscular guard blocked their path.

"They have permission to see Collins," their escort said.

"You sure? He's got someone in there now."

"I'm sure."

The large man shrugged and moved aside. Their leader took them to the second doorway and knocked.

Campbell hung back while Nick entered the small room—more like a closet with a couple of chairs, a clothes rack and a vanity—to talk to the musician. A wiry man wearing a cowboy hat slipped out into the hall and walked away.

"Who'd you say you are?" Collins asked, meeting Nick's gaze in the mirror as he wiped traces of makeup off his face.

"Nick Emerson. I'm a private investigator out of Murray."

Collins scowled at him. "What do you want?"

"I was hired by an attorney to find you."

Swiveling around on the stool, he glared up at Nick. "What for?"

"I couldn't say, Mr. Collins. Or should I say, Mr. Capps?"

"All right, that's it! Out of here!" Collins jumped up and nodded to the guard.

"Okay, mister." The guard stepped forward.

Campbell's pulse raced, and she shrank back into the hallway.

Nick said quickly, "Were you aware that your grandmother died a couple of months ago, Barry?"

As the guard seized Nick's arm, Collins held up both hands. "Whoa, whoa, whoa! My grandmother?"

The guard relaxed a little, and Collins eyed Nick keenly.

"Yeah. Sharon Capps."

For a moment, Collins stood still, staring at him. Then he turned away. "You got the wrong guy, buddy."

"I don't think so," Nick said. "By the way, my coworker and I enjoyed the concert."

Collins flicked a glance toward Campbell, who stood outside the doorway. She managed a weak smile.

"Well, thanks, but I can't help you. Now, if y'all give this to the girl at the box office, she'll give you a couple free tickets to our next concert in Nashville."

Nick took the card he handed him but didn't budge. "Look, Barry, it could be important. I don't know, but it's possible."

Collins looked at the guard. "Give us two minutes, Joe."

The guard put his hand on the doorknob and stared meaningfully at Campbell. She hesitated then ducked inside, behind Nick.

"This is your coworker?" Collins asked. "Or your girlfriend?"

Campbell wanted to yell, "I'm not his girlfriend, you rude moron," but she kept quiet.

"She's Campbell McBride," Nick said. "We work together."

Collins frowned but didn't demand to see her license. "Look, I don't know what this is about, and frankly, I don't care."

"It could be in your best interest," Nick said.

"Some kind of an inheritance?"

"I really don't know. I could make assumptions, based on what we usually do for lawyers."

"What would you assume?"

"That Barry Capps was mentioned in his grandmother's will." Nick shrugged. "Or that his family simply wants to let him know about the death."

"No, they wouldn't bother with that, especially if it meant paying lawyer's fees." Collins went to the vanity and stooped to peer at himself in the mirror, poking at a spot on his cheek.

He straightened and turned to Nick. "Like I said, you got the wrong guy."

"Can you show me your I.D.? My boss and our client will want proof."

Collins exhaled testily. "Does the client know you're approaching me?"

"Not yet. We wanted to speak to you first."

"Well, don't tell them, okay?"

"We ... we work for the client," Nick said, "not for you. I'm sorry, but we have to tell them whatever we learn about Barry Capps."

"You're learning nothing about him, you hear me? Nothing."

Campbell studied the young man's face. He was angry, and getting angrier by the minute. She stepped up to Nick and touched his arm lightly. He glanced at her, his eyebrows quirking. After peering at her face for a moment, he nodded.

She cleared her throat and stepped between the two men. Her pulse hammered, but she kept her voice light and steady. "Mr. Collins—Blaze. We understand about stage names. But it seems to me that if you truly had no connection to Barry Capps, you wouldn't be so insistent about it. Now, if you have a legitimate reason not to want contact with the Capps family, we would understand that too."

"Yeah?" He held her gaze, testing her.

"It's not our intention to bring you trouble. If you don't want the family to know where you are, we can tell the attorney, and his office can contact you about this matter of the will. Your family doesn't need to know."

Collins darted a glance at Nick. "But he just said—"

"He said we work for the client. Our client is the attorney, not the Capps family. The lawyer who is probating the will hired us to find you. He's paying us for that, not your family."

"But they're paying him to do it, right?"

"Technically, yes. But if I understand the matter correctly, the money he spends trying to find you will come out of the estate, not from other family members."

Collins's stony expression relaxed. "I get you. But I don't even want my father to know I'm alive, see? If he finds out where I am, it might ruin my career. I could be—" He broke off, shaking his head.

Nick said, "Don't you think that if you don't want them to see your mug, you should move farther away? The band's website is out there for anyone to see, and there are posters with your pictures on them all over Paducah."

That was an exaggeration, but Campbell had seen some in the lobby. Anyway, the attorney had said Barry's family was in Louisville. Five hours or so away, but still, the country music world wasn't infinite. Nick was right about that.

"Look, give us your address and phone number," she said earnestly. "We will give it to the attorney and nobody else. We'll also explain to him that you don't want that information passed on to his family, no matter what."

"Or anyone else?"

Campbell frowned. "We can tell him your wishes. Is there someone in particular, other than your father, that you don't want to find you?" *Like the police, for instance?*

He ran a hand through his hair. "How about you give me the lawyer's number, and I call him tomorrow to find out what this is about?"

"He'd need some identification," Nick said. "He'd probably want you to come to his office, in person. They don't do this kind of business over the phone."

"Where's the office?"

"Murray. An hour or so from here." Nick took out his pocket

notebook. "Here. Give us your deets. We don't get paid until we bring the lawyer a way to contact you."

"Would I have attorney-client privilege?"

Nick looked helplessly at Campbell.

"I don't know," she said. "Technically, you're not the client. The estate is."

"Isn't someone in the family in charge of the estate? The whattayacallit—executor or something like that?"

"Maybe. You could ask the attorney. If you're named in the will, I'm sure they'd tell you about the estate's management."

"But why are they using a lawyer in Murray? My family's in Louisville."

"Because the last address they had for you was over here. The actual attorney handling the probate is in Louisville, but he's got one over here looking for you because you lived in Murray while you attended college there. They don't have a more recent address."

Collins sighed and took the pen and notebook Nick offered. He paused with the pen hovering over the paper and looked Nick in the eye. "I keep thinking this is all a trick."

"It's not," Nick said gently. "I can show you Mrs. Capps's obituary online if you want."

Someone pounded on the door. "Hey, Blaze! You coming, man?"

"Be right there."

Campbell held her breath as he scribbled in the notebook and returned it to Nick, who scrutinized it for a second.

"Is that a one or a seven?"

"Seven," Collins said. "Look, tell him not to use that name when he contacts me—you know. Address anything he sends to Blaze Collins."

"I'll tell him."

"Thank you," Campbell said. "We'll get out of your hair now."

She and Nick went into the hall, where the guard, another one of the band members, and two long-haired girls were waiting.

"Excuse me," she said, easing past them.

Once outside the building, she and Nick walked quickly across the nearly empty parking lot to his Jeep.

"Thought we'd never get it out of him," Nick said.

Campbell nodded. "I just hope it's the right info."

"He's hiding something."

"I agree."

"An abusive father, maybe," Nick said, hitting the button on his key fob to unlock the doors.

"Or the cops."

"You think so?"

Campbell opened the passenger door and slid inside. When Nick was in and both doors were shut, she reached for her seatbelt. "I think he's afraid of being found. Other than that, I don't know."

———

It was nearly midnight when Nick took Campbell home. He'd intended to drop her off and go get some sleep, but her father was up and pacing, so on her plea, Nick went inside with her. She let him do most of the talking.

"So that's it." Nick handed over the slip of paper from his notebook. "He definitely doesn't want his family to find him, but he did finally give us an address and phone number."

Bill frowned down at it. "I think I'll have you go with me Monday morning to deliver this. It's possible they may want us to do a little more."

"I suppose he's on the road a lot," Campbell said. "The address is just outside Nashville, though."

"How long are they playing in Paducah?" her father asked.

"Tomorrow night's the last performance there." Campbell had checked that out when they first arrived at the auditorium.

"Okay, good job. You guys get some sleep. Nick, I'll see you Monday morning. Be here by eight thirty."

"Will do." Nick sauntered out the front door.

Bill sat staring at the framed photo of Campbell's mother. It stood on the mantel, over the empty fireplace.

"What's the matter, Dad?"

"Oh, nothing. Just thinking."

She walked over to his chair and put her arm around his shoulders. "Everything go okay today?"

"Yes, fine."

Even so, she hated to break the moment. They didn't seem to connect deeply very often. She rubbed his shoulder. "You must be tired."

"I am." He let out a big sigh. "There's something about that Galt guy."

"Why do you say that? Is he stalking her, like she thought?"

"I'm pretty sure he had that P.I., Maguire, following her. But tonight, she turned on a radio, and they mentioned Weylan Osgood's name. Well, her reaction ..." Bill propped his elbow on the chair arm and rubbed his head.

"She hadn't heard about the press conference?"

"Apparently not. She was in Bowling Green for a couple of days. Either she didn't hear the local news, or they didn't mention it over there."

"What did she say when she heard it?"

He sighed. "Not much. She said the name was familiar but she didn't know him."

"That's it?"

"Well, she started in on how maybe it wasn't Sid after all who put the P.I. on her. Maybe it was someone else."

Campbell frowned, but her dad wouldn't look at her. She went around to the sofa and sat down kitty-corner from him. "Dad."

"Yeah?" Finally he raised his chin and met her gaze. "Maguire told you he was there for Sid Galt, right?"

"No. That would be breaking client privilege."

"But he didn't disagree with you when you said it. Isn't that right?" Nick had detailed Bill's conversation with Maguire to her, and she was pretty sure her dad had leaned on the P.I., accusing him of surveilling Jackie on Galt's behalf.

"No, he didn't contradict what I said, but maybe he was smarter than I thought. Maybe he just clammed up and let me think whatever I wanted. Then he left the scene to get away from me. What if he went back later?"

"Lucy would have called you."

"I suppose." Bill drummed his fingers on the chair's arm for a moment. "Unless he's *a lot* smarter than I thought."

Campbell stood. "Come on, Dad. You can't sit up all night fretting over it. Go to bed, and we'll pick it up in the morning."

"You're spending the day with Keith."

"Are you going back to Jackie's?"

"I dunno. We didn't say for sure. I figured she'd want a day to herself, to settle in and finish unpacking the way she wants to. She had most of the kitchen stuff to do, and I wouldn't be a whole lot of help on that."

Campbell nodded. A woman liked to arrange her own kitchen cupboards and drawers.

"Well, you can do some more research on Maguire and Osgood and ... and whoever else you think you should. I'll help you in the morning. Keith's not coming for me until eleven."

"You're right." Bill lumbered up out of his chair, and they headed for the stairs, turning out lights as they went.

At the top of the flight, Campbell said, "Goodnight, Dad."

"Hmm? Yeah, goodnight." But as he turned toward his own room, he was still muttering under his breath.

18

Campbell rose early on Saturday, even though she'd been up late. Something was nagging at her, and she sat cross-legged on her bed with her laptop open on her knees. She opened the Kellum file. Her dad had added the information they had so far about Weylan Osgood. As she'd recalled, he was employed in maintenance and grounds at MSU, and his house was not far from campus.

Next, she opened Nick's file on Barry Capps, aka Blaze Collins.

"Yes!" The young man had attended Murray State for four semesters, but he'd given up his apartment and left Murray in early June and hadn't returned for classes when the fall semester opened. Was it possible Barry knew Weylan Osgood?

She hunched over the laptop, frowning at the screen. Someone else they'd discussed recently was also connected to the university.

Of course, thousands of people had some sort of connection there. Students, faculty, staff, alumni ...

She snapped fingers. Her father had been over there

Thursday, when the private investigator from Clarksville showed up outside Lucy Holm's apartment. Lucy's husband, Garrett, worked for Murray State, she was almost sure.

Jumping up, she left the laptop on her bed and padded down the hallway to her father's room. Was it too early to wake him up on Saturday? With her ear to the door, she could hear him moving around. A dresser drawer creaked open. She smiled and gave a swift knock.

"Yeah?" Bill called.

"Dad, can I come in? I want to ask you something."

A moment later, he opened the door, clothed in a pair of old pants and a T-shirt. "What's up?"

"Dad, how many people involved in the cases we're working on are connected to Murray State?"

"I don't know." He shrugged but suddenly his features sharpened and he zoned in on her eyes, as though he realized it wasn't a casual question. "What are you thinking?"

"Well, we know Weylan Osgood worked there on maintenance, right?"

"Yes, he was a supervisor."

"Okay, good. Now, Barry Capps went to school there for two years, but then he left. In June."

"Right." Her father eyed her closely. "So? It's a fairly large campus."

"It is. But what about Garrett Holm? I've never met him or Lucy, but they live near campus, in an apartment. Are they students?"

"No, Lucy is a dental hygienist. As I understand it, Garrett helps run the school farm and teaches a couple of classes in the agriculture department."

"Really. How old is he?"

Bill shrugged. "Thirty, maybe."

"And Lucy's ...?"

"About your age, within two or three years."

"I'm surprised they're living in an apartment."

"It's my understanding they're saving for a house."

"What about Mr. Kellum?"

"No, he works for the city, remember?"

"That's right, public works." She nodded slowly. "Is it possible either Barry Capps or Garrett Holm knew Weylan Osgood?"

Bill's shoulders slumped. "Sure, anything's possible. But how often do students get to know groundskeepers? Maybe a football player would get to talking with one, but Barry wasn't an athlete."

"No, he was into music. Do we know if he was a music major?"

"I'm not sure. Ask Nick. But that's a totally different case, remember."

She nodded. "Yeah, but he acted really weird last night. And what about the aggie guy, Garrett ... I don't suppose there's a connection there?"

"There could be. But honestly, half the people in Murray have either gone to school there or worked there in some capacity."

"Surely not."

"Okay, not half, but a lot. And those who haven't actually attended the university have gone to basketball games or theater productions on campus, at the very least. A lot of community events are held there."

She let out a sigh. Keith had taken her to a student play there. "I guess you're right. It was a thought. But the pool of possibilities is too large."

"Maybe not. We know Garrett Holm knew Sid Galt, through Jackie. And I don't deny that Jackie's reaction to Osgood's name made me uneasy." His mouth skewed. "Okay, put the coffee on and let me finish getting dressed. It's Saturday, but I know a couple of people at the university I can probably track down and talk to. You may be onto something."

"You don't really think so."

"You never know, kiddo."

————

Nick wasn't due to work for the weekend. Campbell and Bill enjoyed a cozy breakfast together, seated at the small kitchen table. The urge to set up her laptop on the surface was strong, but Campbell resisted. Even though they lived together, she and her dad didn't have that many chances to give each other their undivided attention.

After breakfast was a different story. She took her laptop into Bill's office and sat across the desk from him.

"I don't think it's too early to call Bob Hunter now," Bill said. "Meanwhile, try searching for Galt and Osgood together. You probably won't find anything, but it would be a shame if we missed something obvious."

She started in, trying to think of ways to coax the server to bring up information that would be useful.

"Hey, Bob," her father said. "It's Bill McBride. I hope it's not too early. Oh, heading for the lake, are you? Well, I've just got a quick question. You knew Weylan Osgood, didn't you? Yeah, that's right. Okay. Does the name Sidney Galt mean anything to you? Uh-huh. And how about a student from last year named Barry Capps?"

He hung up a minute later, wishing his friend good luck fishing.

"Nothing there," he told Campbell. "He knew who Osgood was but didn't claim to actually know him. He had a vague memory of Capps, but he drew a blank on Galt."

"We don't know much about Sid Galt, do we?" Campbell frowned. "What he does for a living, for instance."

"I don't think Jackie ever said." He rubbed his chin. "She did mention a letter she saw by accident—a past due notice on something he'd bought with the previous Mrs. Galt. I assumed it was something like a refrigerator, or maybe even a car. But maybe not."

"Can your special websites help you find out?"

"Maybe, if he's defaulted on a loan or something like that. The bank would have to file certain paperwork ... Give me some time."

She got up and carried her laptop out to her desk across the hall. Her father had already added Sid Galt's previous wife's name to their file—Alanna. She started searching for information on the woman. What if Sid wasn't the one spying on Jackie? What if it was Alanna?

It didn't take long for her to find a failed restaurant called "Lanie's" in Bowling Green. The owner, Alanna Galt, had filed for bankruptcy two years ago. Another search told her that Alanna had been married to Sid for three years at the time. However, the restaurant had been operating for more than a decade. Campbell almost thought she remembered it, but she was sure she'd never eaten there. She'd passed it, though, back before her college days.

Fascinated, she started pulling up old articles mentioning Lanie's Restaurant. It had good ratings up until a year or so before the bankruptcy. In fact, it seemed to thrive, and Alanna had opened a second location in Elizabethtown. That branch was still operating, but it had been sold within the last year. Was Alanna getting out while she could?

She copied some articles and made a few notes.

Half an hour later, Bill emerged from his office, his face eager and ready for action.

"I found some dynamite. Sid Galt definitely knew Weylan Osgood."

"Oh yeah?"

"I found a mutual acquaintance—or rather, someone Osgood introduced to Galt."

Campbell let that sink in. "I guess that torpedoes my little theory."

"Which one?"

She laughed. "I had started to think it was Sid's ex—that is, Alanna Galt—who was stalking Jackie, not Sid."

"She thought she saw Sid."

"Would she recognize Alanna?"

"I don't know, but ..."

Campbell swiveled her chair around. "Okay, supposing it was Sid following her around and then hiring the P.I. What if Sid was following Jackie the day she went house hunting—the day she went to the lake to view the Laffertys' cottage?"

Bill started to speak and stopped. His face took on a somber set. "That could explain why the body was planted in the cottage debris. If he'd been out there—whoever the killer was —because he was keeping an eye on Jackie, and then, when the need arose, he thought it would be a fairly isolated spot to dump the evidence ..."

Campbell's mind whirled a mile a minute, and she was sure her father's did too. She pulled in a deep breath. "Okay, I'm not saying it was Sid, but whoever was with Osgood the night of the tornado may have shadowed Jackie while she was staying with Lucy and Garrett and shopping for a house over here."

Bill nodded slowly.

"But wouldn't she have seen him that day?" Campbell squinted, remembering. "Jackie viewed that cottage a day or two before the tornado. It would have been broad daylight when Nell showed it to her. You said Jackie thought she recognized Sid's vehicle the day you ate lunch with her and Lucy."

"Right."

"Surely she'd have noticed it even more, out there on a dirt road with not many cars passing."

Bill frowned. "If he was smart, he'd have hung back. He could even have hidden his car when he saw her and Nell stop, and then walked toward them, keeping out of sight. Or maybe he had a rental car that day." He shrugged. "I don't know. There are lots of options. I do know he's crafty."

"Yeah. Take a look at these stories I found about Alanna Galt, Dad. She owned a trendy restaurant in Bowling Green until she got mixed up with Sid."

He leaned in and looked at the article she'd brought up on her screen. "Lanie's. Sure, I know the place. Emily and I ate there a couple of times."

"It went bankrupt a couple years ago, and it had been doing well."

"Ouch."

"Not only that, she'd opened another one in E-town, and she sold that last winter."

Bill frowned, still skimming the news story. "You think Sid was the cause of her business failing?"

"I didn't say that. But it was doing well until he came along."

Bill frowned and continued reading. After a couple of minutes, he lifted his chin and met her gaze. "Okay, so let's assume Sid had financial problems with the last wife, and again with Jackie. Only Jackie didn't have a business to drain, so he stooped to stealing her credit cards out of her purse."

"That's awful."

He nodded. "But she still had enough to buy a new house. Not a very fancy one, but still ..."

"Dad ..."

"Yeah?"

Campbell glanced up at him, agonizing over whether to reveal everything. "I heard Jackie on the phone once. It was in the church parking lot. She was yelling at someone, telling them that some money had better be in her account soon or else."

"Or else what?"

"I don't know." She frowned, trying to remember. "I don't think she said. I figured it was her ex or somebody in the family. I didn't know much about her at the time."

"Okay, I'll think about that."

Glancing at the corner of her screen, Campbell said, "I've got to get ready. Keith will be here soon."

"You go ahead. I'm going to do some more digging here. And I may call Jackie to see if she's all right."

Campbell saw deep concern in his eyes. "You like her, don't you, Dad?"

"Yeah, I do." He hesitated. "It's nothing serious at this point, you know."

"She's not like Mom."

"Nobody's like your mother." He let out a puff of breath. "Jackie doesn't know her neighbors yet. I've got a feeling this Sid guy is more sinister than we thought, and I don't like the idea of her staying alone in the new house."

"I don't blame you." Jackie was lucky to have someone like Bill McBride care about her.

Campbell ran upstairs, trying to put the case out of her mind. She and Keith had decided to eat lunch out before their hike, so she put on jeans and a nice top. The temperature outside hovered near eighty-two, so she didn't bother with a jacket. As she pulled her hair into a ponytail, she heard a car drive in.

They ate at the diner, and a short drive up Route 80 took them to the Land Between the Lakes.

"Be careful," the man in the booth told them when they went to park at one of the campgrounds. "There was quite a bit of wind damage up there, and we don't have it all cleaned up yet. Stick to the trails."

As they started up the trail, Campbell said, "I wonder if they need volunteer workers over here, or if they want their staff to do it."

"We can ask when we go back down."

Keith took her hand on the lower part of the wooded path. They walked at a leisurely pace, letting others pass them. Two women strode by, trying to keep up with half a dozen excited children.

"Max," one of the moms cried. "Slow down! You need to stay where we can see you."

Campbell smiled at Keith. "They probably brought them here to work off some excess energy."

"Yeah," he said. "But guess who'll be worn out at the end of the day. Not the kids."

As the trail grew steeper, Campbell was surprised at how much damage surrounded them. Downed trees lay thick in the woods, leaving slashes of bright sunlight in the canopy. In several spots, someone had taken a chainsaw to trees and limbs in the path and tossed the wood to the side.

"Do you think all this was done by the tornado last week?" She paused to catch her breath and survey the damage more closely.

"I'm not sure." Keith pointed to a large oak that had toppled, pulling up a huge root ball. "That's new, for certain."

She was about to ask how he could tell when shouting reached them from the path above.

"The kids," she said.

They listened for a moment, and she was sure she also heard a mother's voice raised.

"We may as well go see what's up," Keith said with a rueful grin. "Not the peaceful outing I pictured."

The to-do didn't lessen, and they hurried up the path.

As the group of mothers and children came into view, one mom said bitterly, "Maxwell Austin, I *told* you not to do that."

The second mom stood nearby, her face pale and a hand to her mouth. Five children stood staring at a downed pine tree.

"Hi," Keith said to the quiet mom. "What's going on?"

"One of Sandy's kids was bouncing up and down on that tree trunk." She pointed to the fallen pine. "He fell down under it, and now he can't get out. He said his foot hurts."

"Maybe I can help." Keith gave Campbell a reassuring glance and stepped up beside the boy's mother.

"I'm afraid he's really hurt," the second mother told Campbell. "Sandy was just about to go and try to get to him. I wondered if I should run for help."

"Keith is a policeman. He'll know what to do." Campbell held out a hand. "I'm Campbell McBride."

"Debbie Houston." The woman's face crumpled as they shook hands. "We brought the kids over here for a fun day. My husband had to work, and Sandy's ... well, he's out of the picture."

Campbell nodded, her heart going out to Debbie, who'd thought this outing would distract the children and maybe her friend as well.

"I tried to get to him, but the branches are all broken and mashed together," Sandy gasped, in answer to a question from Keith.

He nodded. "Just wait here while I assess the situation." He waded through brush toward the toppled tree, following the sounds of the blubbering boy. Campbell clenched her teeth and made herself not yell, "Be careful." Keith knew what to do.

A moment later, he called, "Max, can you hear me?"

The boy's muffled response came from the pile.

"My name's Keith. I'm going to try to get you out, okay?"

Max said something, and Keith's face went grim. He spoke quietly to the boy for a moment then climbed cautiously onto the horizontal tree trunk. He disappeared behind it, and Campbell held her breath as Debbie clutched her arm.

They couldn't see anything, but a yelp came from Max, and Keith's head popped up beyond the tree trunk. His gaze homed in on Campbell.

"Can you call an ambulance, to meet us down at the campground entrance? I can carry him down."

"Can you get him out?"

"I think so. I'll clear a path on the far side. It may take a while—"

"Is it bad?" Sandy called.

"Do you know what a compound fracture is?"

Sandy's face blanched, and Debbie hurried to her friend's side. "It'll be all right." She looked toward Keith and yelled, "Is it okay to move him? Maybe you should wait."

Campbell fumbled with her phone, despairing when she saw that she couldn't get cell service in this location.

Keith said, "Someone's going to have to move him, and it could be really hard for the rescue team to get in there. We'd have to get someone up here with a chainsaw, at the least. I'm trained in first aid, and I think I can immobilize his ankle before I lift him."

"Do you need anything?" Campbell called.

"If anyone's got any cordage, or maybe strips of cloth, it

would help. There are plenty of sticks here, and I think I can use a couple of those to stabilize it. But call for an ambulance, okay?"

"I'll have to go down the path," Campbell said. "No service here, and I don't know where I'll be able to get it."

Keith frowned. "You may have to go all the way to the ranger station. Hurry, but be careful."

She nodded and made her way back to the trail. The first bit was steep, and she placed her feet gingerly. She didn't want to go for help and end up needing it herself. When the terrain leveled out, she ran as fast as she could. Reaching another steep spot, she paused for breath and tried the phone again. No such luck.

Fifteen minutes later, when she was sure she was nearly to the trailhead, she at last saw a couple of bars on the screen. She placed the call, telling the dispatcher to which campground the rescue unit should be sent.

Assured the unit was on its way, she walked more slowly to the booth at the entrance. The man they'd spoken to earlier was checking in a couple with an RV, but a woman was behind him in the booth.

"Excuse me," Campbell said to her, "but we have an emergency. A boy is hurt on the trail."

She explained that she'd already called for an ambulance and that Keith was qualified to administer first aid and planned to bring the boy down to their location.

The woman grabbed a first aid kit from a shelf. "I'll head up there. Do you want to wait here for the ambulance?"

Campbell briefly considered going back up the trail with her, but if the woman stayed on the path, she couldn't miss the group. Campbell would be exhausted if she did the hike again. She opted to wait.

After the new campers were checked in and drove off to

find their campsite, the man invited her to come inside the booth and sit down while she waited. Of course, that meant detailing the story to him in between his bouts of serving new arrivals.

A cluster of children erupted from the woods at the trailhead twenty minutes later, with Sandy and Debbie a minute behind and Keith in the rear, carrying the ten-year-old boy. The woman from the booth walked beside him, bringing the first aid kit and keeping up a conversation with Keith and a subdued Max.

In the distance, a siren wailed as Campbell hurried out to meet the group. Keith lowered Max gently to the deck outside the booth, where he sat wincing and snuffling. His mother hovered beside him, anxious to say the right thing and do something that would help lessen his pain.

The ambulance pulled in at last, and Keith strode over to give the EMTs a brief explanation of what had happened. Max howled when they moved him, but he was soon on a stretcher and headed to the back of the vehicle.

Quickly, Debbie arranged with Sandy to keep her two younger children until Sandy could get home from the hospital. Campbell helped Debbie round up the five remaining kids, and they drove off with many shouts of thanks and goodbyes.

Campbell waved as the minivan disappeared and let out a big sigh. She looked up at Keith. "You okay?"

"Oh, yeah. How about you?"

"I'm fine."

He took her hand, and they walked slowly toward his black SUV.

"Not your usual off-duty happening," she noted.

"It wasn't, but ... I don't know. I'm glad we were out here. It's sort of a reminder of why I do what I do." He looked down into her eyes as he opened the passenger door for her. "You and your dad, too. We're all here to help people."

She nodded, thinking about that.

"By the way," he said, "good job."

Campbell smiled. "You too, Detective."

They arrived at her house half an hour later. Campbell left Keith chatting with her dad and went to the kitchen to fix glasses of iced tea. When she came back, Keith was in Bill's office and both were looking at his desktop's monitor.

Keith straightened and eyed her tray with approval. "That looks great."

She served them and then, curious, edged around Bill's desk. She glanced at the screen and froze. "Who's that?"

"Maguire," her father said. "The private investigator out at Lucy's the other day."

"No." Campbell pointed at the driver's license headshot, her finger shaking. "You can ask Nathan to be sure, but that's the volunteer who threw the wrench out of the cottage cellar on Thursday."

19

In the car on the way to church Sunday morning, Campbell asked her father if he was going to show Jackie the photo of Maguire.

"No need. I saw Maguire at Lucy's place, but Jackie didn't. I know he's the one who was there. And you and Nathan agree he was the one at the cottage. So we have a solid I.D. on him. No need to ask Jackie."

"But what if ...?"

"What if she knows him?"

"Well, yeah, or what if she's seen him around? If Galt's hired him to follow her, she needs to know what he looks like."

He sighed. "You may be right. I'm thinking about it."

Campbell took that to mean she should keep quiet about it for now. When he was ready, her dad would share it with Jackie, she was sure.

Jackie came to the service, which didn't surprise Campbell, since she'd had been volunteering in the church's tornado relief effort. Why shouldn't she attend services here?

When her dad didn't intercept Jackie in the aisle and

invite her to sit with them, Campbell didn't comment. Instead, she started a conversation with the woman in the pew in front of her until the music director rose to lead the opening hymn.

After the worship service, they joined the throng headed for the door. Jackie moved into the aisle next to her and gave her a tentative smile.

"Well hi, Campbell. How's everything at True Blue?"

"Fine. Are you getting settled in your new place?"

"Trying. Your dad's been a big help." She tilted her head, looking across Campbell to Bill.

His lips quirked. "It's nothing."

"No, it's a lot," Jackie insisted.

Bill cleared his throat. "So, have you got everything in place now?"

"Not by a long shot. But it's coming."

They'd reached the door. Bill waved Jackie forward, and she shook Pastor Flynn's hand and greeted Nancy warmly. Campbell stepped up for her own moment with them then followed Jackie down the steps.

She turned toward her, feeling she ought to say something friendly. "How's the new house feel?"

"Good. Snug, but I like it. I'm picking up my cat this afternoon."

"Oh. I love cats."

Jackie nodded. "Me too. This one's an indoor cat, and I didn't want to move her until things were settled."

Bill came down the steps and joined them.

Jackie turned a high-beam smile on him. "I don't suppose you'd be available tomorrow?"

"Actually, I have an early appointment with a client and court in the afternoon," Bill said.

Campbell blinked, but then she remembered her dad

telling Nick to come in early so they could see the attorney on the Capps case together.

"No problem," Jackie said. "I can get Lucy to help me after she's done work. I just have a couple of dressers to move, things like that."

"I could help you," Campbell said. She glanced at her father, who looked as surprised as she was at the offer. "That is, if Dad doesn't need me at the office," she finished feebly.

"No, you can go. I'm sure you can be a big help to Jackie."

"Thanks," Jackie said. "Maybe come around tenish? I'm sure an hour would be plenty, and it would be a big help. It's just a few things that are too awkward to move by myself. I can ask Lucy and Garrett, but they both work all day, and I know they're tired in the evening."

Campbell agreed to be there at ten, and they all said goodbye and headed for their vehicles.

"I'm surprised you volunteered," Bill said as he started the engine.

"Well, I ... I don't know. It seemed like a good thing to do." She made a face at him. "Did you not want me to get involved with Jackie?"

"What? No, it's fine. Maybe you can get to know her a little better. She might even be willing to talk to you about the names we mentioned. I suspect she knows Osgood, but I'm not sure how. It didn't seem like a happy memory for her." He drove slowly to the parking lot's exit. "Want to eat out today?"

"Not really. We have plenty of leftovers."

"Leftovers it is." Bill turned toward home. "You know, I've been thinking. We should clear out that storage unit. It would save us money not to keep renting it, and if there were things we don't want to keep, we could donate them."

"Great idea, Dad. But did you mean today?"

"You got something else planned?"

"No." She considered tackling the remaining boxes and bric-a-brac in the storage unit. They had plenty of room in their new home. "You just spent one day moving stuff. Are you sure you want to do it again?"

"Oh, we can make it in two trips with our cars, easy. There's not that much stuff."

"Okay. Let's go eat lunch and change into our grubbies an' get 'er done."

Three hours of hard work and two trips back and forth allowed them to clear out Bill's storage unit. To Campbell's delight, she rediscovered the baby book her mother had kept for her, a tiny dress she'd worn on her first visit to church, and more old photos. Her mother's desk and a chair she had stenciled were now in her bedroom. A plant stand from her grandmother's house now stood in their sitting room beside the old rocking chair, and more than a dozen cartons now rested in the attic, awaiting her attention.

She fixed iced tea for herself and her father, and they sprawled in their upstairs living room.

"Thanks, Dad," she said. "I feel good about today."

"So do I. I'm tired, but I'm glad we did it."

Campbell picked up a snapshot of herself and her mom on the day of her high school graduation. Cheek to cheek with Emily, she sported a silly grin as her mortarboard threatened to fall off. "May I put this in my room?"

"Of course you can." Bill took a long drink from his glass and sat back with a sigh. "I wish we could have wrapped up the Osgood case."

"The police are still working on it." Campbell leaned her head back and shut her eyes. Lethargy had overtaken her since she sat down.

"I know, but it still feels like we're missing something."

Campbell jerked awake sometime later when her dad's cell

rang. As she straightened her crumpled body and stretched, he answered it.

"Yeah, Keith."

She perked up, and Bill looked over at her.

"Keith, let me put you on speaker. Campbell's with me."

Immediately Keith's voice came into the room. "Yeah, as I was saying, I just had a report from the state police. They talked to Stephen Maguire in Clarksville, but they didn't hold him."

"They think he's out of it?" Bill asked.

"Not completely, but they're not ready to charge him with anything. Maguire admitted that Sidney Galt hired him, but he maintains he did nothing illegal. He surveilled Jackie—Galt told him she was his wife and they were going through a divorce. Maguire didn't question that. Says he never knew they weren't legally married."

"That sounds about right for Galt, from what little I know of him," Bill said.

"Well, Maguire says that he went to volunteer for the debris cleanup under Galt's instructions. Galt told him his wife —Jackie—had stayed in a certain cottage with another man, which was a lie. We know she was only there to view the Laffertys' house with a real estate agent. But Galt told Maguire not to let on who he was, and to look for a couple of specific items."

Campbell frowned. "He managed to get on the crew doing that specific area?"

"Yeah. He hung out with the secretary who was making up the schedules, took her to lunch, sweet-talked her a little."

"What things did Galt tell him to look for?" Bill asked.

"He described a couple of items he said Jackie kept in her purse—a lipstick of a certain shade, a compact he'd given her as a gift. And a Crescent wrench."

"What?" Campbell nearly shrieked. "He asked him to look for the wrench?"

"Yeah. We figure the cosmetic items were a blind. The wrench was what he really wanted."

Bill said slowly, "I'm guessing he didn't find the other things."

"Nope."

"What kind of excuse did he give Maguire for the missing wrench?"

"As I understand it, Galt wove a tale about him leaving his toolbox in Jackie's car. He wanted it back, and she gave it to him, but it was minus the wrench. He claimed he wanted Maguire to look for it every place he knew she'd been the previous week."

"Oh yeah? Where else?" Bill demanded.

"He did some poking around Lucy's apartment. In fact, he says he picked the lock on Garrett's pickup cap and sorted through the tools Garrett was carrying around in there, without taking anything."

"Did they check with Garrett?" Campbell asked.

"Yeah. He says he's not missing anything from his toolbox."

"Why was Sidney Galt so eager to get the wrench back?" she said slowly.

Her father seemed to agree. "Yeah, he could have just thrown it in the lake, or even driven out on the bridge and thrown it in the Tennessee River."

"I don't know what Galt's reason is, but Maguire says he was just following orders and didn't ask why. He also promised not to do any more work for Galt."

"Have they pulled Galt in?" Bill asked.

"Not yet. The Kentucky State Police went to his house yesterday, but he wasn't there. They've got a warrant out on him."

Campbell blew out a big breath. "That's really something."

When Keith had hung up, she looked at her father. "Jackie needs to be extra careful."

He nodded. "Keith says the police will speak to her."

"Maybe you should give her a call." Campbell stood and reached for their empty glasses.

———

Hurrying through her morning routine, Campbell paused for a moment and picked up the small framed photograph she'd perched on her dresser the previous evening. She liked this one even better than the one in her graduation gown, with her mother.

In this shot, her mom smiled out at her, sincere, trusting, and totally in love. Standing close, with his arm holding her against his side, was her father in his patrolman's uniform. His expression was more serious, as though he knew he was taking on grave responsibility, both with his job as an officer and his commitment to Emily. The photo was snapped shortly after he'd proposed to her. Marriage. A family. Protecting them, as well as the citizens of his city.

Campbell turned the frame over and slid down the backing. Yesterday she'd done that when she'd discovered the photo in the last box marked "Em's stuff." She just wanted to see if her mother had written anything on the back before inserting the picture in the frame.

And there it was. "My one and only." Emily had declared herself in writing. Campbell sighed and met her own eyes in the mirror. She had a dreamy smile on her lips.

With a silent, but not too harsh, rebuke for daydreaming when she had work to do, she replaced the photo and hurried downstairs. If all went well, she could cap off one of those reports for the insurance company before leaving for Jackie's house.

Her father and Nick had already left for the attorney's office. Campbell enjoyed a quiet hour of solitary work. Only one phone call interrupted her—a potential client who wanted someone to discreetly check into his son's finances. The man suspected a gambling problem. Campbell assured the caller that Mr. McBride would meet with him the next day. She wrote out a detailed message for her father and placed it on top of her finished report.

She returned to her browsing. Her father had introduced her to a website where she could poke around for connections that might not surface with the usual browsers. To her surprise, after twenty minutes of concentrated effort, she found Weylan Osgood's name among the financial backers for Alanna Galt's restaurant in Elizabethtown. That seemed ambitious for a man who worked in the college maintenance department. If she could find a definite link between him and Galt …

No putting it off any longer. Jackie expected her in fifteen minutes, and it could take all of that for her to get there. Traffic in Murray was much heavier than it had been in the summer. Once the university semester was in full swing, Twelfth Street and everything on the side of town near the MSU campus swarmed. She sent a quick email to her father's account and gathered her things.

After locking up the house, she set out, avoiding the main streets and wending her way to Almo on the north edge of Murray. With her phone's GPS app guiding her, she found Jackie's house easily. The garage was closed. She parked in the driveway and got out, assessing the little ranch house. Cozy, and a good size for a single woman. The roses were in full bloom, and flower beds along the front of the house promised lots of color next spring.

She rang the bell, and Jackie opened the door almost immediately.

"Hi! Thanks for coming. It's silly, really. I feel like I should be able to do this by myself. Oops! Watch the cat."

Campbell quickly stepped in and let her shut the door a second before the long-haired calico reached it.

"That," Jackie said, "is Miss Pepper."

Campbell crouched and held out a hand for the cat to sniff, then patted her head. "Hello there, Miss Pepper. You're not shy, are you?"

"She loves people. And other cats. Every time she hears the door open, she comes running. I don't dare let her out for fear I'll never see her again."

Campbell could see that Miss Pepper was a special cat, and one her owner would not want to lose, especially when she'd already lost so much.

She stood and smiled at Jackie. "So, what are we moving?"

"Oh, it's mainly the dressers. Somehow the movers got mine in the wrong room. I tried putting my stuff in the one that's in there, but it just didn't feel right, you know? So I'd like to swap it with the one in the spare room. I should have noticed it the day Bill was here. Well, I did, but not until it was getting late. I didn't want to ask him to stay longer."

"We should be able to do it," Campbell said. "Lead the way."

Jackie's dresser of choice was a heavy, antique oak unit. They removed all the drawers and were able to maneuver it without too much trouble, down the hall and through the doorways. Then they took the lighter maple dresser to the other room and took the drawers to the correct places, passing each other in the hallway and laughing.

When it was done, Campbell met her in the living room. "What else can I help you with?"

"Oh, let's sit down for a minute and have something cold to drink."

She followed her hostess cautiously to the kitchen. Jackie's preferred cold drink turned out to be Diet Dr. Pepper. Campbell wondered if the cat's name had anything to do with that.

"Looks like you've got things pretty well under control," she said, noting several collapsed cartons standing behind the wastebasket.

"I think so. I've still got books to shelve and a few other things. Oh, the drapes. That box finally turned up. I'd mismarked it for the bedroom." Jackie rolled her eyes. "When those things are finished, I'll be done. I think. Then I'll just have to remember where I put everything." She chuckled and handed Campbell a bottle of pop. "Want a glass?"

"I can drink out of the bottle."

They both unscrewed the lids and took a sip.

"Have a seat." Jackie sat down at the kitchen table, so Campbell took a chair opposite her. "You know, your father put this table together using his pocketknife."

"I'm not surprised," Campbell said with a chuckle. "He's a very resourceful man." After a moment, her curiosity got the better of her, and she ventured, "So, have you had any trouble with ... you know, anyone following you since you moved over here?"

Jackie's mouth tightened and she shook her head slightly. "You know, I told Bill about how Sid—my ex—was making use of my accounts. It was my own fault really. Maybe he told you."

Campbell gave a little shrug. "He did mention it, since he was worried about you."

"Well, I'm embarrassed to admit it, but I let Sid get away with some things that I should have put a stop to earlier. I had no idea he had a history of—of bilking people." Jackie huffed out a breath. "Red flags, you know? Anyway, I had put his name on my checking account, with the understanding that we'd go to his bank and put me on his too. But we didn't get around to that somehow."

Campbell nodded sympathetically. "And he used your money beyond what you intended."

"Way beyond." She held her cold bottle up to her reddened cheek. "He actually bought himself a car! A used one, but still ... Anyway, I'm so glad I never put him on my savings account. That's what I used for the down payment on this house. But he took nearly as much from my checking, and he used a couple of credit cards to run up some big bills. I was devastated when I realized what he'd done."

"Any hope of getting it back?"

"I don't know. The lawyer in Bowling Green wasn't too optimistic." Jackie tipped her bottle up and took a drink. "After all the shouting was over, we—that is, the lawyer and I—learned someone was trying to get him to be a partner in a housing development scheme."

"Scheme? It wasn't legitimate?"

"I don't think so. I mean, Sid would have to make a hefty investment to be a partner in that sort of deal. Where would he get that kind of money? Not from me."

Maybe from his ex-wife, Campbell thought. Was that where Alanna's capital went, forcing her to sell her restaurants?

"He even tried to drag Garrett into it," Jackie said bitterly. "He backed out, though, when things blew up with Sid and me."

"Wow. You must be glad he and Lucy didn't get mixed up in that."

"I am, believe me."

"Why do you think he's been following you around?" Campbell asked.

"Honestly? I think he's mad. That, and he might be able to squeeze a few more dollars out of me. I told the police what he'd done, but so far the only satisfaction I've gotten is a restraining order. But I had to change all my accounts and my phone number—lots of things. I totted things up, and he took over thirty grand from me. That may be small potatoes to some people, but to me it's a year's income."

Campbell nodded. "Still, he wanted to marry you."

Jackie's lips skewed. "He *said* he did. But it was a fake marriage—did Bill tell you?"

"He did, but only because he thinks maybe I might be able to help him help you. He's concerned about the legalities you've got to untangle. Jackie, he cares about you."

"I think that Sid never intended a legal marriage at all. He just wanted me to trust him long enough for him to take whatever he could." She pressed her lips into a thin line. "I wonder if Bill thinks I'm stupid."

"No." Campbell reached across the table and touched her hand.

"I was an easy mark."

"I won't deny that, but Dad sees you as a lot more than that, Jackie."

"Thanks for saying so."

"Well, I'm not just saying it. It's true. So ... I take it you have to work?"

She nodded. "I've been a receptionist at an eye doctor's practice in Bowling Green since right after Phil died. I'm starting a similar job with a family practice over here next week."

"It's good that you found a job right away."

"Yeah, my old boss recommended me. I'm thankful I could move and not worry about employment."

A new empathy for Jackie sprouted in Campbell's heart. She'd accepted the fact that she'd gotten herself into a dicey situation, and now she was taking the initiative to get out of it. She wasn't afraid to work hard in order to put things right.

Campbell looked around the kitchen. Everything looked tidy, and Miss Pepper was lapping water up from her bowl near the refrigerator. "What do you say we get those last few things done?"

"Are you sure?"

"Why not?" Campbell said. "I'd like to leave here thinking you're all settled."

"You don't have to."

"I know."

Half an hour later, they'd finally figured out the tricks to hanging the living room drapes so that the pull cords worked.

"Thanks so much for staying," Jackie said, surveying the perfectly hanging blue-gray cloth. "I really didn't expect you to be here this long, but I doubt I could have got those up alone."

"No problem." Campbell stood back to eye their handiwork. "They look really good in here."

"Do you think so? I was afraid they'd be too long, and my old living room was smaller. I don't want to overwhelm this one." Jackie frowned. "Maybe I should just buy new ones."

"No, these are great. I really like the texture, and the color's terrific with your upholstery. That print ties it all together." Campbell nodded toward a large, framed picture that Jackie had stood on the mantelpiece. She wasn't a big fan of abstracts, but this one was warm and reminded her of the moment just before sunrise. The background, which she saw as sky, harmonized with the drapes, and Jackie's throw pillows picked up the hue of the scarlet slashes in the print.

"Phil hated it," Jackie confessed.

"But you loved it. You kept it all this time."

"I put it away for a while. But after he died, I got it out again." Jackie shrugged. "You're not a picture hanging expert, are you?"

"Afraid not."

"I'll ask Garrett and Lucy to help me. I'm afraid I'd make a big hole in the wall." Jackie pulled her phone from a pocket and looked at the screen. "You know what? It's almost noon. Do you have to go back to the office? We could eat out—my treat."

"We were going to unpack your books."

"They can wait."

Campbell considered the options. "Tell you what, I'll call Dad and tell him I'm not coming home for lunch. You go grab some takeout—whatever you like—and I'll stay here and uncrate the books."

"You don't have to!"

"I love books. Do you want them in order by author's last name?"

"Well, yeah. The fiction, anyway. I was going to put them there in that bookcase." Jackie pointed. "As for the craft books, there's a smaller shelf unit in the spare room. You could group them by subject."

"Got it. Go on—I'll enjoy myself while you're gone."

"Okay. Is pizza all right?"

"Perfect. And anything diet to drink."

The kitchen door to the garage closed behind her, and Campbell took out her cell. Best to call Dad before tackling the books. Should she have brought up the private investigator's name in her conversation with Jackie? She was dying to know if Jackie would recognize Stephen Maguire's name. But her dad had said to keep quiet for now on the fact that Maguire had handled the wrench at the crime scene near the lake.

On the other hand, he'd said Jackie reacted when he mentioned Weylan Osgood's name. Maybe she'd work the dead man into the conversation when Jackie returned.

She strolled into the living room and told her phone, "Call Dad." She glanced out the window. A white vehicle came slowly down the street. Not Jackie's green Camry. The fact that it crept past the end of the driveway made Campbell shrink back and close the drapes. Was Jackie's stalker still at work, or was she being paranoid?

20

Bill took Campbell's call as he and Nick left the attorney's office.

"I won't get home for lunch, Dad," she said. "Jackie's getting some pizza, and we'll do a little more here. Then I'll come back—unless you need me right away."

"No, that's fine. We're done with the Blaze Collins case, and Nick will stay at the office. We'll grab something to eat on the way home, and then I'll change and get over to the courthouse."

"Oh, that's right. Sorry, I forgot you had court today."

"It's okay. I don't have to be there for another hour."

"How'd it turn out about Collins?"

Bill sighed. "The lawyer will relay the contact information you two got to the executor, and he'll try to contact the kid. It's out of our hands now." He could tell Campbell was as disappointed as he was. When he'd signed off, he said to Nick, "She'll probably pump you for details later."

"There's nothing she doesn't already know." Nick scowled

and slumped in the passenger seat of Bill's car. "I wish we coulda tied it up better."

"Not everything gets gift wrapped and tied with a bow," Bill said.

"I know." Nick was still frowning.

"Okay, buddy. What's up?"

"Nothing."

"Something." Bill pulled up at a stoplight, and Nick met his gaze for an instant.

"I've just been feeling down lately."

"Anything specific?"

"Not really."

"You getting tired of the job?"

Nick shrugged. "Nah. It's boring sometimes, but other times it's exciting. I guess I'm really disappointed in the way this case turned out."

Bill thought about that as he turned onto Willow Street. They were all a bit deflated today. "I'll try to come up with something more exciting for you next time."

Nick was silent.

As he pulled into the driveway, Bill said, "You sure it's nothing else? No girl trouble or anything like that?"

Nick shook his head.

They rolled into the garage, and Bill switched off the ignition and faced him. "I try not to push it with you, Nick, but I do get concerned about your spiritual condition. You're a great employee and a good friend, but you always shut down when I mention God. I've tried not to badger you about it."

"I know you have." Nick's eyebrows morphed together. "I think when you don't mention it for a while, I feel like maybe you don't care anymore."

"What? No! Just the opposite."

Unbuckling his seatbelt, Nick said, "Maybe it's just Campbell."

"Campbell?" Bill put a hand on his arm to stop him from getting out of the car. "Did I miss something? Has she been uppity to you?"

"No, no."

"Oh." Bill studied his profile for a moment. "When you two went to the concert Friday night, did something happen?"

"Uh-uh. She was good. In fact, I might not have gotten as much out of Capps-Collins without her. She's got a knack for questioning."

Bill nodded slowly. "So...?" Was it possible that Nick had a crush on Campbell, who was only a couple of years older, and she didn't reciprocate?

"Aw, it's stupid." Nick turned and looked him full in the eyes. "If she finds out she passed her exam, she's going to stay on, right?"

"That's the idea."

"I feel like she'll be your righthand man then. Or woman. Whatever."

Bill was silent for a moment. "Nick, she's my daughter. I love her more than anything on this earth. But I won't give her preference in the business. I won't give her all the plum assignments."

Nick's mouth twitched, but he didn't say anything.

"I've been training her, the same as I trained you three years ago. She needs more guidance right now than you do. And there are a lot of things in this business that you're better at than she is. Computer searches, for instance. Skip traces. That's why I put you on the Barry Capps case. I didn't think Campbell was ready to handle that alone. But I was pleased when you included her the night of the concert."

"Really?"

"Yes, really."

"Okay. Thanks. That makes me feel—not worthless."

"Aw, Nick. Don't sell yourself short. Your help is extremely valuable to me." Bill slapped his forehead. "I forgot to stop for lunch."

"You've got court," Nick said. "I'll go get something while you get ready. Burgers okay?"

"Sure."

"And maybe sometime we can talk about, you know, the other stuff."

Bill eyed him keenly. "Spiritual stuff?"

Nick nodded. "I ... I think it's something else I could learn about from you."

———

After settling the lunch question with her father, Campbell turned to the three large cartons of books. She was surprised they were still in boxes. Those were the items she would have unpacked first, but Jackie seemed to have thought dishes and clothes were more urgent.

The first box was full of craft books. Campbell hoisted it and managed to plod down the hallway with it pressing against her stomach. When she reached the guest room, she set the box carefully on the chair near the bookcase.

On top of the shelves, Jackie had already set a potted philodendron and a framed photo from her wedding to Philip Fleming. Campbell picked up the frame and studied the picture. A more mature version of her mom's prom date smiled out at her. Nice-looking man.

She tried to remember what Sid Galt looked like. She'd seen a couple of pictures of him online, but her memory was vague. Was he as handsome as Phil? Maybe. Probably every photo of

Galt had been destroyed and deleted from Jackie's phone. She certainly wouldn't want any pictures of the man who betrayed her in her new home.

Campbell pulled the box to her and sat down in front of the shelves. Arranging the colorful books by topic was enjoyable. Cross stitch patterns here, knitting below it, then needlepoint and decoupage.

When she pulled a couple of quilting books from the box, she frowned and looked over at the quilt on the back of the convertible sofa. It was sewn in the same pattern shown on the front of one of the books. Jackie had probably made it and several other decorative items she'd seen scattered around the house, including the cross-stitched guest towels in the bathroom and a knit afghan draped over the back of the living room sofa.

When the carton was empty, she untaped the bottom, collapsed the box, and carried it to the kitchen. Jackie had taken the stack of empty boxes from there to the garage and added the one the drapes had been in after she broke it down. Campbell opened the door to the garage and was surprised to find the overhead door open. Jackie must have left it that way when she drove out. The trash can bulged with full bags, and the lid didn't quite fit down over them.

She fitted the folded carton behind it with half a dozen others and turned to the steps leading up into the kitchen. She hesitated and glanced up to find the button that would activate the big door. Should she close it?

With sudden decision, she pushed the button and let the overhead door creak and whine its way down. Dad could fix that so it didn't make so much noise. And her hostess could hit the remote on her sun visor when she got home.

Inside, Campbell walked through to the living room and sidled up to the drapes they'd hung earlier. She used one finger to push the fabric aside and peered out from the side, rather than standing in front of the large window.

The boxy white vehicle hadn't moved on. It had pulled in just past Jackie's drive and sat motionless by the curb. Was anyone inside? She couldn't tell from this angle, with the headrest blocking her view.

A faint meow reached her, and she turned around, looking for the cat.

"Miss Pepper?" She listened carefully until another meow came and headed back to the kitchen. Could she have shut the cat in the garage? She opened the door.

"Miss Pepper, where are you?"

The next plaintive meow came from behind another door inside the kitchen. Campbell closed the garage door, walked over to it, and turned the knob. The calico cat scampered out past her feet and trotted into the living room.

Campbell frowned and looked into the recess. She stood at the top of the cellar stairs. *That's odd. I could swear the cat was up here when Jackie left.* Would Jackie shut her cat into the basement when she was still unfamiliar with the house?

She walked around, looking carefully into each room. Miss Pepper's litter box was in the laundry room. The cat had settled in an armchair opposite the sofa, already nestled down for a nap.

Uneasy, Campbell went back to the front window. The white SUV was still out there, motionless.

Jackie would be back soon with pizza. She made herself turn away and returned to the kitchen, where she explored the cupboards until she found plates and glasses. She was counting out the silverware when she heard movement in the living room.

"That you, Jackie?" she called, turning toward the doorway.

No answer. But the sound wasn't right for Miss Pepper.

With two forks in her hand, Campbell walked around the island and peeked into the next room.

At first she didn't see anything, but then she heard a quiet sound from down the hallway. Someone was in Jackie's bedroom. She tiptoed across the living room, to the opening into the hall. The bedroom door was open. Campbell stood still, listening, her gaze riveted to the door. A shadow flickered across the panels, and then she heard a drawer open or close.

Her heart raced. That couldn't be Jackie. She'd have come in through the garage and taken the pizza directly to the kitchen. Just to be sure, Campbell sniffed. Nope, no pizza. She'd smell it if there was any in the house. Had someone managed to slip in before she closed the garage door and stay out of sight while she unpacked the books?

She hesitated. Should she confront whoever it was? Maybe Lucy had dashed over on her lunch hour. But the vehicle outside made her believe it wasn't Lucy. *Lord, make me wise!* She didn't feel any bolts of wisdom.

In the recliner, Miss Pepper stretched, rose, and hopped to the floor with a quiet thud. Campbell caught her breath and froze. Why couldn't Jackie have a Doberman, instead of a calico cat?

The noise in the bedroom had stopped. Campbell's chest tightened. She had to get out. Tiptoeing across the carpet toward the kitchen, she looked back. The shadows in the hall stirred. Someone was coming out of the bedroom. She ran into the kitchen.

Her phone was in her side pocket, but the forks were in that hand. She plunked them on the counter and flinched at the sound they made.

She should have gone out the front door. With a gulp, she managed to extract the phone.

Footsteps. Whoever it was didn't try to silence them. Clutching her phone, she ran to the garage door and flung it open.

It took a second for her fingertips to find the control button. As the overhead door began its slow journey upward, the heavy footsteps reached the bare kitchen floor. Campbell sucked in a breath and poked at her phone to hit her father's contact.

"Hey, Soup."

Before she could say a word, a hand clutched her shirt and jerked her backward. Another slammed down on her forearm, and her phone flew from her hand and clattered on the cement garage floor.

She pitched backward, landing with a hard thud on her hip and her left arm. Her head impacted the tiled floor more gently and rebounded. She rolled onto her back and stared up at her assailant.

She'd expected to meet the brown eyes she'd seen after she picked up the wrench near the ruined cottage. But no, this wasn't the investigator working undercover as a volunteer. The fragmented images she'd tried to recall and piece together had coalesced. Staring down at her with calculating gray eyes was a very cynical and determined Sidney Galt.

———

"Campbell?" Bill hit the brake and checked his rearview mirror, straining to hear his daughter's voice over the phone. Nothing. "Campbell, are you there?"

He managed to steer into the righthand lane and hit the turn signal. He took the first right, into a parking lot and ground to a halt as soon as he was out of traffic.

He could hear something over the phone, but it wasn't his

daughter's voice. A rumbling sound. Traffic, maybe? The vehicles around him camouflaged what little he could hear from Campbell's end.

"What's going on, kiddo?" His pulse picked up. Was Campbell driving? Maybe she dropped her phone on the car floor and couldn't reach down to get it. He was pretty sure the connection was still open. He looked around and turned the car so that he was facing out of the parking lot.

Campbell still wasn't talking. The call was probably dropped, but it was so hard to tell without a dial tone these days. He swiped the screen, eyed the icons, and hit contacts to call her back. The recorded voice that greeted him advised him to leave a message, as Campbell McBride was not available. He said, "Hey, it's Dad. I think we lost our connection. Everything okay? Check in with me."

He clicked off and waited a few seconds. When nothing happened, he pocketed his phone and headed for the street. Just before pulling out, he hit Jackie's number. She answered on the second ring.

"It's Bill. Is Campbell with you?"

"No, I'm at Little Caesar's on Twelfth Street, waiting for a pie."

"Where's Campbell?"

"Back at my house."

Bill pulled in a careful breath. "She called me, but when I answered, she wasn't there."

"Probably just a glitch. Try calling her back."

"I did." Bill clenched his teeth. "I'm heading over there."

"Great. I'll see you as soon as I get my pizza."

Bill tossed the phone onto the passenger seat and concentrated on driving fast but with precision toward Jackie's little house. He'd be late for court, but that was no reason not to make sure his daughter was safe.

21

"Who are you?" His eyes drilled into her.

Campbell lay helpless, breathing in quick, shallow gasps. "Jackie's friend."

He shook his head. "I know Jackie's friends."

"Ever think she might make new friends on this side of the lakes?"

The wrinkles in his forehead deepened. "You're too young. A friend of Lucy's maybe?"

Trying to project more confidence than she felt, Campbell barked out a laugh. "What, Jackie can't make friends from another generation? You *are* arrogant, aren't you?"

His eyes narrowed.

Campbell pushed upward, in an effort to sit. If she had to face a jerk, she didn't want to be sprawled on the floor. Her head ached, and pain seared her hip. She bit back a moan and sat straighter.

"I know who you are. You're Sidney Galt."

He said nothing, but his chin lifted an inch, and he looked down his nose at her.

"So, what are you doing here?" Campbell demanded. She'd faced down an adversary before. *Don't let him see that you're quaking in your sneakers.* Or, as Nick would probably say, spit in his eye. Her lips twisted in a sour frown. "Did you come to see Jackie?"

"Not exactly."

"Good. Because she has a restraining order on you. You could go to jail just for being here."

Was he surprised that she knew about that? If so, he did a good job of hiding it.

They stared at each other for ten seconds. Campbell suspected he'd watched the house and saw Jackie leave before he broke in. Apparently he hadn't worried about Campbell's Fusion, parked in the driveway. But he must have heard her call out to Jackie, and he didn't care.

"Get up." His voice was low and guttural now, sending a shiver through her.

As far as she could see, he had no weapons. She fought the instinct to look around the kitchen for something with which to defend herself. Jackie's knife block was across the room. Her purse with her pepper spray was tucked below the plant stand in the living room. She'd tossed two forks on the counter, but no way would he let her leap over there and grab one.

"Now!"

As she struggled to get up, she thought she heard a faint sound but couldn't place it. Where was Miss Pepper? Was that a cat noise?

She rolled to her knees, moving as slowly as she dared.

"Where's the gun?" His voice held a snarl that made her shudder.

"Gun? I don't know anything about a gun." She stopped moving, still on her knees.

"Jackie's gun. She always kept it in her top dresser drawer, but it's not there now."

Campbell shook her head helplessly. "I didn't know Jackie had a gun. But the moving men put her dresser in the wrong room. I came over today to help her get the one she wanted into her room. There wasn't any gun in the drawers. I'd have seen it."

He swore.

She prayed silently, frantically, and thought she heard the faint crunch of tires on the driveway. She listened for the garage door to go up, but no sound came from the direction of the door behind Sid. Even so, she was certain an engine died outside the house.

He was listening too, tilting his head slightly toward the kitchen window.

"Get up!"

"Why should I?" Campbell's heart thudded. As long as Galt didn't have a weapon in his hands, she figured she had a chance. She might be able to outrun him, or at least wrestle with him long enough for someone to arrive. She spared a pang of regret for the phone she'd dropped onto the garage floor.

He drew back a foot and aimed a kick at her.

"Because I said so!" He swung, but before his kick could land, she flung herself backward and once more lay on the floor, looking up at him. His face turned a violent shade of purple and he strode toward her.

Ding-dong!

Galt froze at the sound of the doorbell. "Who's that?"

"How should I know?" she gasped. She could almost read his mind as his eyes darted to the doorway and back to her. Jackie wouldn't ring the bell. Jackie would come in through the garage.

He edged toward the window and squinted out at the driveway. After a moment, he said, "The white car's yours?"

"Yes." Campbell clamped her lips together to stop their trembling.

"There's a blue car behind it." Galt squinted into the glaring sunlight. "Looks like a Camry."

Her hopes surged. *Thank You, Lord!* At once her fear peaked. *Protect my dad! Please don't let him get hurt.*

The doorbell chimed again, and Galt's eyes locked on hers. "Get up. Go answer the door. And not a word about me. Whoever it is, send them away."

Campbell rose slowly and walked on wooden legs into the next room. Her dad wouldn't be sent away easily.

She opened the door and stared into his eyes.

"What's going on?" he asked softly.

She licked her lips.

"You okay?" Bill peered at her.

For a moment, Campbell closed her eyes. Then she opened them, hoping he understood. She remembered that from somewhere—patients who couldn't speak could use their eyes to blink yes and no. But which was one blink and which was two?

Bill's right hand went inside his jacket. "Get down."

Her throat dry, Campbell dropped to the floor. Her dad pushed past her, slamming the door all the way open, but it didn't crash against the wall. Sid Galt pushed from behind it and grabbed Bill's arm. She skittered to her feet and jumped back to avoid the two men tangling over the gun.

"Dad!"

With his foot, Bill swept Galt's legs from under him, and the two fell heavily. "Call backup," he ground out.

Campbell's hand went to her throat. Jackie had no landline, and her cell was on the garage floor, probably useless.

She bolted to the kitchen. A fleeting thought told her to stop and grab a knife—a skillet—a rolling pin—anything. She kept on to the door leading into the garage, expecting to hear any moment the roar of a gunshot.

The overhead door was rising. She didn't stop to ponder that but leaped to the concrete floor and grabbed her abandoned phone. The screen was cracked but not broken out.

A car door opened, and she looked up. Jackie had her driver's door open and was halfway out. "Campbell, what's going on? Is that Bill's car?"

A living room window beyond her car shattered, spewing glass outward, as a shot fired. Jackie stared at Campbell, her mouth and eyes wide.

"It's Sid Galt," Campbell managed. "He and my dad were fighting over Dad's gun."

Jackie dove back into her car and emerged at once with her purse. She ran past Campbell, fumbling with the clasp. "Call the cops!"

Unable to pull in a deep breath, Campbell tapped her fractured screen. To her relief, it responded. Keith or 9-1-1? This time she chose the emergency number.

She stammered out the information, blanking on the address.

"I—I—it's in Almo. Hold on." She hauled in two shaky breaths, exhaling slowly through her mouth and hoping they could track her phone if she couldn't remember.

"We've got you."

"Hurry!"

She hopped up the steps and through the kitchen. Jackie stood in the living room doorway, holding a small automatic pistol pointed into the living room.

"I mean it, Sid! Drop it now, or I'll kill you."

Campbell's heart lurched. If Sid had the gun, did that mean—

"Smart choice," Jackie said. "Keep your hands high."

"Cops are on the way," Campbell said softly. She tried to see over Jackie's shoulder. Where was her father?

"Get over to the couch and sit," Jackie said in harsh tones.

His hands at shoulder height, Sid Galt edged sideways toward the sofa. Jackie took a step into the room, and Campbell squeezed past her in time to see her father standing shakily, using the wall beyond the open front door for support.

"Dad! Are you all right?" She hurried to his side. "Are you hurt?"

"Just my pride, kiddo. I shouldn't have rushed in like that. Seeing you so upset made me see red."

"Are you sure you're okay?" She put her arm around him.

"Yeah. A few bruises, and I skinned my knuckles. If Jackie hadn't come in—well, we won't go there." Bill took a step and stooped to retrieve his gun.

Campbell stood still, trying to calm her choppy breathing. Her father holstered his pistol and walked over to Jackie.

"Are you all right?"

"I'm fine," Jackie said grimly. "What were you doing here?" she asked Sid.

"He was looking for your gun," Campbell said. "I didn't see him come in, but he shut Miss Pepper in the cellar."

"In the cellar?" Jackie's cheek twitched. "Where is she now?"

Campbell looked around. A siren blared down the street, growing rapidly louder. A blur of black, white, and orange tore past her and out the open door.

"Miss Pepper!" Jackie stared after the cat.

Galt took advantage of her distraction and leaped off the couch toward her, reaching for the gun.

Bill was quicker. He had his pistol out as Jackie jumped away from Galt and he tripped over the leg of the coffee table.

"Back on the couch," Bill said. "Campbell, take Jackie outside to meet the officers and explain to them what happened. Then ask the neighbors to keep an eye out for a scared calico cat."

———

Campbell sat at her desk, cueing in keywords for a background check. Three days had passed since her confrontation with Sid Galt. She still flinched occasionally when her bruised hip brushed against furniture, but she was otherwise okay. By the grace of God, she thought.

"Breaking news." Her father stood in the doorway, his eyes sparkling.

"What is it?" Campbell and Nick asked at the same time.

"Keith just called me. Jackie went in this morning to answer a few more questions about Galt. She told Keith that when Sid told her about his financial investment plan, he told her someone in Murray wanted him to come in on it as a partner."

"We knew that," Nick said.

"Yes, but not who."

Campbell drew in a sharp breath. "She told you she recognized the name."

Her dad nodded. "Weylan Osgood was the one heading up the scheme."

She exhaled slowly.

Nick grinned at the boss. "I guess this means we're done with the Kellums' case."

"It sure does," Bill said. "I'll set up a final meeting with Drew and Marnie."

As he left the office, Campbell's computer pinged, and she couldn't resist taking a look at her email account. She caught her breath, her hand lingering on the mouse.

Nick was staring at her. "You okay, Professor?"

"Uh, yeah, I just ... It's my test results."

He jumped up and hurried across the room. "Open it."

"I don't know."

"What, you're still scared you flunked?"

She glared at him. "No, I just want someone more supportive than you beside me when I do it."

He backed off a step and glanced away. "Want me to get your dad? He's in his office."

She swallowed hard. "I'll tell him when I'm ready."

Nick threw his hands up. "Okay. Have it your way. I wasn't trying to make you feel uncomfortable."

Ha, Campbell thought. Nick always wanted her to be uncomfortable. She squirmed inside, knowing that uncharitable thought wasn't entirely true.

She considered her options. Did she want to be alone when she opened the email? If not, who did she want next to her? After a moment, she picked up her cell and texted Keith.

Test results in. Are you available?

To her surprise, in thirty seconds, she received a reply.

Can come at noon.

She smiled and sent a note back.

Great. Lunch included, of course.

A smiley face came in on the screen. She got up and walked across the hall. Her father's door was open.

"Hey, Keith's coming for lunch."

"Good. Tell Rita." He turned his attention back to his computer.

"I will. Oh, and Dad ..."

He looked up at her and waited for her to go on.

"My test results are in. I haven't opened them yet."

After a moment, he said, "And when do you plan to open them?"

"When Keith gets here."

Bill nodded. "I guess in the interest of fair disclosure, I should tell you that I'm having dinner tonight with Jackie."

Campbell smiled. "Great. I'm so glad Miss Pepper came back."

The cat had eluded the searchers all afternoon on the day she escaped, but at twilight, she'd found her way back to Jackie's door and sat meowing on the front steps until her owner heard her and let her in.

"So am I," he said. "That would have been one loss too many for her right now."

Campbell gave Rita an update on their meal plans and went back to the main office.

"Keith's coming over for lunch," she said to Nick. "I'll open it then."

When he arrived an hour later, she met him at the door. He kissed her and walked into the office with her.

"Still haven't peeked?"

"Nope. I decided to wait for you."

"Hi, Keith," Nick said.

Campbell was going to ask him to give her a few minutes alone with Keith, but Nick pushed his chair back unprompted.

"Excuse me, I need to check with Bill on something," he said.

"Sure." Keith stood aside to let him leave the room. He looked down at Campbell. "Is Nick being diplomatic?"

"I think so, incredible as that might be." She took his hand and led him over to her desk. "Dad told us that Jackie made the connection between Sid Galt and Weylan Osgood."

"Yes. Detective Roland had another session with Galt, and I sat in. We've got him, Campbell."

"You mean, he confessed?"

"After some heavy pushing on Roland's part, yeah. He said he was at Osgood's house the night of the tornado. They had a big fight over their methods of getting investors. I'm guessing Galt wanted to use some shady tactics. Osgood actually hoped to build a nice development that would be an asset to the community."

"Sid just wanted to get his hands on the money," Campbell said.

"He didn't admit to it, but that's what it boils down to. Roland told him we found his prints in Osgood's basement and on the wrench."

Her gaze sprang to his eyes. "Did you?"

Keith winced and shook his head. "Roland's ideas of fair play in interrogation are different from mine. Anyway, his lawyer advised him to take a plea bargain, and he did. He said they took shelter from the storm and continued their fight in the basement. Osgood's toolbox was there, and Sid killed him with the wrench."

Campbell sucked in a breath. She'd suspected it, but hearing Keith say it made it real.

"After the storm, Sid decided he needed to get rid of the body. Someone might have seen him going into Osgood's house, so he felt he had to get it out of there. He heard on the radio that there was a lot of damage out near the lake, so he loaded the body in his trunk and drove out to the lake, where he'd followed Jackie when she looked at the cottage. He spotted a house nearby that was hit hard and unloaded the body into the debris."

"What about the wrench?" she whispered.

"He saw lights at my dad's house—he told me he and Mom lit a lantern after the tornado went through and knocked out the power. Galt started to leave then remembered the wrench. When he'd hidden it in the debris at Laffertys', he hightailed it out of there."

"Whew. That's a lot."

"Yes. And you helped solve the case." He squeezed her hand and nodded toward her laptop. "Now, are you ready?"

She was. No matter what future God had in store for her, she knew she could cope with it. "If I wait any longer, I'll burst."

"Okay. I'm here for you."

She sat down but hesitated. "Listen, if it's bad news, I'll probably cry. I mean, Dad is so set on me passing and being an investigator."

"What about you? Are you set on it?"

"Yeah. I really want this."

He smiled and laid a warm hand on her shoulder. "There's only one way to find out."

"Right." She pulled a deep breath, straightened her shoulders, and reached for the mouse.

Her lungs felt odd, as though the air she breathed was different somehow, and her head whirled. Steady, she told herself.

She clicked.

Staring at the screen, she couldn't move for a moment. Then she grabbed his hand. "Oh, Keith." She sobbed, and tears welled in her eyes and spilled over, streaming down her face.

He knelt on the rug beside her and pulled her into his arms. She clung to him, shocked by her own reaction.

"I knew you could do it," he whispered.

"I missed two questions."

He chuckled. "I doubt anyone gets them all. Look, sweetheart. It says your score is exceptional. Congratulations."

She turned her head and read the message again, gave a sob, and stretched for the box of tissues on the corner of the desk. Keith snatched it and held it for her. Campbell pulled one out and wiped her face.

"Sorry," she whispered.

"No need to be."

"I'm not usually this emotional."

He wagged his head back and forth. "You've been under a lot of stress. And besides, sometimes it's good to let the feelings out."

"Yeah." She hated feeling weak, as though she'd let her dad down and not carried well the load assigned to her.

He pulled her in for another hug. "I love you, Campbell."

She jerked away from him and stared at his face. "You do?"

"Definitely, I do. And I'm sorry I haven't told you before."

She sniffed. "I ... I love you too."

His smile grew. "I thought so, but it's great to hear you say it."

She took a couple of shaky breaths. "I'm a mess."

"No, you're beautiful."

That was hard to believe, even without the blotchy face and swollen eyes. She reached for another tissue. "Let me go wash my face, and then we'll tell Dad?"

"And Nick?"

"Yeah, him too." She scrunched up her face. "I haven't been very nice to him lately."

"I don't know about that, but you can always start now."

Campbell smiled. "Yes." She got up and hurried to the bathroom down the hall.

She returned a few minutes later, still a bit puffy-eyed but more in control of herself.

With a smile, Keith took her hand. "Ready now?"

For her answer, she led him to her dad's closed door and tapped on it.

"Come in."

When she swung the door open, Bill was sitting at his desk with Nick at his elbow, looking over his shoulder at the desktop screen.

Her father rose with a quizzical smile.

"I passed," Campbell said.

"I knew it!" Her dad swerved around the desk and gave her a bear hug.

Pulling away, she took Nick's outstretched hand.

"Congrats, Professor," he said. "Or should I start calling you Sherlock?"

"Please don't. That would make me start looking for a derogatory nickname for you, and I don't want to do that." She looked into his dark brown eyes. "Let's just be friends, okay?"

Nick laughed. "Sounds good to me."

"Oh, just a sec." Bill retreated behind the desk and opened a bottom drawer. He took out a desk plaque with her name engraved on it. Beneath, in smaller letters, were the words "Certified Private Investigator."

Campbell took it in both hands and blinked back the tears springing to her eyes. "Thanks, Dad."

Sheepishly, Nick held out a magnifying glass with a golden rim and a wooden handle. "Congrats, friend."

"Oh, thank you. I love it." She gave him a quick hug.

"I feel like a cheapskate," Keith said.

Nick eyed him with arched eyebrows. "I thought you told me you were bringing her a dozen roses."

Keith chuckled. "Thanks for spilling that, Nick. I was going to bring them tonight, when I take Campbell out for dinner."

"I'm ... overwhelmed." She looked around at the three smiling men. "Thank you *all*. Now ... lunch, everybody?"

"Rita tells me it's ready," Bill said, "and she made a special celebratory dessert."

"Wow. What if I'd failed?"

"Then it would be a consolatory dessert," Nick said.

They moved into the hallway, and she tugged Keith's hand to hold him back for a moment.

"Your gift is the best," she whispered, "and I don't mean the roses."

The end

ABOUT THE AUTHOR

Susan Page Davis is the author of more than 100 novels and novellas. She's a winner of the Carol Award, the Will Rogers Medallion, and the Faith, Hope, and Love Reader's Choice Award. Her books include the Homeward Trails, Skirmish Cove Mysteries, the Maine Justice series and Hearts of Oak series. A Maine native, she now lives in western Kentucky with her husband, Jim, and one very naughty cat. They also have six grown children and eleven grandchildren.

MORE MYSTERIES BY SUSAN PAGE DAVIS

True Blue Mysteries

Blue Plate Special—Book One

Campbell McBride drives to her father's house in Murray, Kentucky, dreading telling him she's lost her job as an English professor. Her father, private investigator Bill McBride, isn't there or at his office in town. His brash young employee, Nick Emerson, says Bill hasn't come in this morning, but he did call the night before with news that he had a new case.

When her dad doesn't show up by late afternoon, Campbell and Nick decide to follow up on a phone number he'd jotted on a memo sheet. They learn who last spoke to her father, but they also find a dead body. The next day, Campbell files a missing persons report. When Bill's car is found, locked and empty in a secluded spot, she and Nick must get past their differences and work together to find him.

Get your copy here:

https://scrivenings.link/blueplatespecial

————

Ice Cold Blue—**Book Two**

Campbell McBride is now working for her father Bill as a private investigator in Murray, Kentucky. Xina Harrison wants them to find out what is going on with her aunt, Katherine Tyler.

Katherine is a rich, reclusive author, and she has resisted letting Xina visit her for several years. Xina arrived unannounced, and Katherine was upset and didn't want to let her in. When Xina did gain entry, she learned Katherine fired her longtime housekeeper. She noticed that a few family heirlooms previously on display have disappeared. Xina is afraid someone is stealing from her aunt or influencing her to give them her money and valuables. True Blue accepts the case, and the investigators follow a twisting path to the truth.

Get your copy here:

https://scrivenings.link/icecoldblue

Persian Blue Puzzle—Book Three

An antisocial cat, an elusive investment broker, and a hope-selling psychic
raise suspicions in a western Kentucky community.

Someone's broken into Miss Louanne's house. Campbell McBride
and her father Bill have moved their home and detective business
into an old Victorian house. Their new neighbors bring in
unexpected cases for True Blue Investigations to unravel.

While helping Miss Louanne look for her missing cat, Campbell
learns of other suspicious activities in Murray. Another neighbor
tells the detectives about a stranger in town who's peddling an
investment plan. They aren't sure any crimes have been committed,
but they're intrigued enough for Campbell to visit a psychic along
with police detective Keith Fuller's mom and to start checking up on
the financier.

Things heat up when a customer threatens the psychic and then she
vanishes.

Get your copy here:

https://scrivenings.link/persianbluepuzzle

————

Skirmish Cove Mysteries

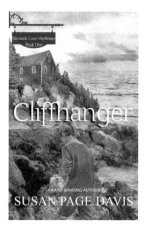

Cliffhanger—**Book One**

A charming themed inn, breaking waves, and a missing guest. What more could one ask?

The Novel Inn's reopening goes smoothly until a guest vanishes. The new owners prepare for their first large group—a former squad of cheerleaders meeting for a reunion. Things go awry when the head cheerleader fails to show up. Sisters Kate and Jillian, the innkeepers, enlist the help of their brother Rick, a local police officer. They're confident the missing woman will be found, but they soon learn to expect the unexpected, even during a walk on the beach.

Get your copy here:

https://scrivenings.link/cliffhanger

The Plot Thickens—Book Two

Jillian only wants to redecorate one room at the Novel Inn—but first she has to deal with murder.

Murder strikes Skirmish Cove during the coastal town's winter carnival. Jillian Tunney, part owner of the nearby Novel Inn, discovers the body of a clerk at her favorite bookstore. With her sister Kate and brother, Officer Rick Gage, she tries to find out who killed him.

Meanwhile, Jillian is immersed in redecorating one of the themed rooms, but Kate is annoyed when a mysterious guest at the inn doesn't want to leave his room. The innkeepers find they have way too many secrets to solve.

Get your copy here:

https://scrivenings.link/theplotthickens

HISTORICAL ROMANCE BY SUSAN PAGE DAVIS

Homeward Trails

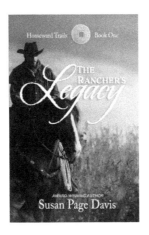

The Rancher's Legacy—Book One

Will Rogers Medallion—Copper Award Winner

Matthew Anderson and his father try to help neighbor Bill Maxwell when his ranch is attacked. On the day his daughter Rachel is to return from school back East, outlaws target the Maxwell ranch. After Rachel's world is shattered, she won't even consider the plan her father and Matt's cooked up—to see their two children marry and combine the ranches.

Meanwhile in Maine, sea captain's widow Edith Rose hires a private investigator to locate her three missing grandchildren. The children were abandoned by their father nearly twenty years ago. They've been adopted into very different families, and they're scattered across the country. Can investigator Ryland Atkins find them all while the elderly woman still lives? His first attempt is to find the boy now called Matthew Anderson. Can Ryland survive his trip into the wild Colorado Territory and find Matt before the outlaws finish destroying a legacy?

Get your copy here:

https://scrivenings.link/therancherslegacy

———————

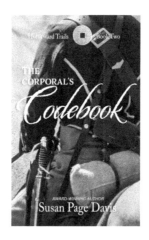

The Corporal's Codebook—**Book Two**

Jack Miller stumbles through the Civil War, winding up a telegrapher and cryptographer for the army. In the field with General Sherman in Georgia, he is captured along with his precious cipher key.

His captor, Hamilton Buckley, thinks he should have been president of the Confederacy, not Jefferson Davis. Jack doubts Buckley's sanity and longs to escape. Buckley's kindhearted niece, Marilla, might help him—but only if Jack helps her achieve her own goal.

Meanwhile, a private investigator, stymied by the difficulty of travel and communication in wartime, is trying his best to locate Jack for the grandmother he longs to see again but can barely remember.

Get your copy here:

https://scrivenings.link/thecorporalscodebook

———

The Sister's Search—Book Three

A young woman searches for her missing brother and finds much more awaits her—if she can escape war-torn Texas.

Molly Weaver and her widowed mother embark on an arduous journey at the end of the Civil War. They hope to join Molly's brother Andrew on his ranch in Texas. When they arrive, Andrew is missing and squatters threaten the ranch.

Can they trust Joe, the stranger who claims to be Andrew's friend? Joe's offer to help may be a godsend—or a snare. And who is the man claiming to be Molly's father? If he's telling the truth, Molly's past is a sham, and she must learn where she really belongs.

Get your copy here:

https://scrivenings.link/thesisterssearch

MORE MYSTERIES FROM SCRIVENINGS PRESS

Not a Good Day for Namaste

by Keri Lynn

A Texas-Sized Mystery—Book Two

Witnessing the hit and run of fellow Flamingo Springs resident Ryan wasn't how yoga instructor Misty Van Oepen planned on starting the Thanksgiving holidays.

When Ryan's mysterious brother shows up along with a spree of crime, she decides it's up to her and fellow business owners Lacey and Jeni, to find out what's going on. After an attempt on Misty's life lands her in protective custody at deputy Stetson Owens' ranch, she finds herself in danger of losing her heart to the former bull rider.

With time running out, will Misty succeed in discovering who's behind the attacks? Or will she fail and become the next victim?

Get your copy here:

https://scrivenings.link/notagooddayfornamaste

———

The Gold Doubloons

by Suzanne J. Bratcher

Jerome Mysteries—Book Three

When Coronado marched through the Verde Valley in 1542 looking for the Seven Cities of Gold, Yavapai scouts took him to a mine near present-day Jerome. Coronado didn't find what he was looking for, but a persistent legend says he left behind a bag of gold doubloons. Now, almost five hundred years later, Reed Harper, Paul and Marty Russell's foster son, needs those precious coins to finance the future he dreams of.

But Reed isn't the only one determined to find the gold doubloons. As the search intensifies in the caves around Jerome and extends to the ancient cliff dwelling called Montezuma Castle, a young Yavapai person dies. Was the fall from a cliff that borders Montezuma Well an accident—or was it murder?

When a second fall from the same cliff puts Reed in a coma, the sheriff arrests him for the victim's murder. But Scott Russell knows his foster brother is innocent. Convinced a ruthless killer is after Reed, Scott rushes to protect him. Will Paul and Marty find the teens in time to rescue them, or will the murderer strike again?

Get your copy here:

https://scrivenings.link/thegolddoubloons

————

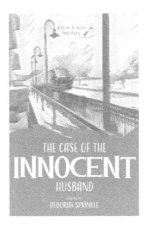

The Case of the Innocent Husband

by Deborah Sprinkle

A Mac & Sam Mystery - Book One

Private Investigator Mackenzie Love needs to do one thing. Find out who shot Eleanor Davis. Or else.

When Eleanor Davis is found shot in her garage, the only suspect, her estranged husband, is found not guilty in a court of law. However, most of the good citizens of Washington, Missouri, remain unconvinced. It doesn't matter that twelve men and women of the jury found him not guilty. What do they know?

And since Private Investigator Mackenzie Love accepted the job for the defense and helped acquit Connor Davis, her friends and neighbors have placed her squarely in the enemy camp. Therefore, her overwhelming goal becomes to find out who killed Eleanor Davis.

Or leave the town she grew up in.

As the investigation progresses, the threats escalate. Someone wants to stop Mackenzie and her partner, Samantha Majors, and is willing to do whatever it takes—including murder.

Can Mac and Sam find the killer before they each end up on the wrong side of a bullet?

Get your copy here:

https://scrivenings.link/innocenthusband

––––––––

Printed in the USA
CPSIA information can be obtained
at www.ICGtesting.com
LVHW050332140524
780202LV00036BA/1546